A
Murder
of
Magpies

Also by Judith Flanders

A Circle of Sisters: Alice Kipling, Georgiana Burne-Jones,
Agnes Poynter, and Louisa Baldwin

The Victorian House: Domestic Life from Childbirth to Deathbed

Consuming Passions: Leisure and Pleasure in Victorian Britain

The Invention of Murder: How the Victorians Revelled
in Death and Detection and Created Modern Crime

The Victorian City: Everyday Life in Dickens' London

A
Murder
of
Magpies

Judith
Flanders

Minotaur Books
A Thomas Dunne Book
New York

A THOMAS DUNNE BOOK FOR MINOTAUR BOOKS.
An imprint of St. Martin's Publishing Group.

A MURDER OF MAGPIES. Copyright © 2014 by Judith Flanders. All rights reserved. Printed in the United States of America. For information, address St. Martin's Press, 175 Fifth Avenue, New York, N.Y. 10010.

www.thomasdunnebooks.com
www.minotaurbooks.com

Library of Congress Cataloging-in-Publication Data

Flanders, Judith.
 A murder of magpies / Judith Flanders.—First U.S. edition.
     p.   cm.
 ISBN 978-1-250-05645-0 (hardcover)
 ISBN 978-1-4668-6028-5 (e-book)
 1. Women detectives—Fiction.   2. Book editors—Fiction.
 3. Women authors—Fiction.   I. Title.
 PR6106.L365M87   2015
 823'.92—dc23

                                                    2014034042

Minotaur books may be purchased for educational, business, or promotional use. For information on bulk purchases, please contact the Macmillan Corporate and Premium Sales Department at 1-800-221-7945, extension 5442, or write to specialmarkets@macmillan.com.

First published in Great Britain as *Writers' Block* by Allison & Busby

First U.S. Edition: February 2015

10 9 8 7 6 5 4 3 2 1

For David,
without whom . . .

A
Murder
of
Magpies

O h, just kill me now!" I didn't shriek that out loud, just clenched my teeth more tightly. It was eight thirty, and already the day couldn't get much worse. I'm always at my desk by eight, not because I'm so wonderful, although I am, but because it's the only time of day when no one asks me anything, when I can actually get on with some work, instead of solving other people's problems.

Being a middle-aged, middling-ly successful editor has a downside that no one tells you about when you're starting off. Publishing offices are run by middle-aged women like me. We will never be stars, but instead know dull things like how books are put together. We know how to find reliable proofreaders, what was done on that three-for-two promotion in 2010 and why it failed miserably, and even how to sweet-talk a recalcitrant designer into designing our book jackets instead of tweeting clips of his cat being adorable.

And so people ask you questions. They ask you all day. They

text in meetings. They grab you in the corridor. They stop you in the street on your way to lunch. I'm only surprised that no one has followed me into the loo. Yet.

Luckily, most publishing people are not early risers, and from eight until at least nine thirty, often ten, the place looks like the *Mary Celeste,* and I get through all those jobs that need complete concentration and yet are completely boring—checking jackets (remember the time some squiffy copywriter thought that *The Count of Monte Cristo* was *The Count of Monte Carlo?)* or reading the stuff the marketing department wants to send out (I know they can't spell. It's just always a shock to find they can't cut-and-paste, either). In fact, on a good morning, I should be deeply aggravated by the time my assistant of the week staggers in.

Miranda was the current one, and to be fair to her, she's lasted three months. Before her was Amanda. Then Melanie. Then—well, lots more Amandas and Melanies. Publishing from the outside is so glamorous they arrive in droves. Then they discover that it's just office work, and that I don't spend my days swanning around the Wolseley taking TV presenters for three-hour lunches to discuss their autobiographies. Worse, they discover that I'm *glad* I'm not swanning around the Wolseley taking TV presenters for etc. etc. So they move on, either to the publicity department (more parties), or to the star editors (more everything).

Miranda is impressive. She has mastered such essential skills as getting the right address on the right mailing of proofs. (I know, but the last Amanda looked at me like I murdered kittens when I suggested she give it a try.) She likes reading, not something that always happens. And, bless her tidy little heart, she's a neatness freak, and files everything almost before I've put it down. It's true, she never shows up before ten, and her retro neo-Goth makeup makes some of my authors pause, but it's a small price to pay for someone who not only knows that M comes before N, but actually does something about it.

She wouldn't be in for another hour and a half, though, and my jaw was already clenched tight. My dentist tells me that I ought to have one of those contraptions that you wear to bed, to stop you grinding your teeth. I don't have the heart to tell him it's the daytime that does it for me. Today's gem was lurking for me first thing, a voice-mail message from Breda, left last night after I went home, saying in a faux cheerful voice that she hoped I liked the new book, and when was she going to hear from me?

Good question. Because I hated the new book. David, the editor-in-chief and my boss, hated the new book. The publicity department was frankly appalled by the new book. None of us, in fact, knew what to do about the new book, which was so embarrassing a hot wave of shame washed over me every time I thought about it, which I did as little as possible.

Breda McManus was one of our star authors, and my starriest author. Regular as clockwork, every other January for the last twelve years, she had delivered a nice fat slab of a manuscript, filled with middle-class girls growing into middle-class women, overcoming middle-class problems on the way. We published them in September, ready for the Christmas market, and they paid my salary, many times over.

They did well because Breda was exactly the kind of women she wrote about. She was a secretary in a solicitor's office in

Galway and decided to write in her spare time. She now lived in a Georgian house with her husband, her children were grown, and she had decided that instead of redecorating the house she was going to redecorate her style. I felt exactly like one of those people on a makeover program where they walk in and have to pretend to *adore* the fact that the walls have been covered with aluminum foil.

Because Breda delivered a chick-lit novel.

Not only was chick lit well past its sell-by date, so was Breda's connection to twenty-year-olds. Hell, her children were in their forties. The damn thing was supposedly set in a poly (she hadn't noticed they were turned into universities decades ago), but it was more like a school story. The characters didn't quite have crushes on their teachers, and get up to "japes" in "rec," but it was awfully close.

Lots of readers (including most of my colleagues) despise Breda's books at the best of times. They love the literary fiction that we publish, and think that my sort of book is beneath contempt. I love literary fiction, too, but I also love what are called, usually dismissively, "women's reads." The fact that our literary fiction list has never paid its way, in the entire twenty-eight years of its life, is something we tactfully never mention. Instead the hip twenty-year-old *du jour* gets a huge publicity campaign, and once in forty or fifty writers we strike it lucky. In the meantime, Timmins & Ross makes its money every year on women like Breda.

Until now. So instead of reading proofs, checking marketing and publicity copy, and going through the schedules before our weekly progress meeting, I was on my fifth cup of coffee, which was something of a miracle when you consider how tightly my teeth were clenched.

I smelled french fries, but it couldn't, surely, be ten o'clock already. Then I heard Miranda's computer hum in the space outside my office where all the assistants are shoved in like battery hens. It *was* ten o'clock, and Miranda had evidently been out late the night before—the french fries and a Coke are her hangover cure. I collected the minutes for the meeting and headed out, whispering a tiny hello to Miranda, whose eyes were closed against the glare of her computer screen.

I hadn't gone ten feet when her phone rang, and, wincing, she called after me, "Sam, there's a Jacob Field in reception for you."

"Field? For me? Are you sure?" She stared at me. On hangover days she had the energy to say everything only once. I didn't know anyone named Jacob Field, and I don't make appointments on Tuesday mornings because we always have a meeting then, from ten o'clock until everyone is too bored to go on—usually lunchtime. "I'll go past reception—will you call David and tell him I'll be a few minutes late?" It was probably a friend of a friend, or someone who'd got my name somehow and was trying to flog a manuscript, no doubt about how his mother had abused him, or proving that his great-great-grandfather was Jack the Ripper. We don't have to deal with real live members of the public often, but every now and again one sneaks under the radar. It wouldn't take me long to get rid of him.

I walked briskly in to reception, smiling with my teeth bared. "Mr. Field? How can I help you?"

He was a surprise. No scruffy manuscript, no lost-dog look.

Instead he was conservatively dressed, in student-y sort of way, a short, dark, stocky man in his early forties. He looked, in fact, like a publisher. I hesitated. Maybe he was an ex-colleague, and I was supposed to remember him? I looked again. Well-cut brown hair, nice brown eyes. In fact, generally just nice-looking, although it would have been difficult to put a finger on why.

"Inspector Field."

I was confused. What did he inspect? Drains? Schools? Oh God, not a novel about a schools inspector.

He must have seen that I'd missed a few steps, so he spoke kindly and gently, as one does to the hard-of-thinking. "Inspector Field. CID."

Now I was totally lost.

He went on gamely, although he had realized he was going to get no help from me, as I was too dim-witted to know how to breathe without help. "Can we go somewhere to talk?"

He was right. Whatever he wanted, our reception area was no place to talk. "Area" was really a polite fiction. It was a desk stuck in a niche carved out of the corridor, and as most of my colleagues were only now arriving, dozens of people were pushing past us, reaching over us to collect parcels left overnight, calling back and forth to one another.

I motioned him up the stairs, signaling confusion at Bernadette, the receptionist, whose raised eyebrows signaled in return that this was more interesting than usual.

Once back in my office I gestured to a chair and waited. He took his time, looking at the piles of manuscripts, the acres of files, the almost obsessively empty desk surface, and the absence of anything decorative at all: a blank white space.

He sighed, as though I'd requested the meeting, and this was the last place he wanted to be. When he finally spoke, his voice was as abrupt as his manner. "Ms. Clair, can you tell me if you were expecting any parcels that have failed to appear?"

I mulled this gently for a moment. "Can I tell you about something that hasn't happened?" All right, I was being slow on the uptake. "I'm sorry," I said insincerely, "but could you tell me what we're talking about? And why?" I tried to find a way out. "I'm in the middle of a very busy morning. I should be in a meeting right now." His eyes narrowed at my very overt desire to avoid the meeting I was in, with him, and I softened my slightly schoolteacher-ish tone. "I'm really not sure who you are or why you want to talk to me."

He shrugged, but now he was apologetic, not dismissive. "I'm investigating a car accident."

That was no help. "An accident? CID? I don't know anything about the workings of the police, but it seems, well, an over-reaction?"

He nodded. I wasn't the first person to say that to him today, and his earlier snappish tone was explained: I wouldn't be the last. I gave him that complicated shrug-hand-roll that says, *Sorry your day is crap, but this is really nothing to do with me, now is it?* He seemed to translate it without difficulty. "It's an unusual hit-and-run." He went on, as if slightly surprised himself that he was telling me this. "There was an accident on the Hammersmith flyover, early yesterday morning. A courier was hit by a van that didn't stop. It was wet and it looks like a straightforward hit-and-run, except that there were no parcels on his bike, and his list of deliveries for the day had vanished, too. Maybe the material

7

vanished before the accident. Or maybe someone stole it after-ward—no one saw it."

"What does the courier say?"

"He doesn't. He's dead."

I digested this in silence. Then, "How do I come into the pic-ture?"

"The list and deliveries vanished, but his office had a copy of his schedule. You were on it."

"Who was the parcel from?"

"A mail shop. Without a tracking number or an order refer-ence, they can't tell us who sent it. They have a few thousand items going through every day." He clicked his pen. To business. "I realize this is a nuisance, but we'll have to ask you to list everything that you are expecting."

I gave a snort. "Expecting? Lists? Inspector, this is publishing. Schedules are—" I searched for the word. "They're what we would like to believe might happen." I could see he wasn't following. "I have, I don't know, a hundred, a hundred and fifty authors with contracts that I look after. Some are due to deliver now, but in my business 'now' means . . ." I tried to think how to ex-plain it. "Have you ever watched when parents call their chil-dren in a playground? And the children shout 'Coming!' and keep on doing whatever they were doing before?" I widened my eyes and whispered, "Authors in the making!" He smiled, which was an improvement, but I could see he didn't think I was mak-ing a serious point. "Really. Most authors think that if they've delivered a manuscript within their lifetime it meets the legal definition of 'on schedule.'"

His lips quirked, but what I was saying was also annoying him.

He wanted boxes to tick. *Don't we all, Sunshine*, I told him. But only in my head. Outwardly I tried to look sympathetic and helpful, not merely curious and simultaneously wanting him to go away so I could get to my meeting. I made a helpless gesture. "I don't know how to think about this—you're asking me to tell you what hasn't happened."

He jotted something in his notebook. Thank God, one box ticked, at least. "If you think of anything, will you ring me, please?"

He gave me a card, I pointed him in the right direction down the rabbit warren of corridors and headed off to the meeting room.

As I slipped into my seat, murmuring an apology for my lateness, Ben was saying, "This is going to be really mega."

If anything could have pushed a meeting with a detective out of my mind, it was Ben being mega. I hastily looked down at the minutes, because like Pavlov's dog, all he had to do was say the word and I was ready. But the dogs only drooled when Pavlov rang his bell. I was worried that one more time and I'd roll up my minutes and assault him with them, all the while shrieking "The word is big, you little toad. Big!" As you may be able to tell, Ben and I already have problems. Ben is twenty-six, and this is his first job. He is small, weedy, and terribly, terribly serious about his work. *His*. Not anyone else's. He despises everyone else's. He has, however, produced our only literary fiction in the last two years that has sold over five thousand copies, so people listen to him. Which is a pity, since he doesn't really have anything to say.

I've made an effort with him, truly I have. When he arrived, fresh-faced and eager-beaver-ish, straight down from Oxford, I took him out to lunch. I nearly drowned in my soup as I dozed off while he told me in detail about his life to that point. Even someone as self-absorbed as Ben noticed I was bored, although naturally he didn't think it was anything to do with him. We didn't repeat the lunch.

He is a good reader, and he spots trends, but everything for him is mega. Ben has never bought a book because he thought it would be a nice steady seller. His books either fail miserably (often), or they earn enough to be partly worth the ridiculous advances he pays (sometimes). Ben has major-league Big Dick Syndrome—if a book doesn't cost several times the GDP of many third-world countries, then he doesn't think it can be worth anything.

"Sam?"

I looked fixedly at the minutes, as though still trying to find my place. "Yes, I see your point." Translation: *No, I don't.* "The proposal was quite interesting." Translation: *It was barely three pages long, one entire page of which was about the author. Who was still at school.* "But shouldn't we ask to see a sample chapter?" Translation: *We don't know if the child can write.*

An exasperated sound from Ben. "Look, Sam, there is major interest in this, and we've only got this far because his agent likes me."

Of course the agent likes him. Ben pays top dollar for very little on paper. I'd like him, too, in those circumstances. I don't know why I bother. We're going to buy this book, and I'm going to have to be nice to the little shit, and pretend I like his novel whether I do or not. Then it will fail and the next little shit will be along. Like buses. I stared at the wall behind Ben. I couldn't look at him. I wasn't sure I could look at the wall much longer, either. It was gray and dingy and peeling. Over the years people had pinned up notices and pulled them down again. Dozens of bits of Sellotape were all that remained, gradually yellowing and growing old. I felt the same. Our offices in general were not particularly attractive, but the meeting room was the worst. It was a small partitioned area of what had once been a bigger room. The furniture was all 1960s style, and it must have been described as "fun" or "cheerful" in the furniture catalogue, but in reality orange-molded plastic is never a good look. Orange-molded plastic that had half a century of dirt covering it didn't bear thinking about. I continued to stare at the wall, otherwise I'd have to look at Ben.

A phone was nudged to where I could see the screen without moving my head, and a finger tapped at it to get my attention. Sandra, the publicity director, and one of my closest friends in-house. I let my eyes float down. *Wnkr*, said the text. It wasn't going to change anything, but it made me feel better. I considered. Probably about half the people around the table—maybe eight or ten—thought the same as I did, either about Ben himself, or this book in particular. Of those, possibly four or five had been paying attention, the others either openly doing e-mails or just reading on their iPads until the meeting got around to a book that directly concerned them. Three others were quietly chatting about a lunch they'd all been to, nothing to do with work, officially. But maybe it was—work in publishing is often indistinguishable from chat, and chat was what we did all day.

The two from production, who were there only to deal with schedules, weren't even doing that—even from my end of the table I could see they were playing a rousing game of hangman. And I'd lose a few more if I continued to argue, not because anyone disagreed, just because they were desperate for the meeting to end. I let my attention drift. If you can't beat 'em . . .

"Well," said David brightly. "If we're all agreed."

I woke out of my dream. "Please. We really do need to talk about Breda." I knew I sounded sad and desperate, but that's only because I was. We did need to talk about Breda, but there wasn't anything to say. If we refused this book, she'd go to another publisher; if we published it and it got the reaction it deserved, she would take her next book elsewhere, too, despite the relationship I'd nurtured for over a decade.

Everyone looked embarrassed, and got up to go, as though I hadn't said anything at all.

So we had to buy this book, and it was up to me to turn it into something that wouldn't make her a laughingstock. A success would be beyond me, but maybe I could engineer a quiet, genteel sort of failure.

Miranda had turned up my heater before I came back, which meant she was beginning to recover. Timmins & Ross is in four Georgian houses, which have been knocked together into one highly confusing interior in a turning just off Great Russell Street, behind the British Museum. They are lovely houses from the outside, but the inside has not seen much work done to them in the last century. They *do* have plumbing, it's true, but they don't have central heating, and the beautiful sash windows let in gales even in the summer. In winter it's often warmer outside.

My office is a partitioned bit of what must have once been a drawing room, because it has a huge window, which is great unless you care about your extremities. If I keep an electric fan heater on full blast from eight, which officially we're not allowed to do, by noon I can usually manage with just one sweater.

Before I'd even sat down, Miranda's head was around the door. "So what was that all about?"

"What was what all about?" She's smart, but she can't possibly have known I'd fantasized about assaulting Ben with the acquisition meeting minutes.

She thought I was stonewalling, and wasn't going to have it. "The police?" she nudged.

My eyes popped wide. "Good lord, I'd forgotten." I gestured her in. I outlined the conversation and asked her to check delivery dates for both new manuscripts, even though most came electronically, and proofs, which didn't. She nodded, but her mind wasn't on it. "A hit-and-run? Really?"

"That's what I said. But maybe that's the way the police work. God knows, he didn't believe me when I told him how publishing worked."

I shrugged and turned to my desk. And then swore comprehensively when I saw my e-mail was down. Already on her way back to her desk, Miranda called through the wall that it was the entire company, so it should be fixed relatively quickly. Meanwhile my voice mail was stuffed, in only an hour. Breda. Breda's agent. Marketing, asking why I hadn't approved copy they'd sent down a whole ten minutes earlier. Two copy editors who weren't going to make their deadlines. A proofreader touting for work. My mother. And Kit, three times.

Kit Lovell is one of my favorite authors. He is a fashion journalist, he is efficient, he is professional, he meets his deadlines, and he is the best gossip on the planet. I don't usually do his sort of book—quick-and-dirty low-downs on the rich and famous—but he came to me through a friend, and he's been a constant delight. But it was unlike him to keep calling. If he had got some really hot gossip, he'd leave a message and then I wouldn't be able reach him because he would be busy calling the immediate world while it was still fresh. Maybe that's why we'd become friends so quickly—like publishers, Kit lived off chatter.

I had his latest manuscript, which his typist e-mailed to me two weeks earlier—Kit was above such mundanities as computers—and I'd already told him how much I loved it, so it couldn't be that. Whatever it was, he took precedence over my mother, and he absolutely took precedence over Breda that week. I put the phone on automatic redial, hoping his gossip wasn't so hot that it took him the whole morning to work through his contacts list.

In the meantime, I had to start preparing his book. It didn't need much editing from me—Kit's work never did—but like all of his books it would have to go to a libel lawyer before we sent it out for copyediting. It was not that Kit was reckless, it was just a by-product of the kind of books he wrote. Most people in business have things that they don't want the world to know, even if they've never so much as crossed the road against the lights. People in the fashion business, which is built entirely on appearances, *really* don't want the world to know how they got to where they were. What Kit supplies is the true story, which as he says sweepingly, "everyone" knows. But the "everyone" of the fashion business, and the "everyone" who reads a Sunday newspaper, where Kit's books usually get serialized, are not the same thing, and his subjects often objected. Strenuously. With lawyers.

The three rules of checking for libel are short and sweet. Is the reported incident true? Can we prove it? Then the most important one: Can the subject afford to sue, whether it's true or not? With fashion houses owned by multinationals, the answer to the questions were yes, yes, and *yes*. So far as I could see, taking a dispassionate look at it, our troubles with this book began on the title page. Kit had called his biography *The Gilded Life and Tarnished Death of Rodrigo Alemán*. Alemán was Spain's most prominent (only?) international star on the fashion scene. He had been brought in to put the ailing French couture house of Vernet back on its feet after Jules Vernet's retirement. And he did, although in a way that probably hastened Vernet's death—hip-hop and trance at the shows, ads featuring semi-naked models in soft-core pornographic poses. He'd created a diffusion range, with lower-priced clothes than the standard prêt-à-porter, and then began opening boutiques across the world to sell them in.

Most of this was no different from any other fashion house, but everything Alemán did was brasher, brighter, bolder—and bigger. There were questions about how the gigantic warehouses he called boutiques managed to survive, given that most days you could shoot a cannon off in any one of them without risking harm to a paying customer. His lavish parties always got into the glossy magazines, but the actress-model-whatevers all borrowed his dresses, they didn't buy them. And short of hookers, who couldn't afford them, it wasn't clear to anyone who would want to.

All fashion stories are stories of money and excess. And money and fame. And money. And, in this case, violent death.

I tried Kit one last time. Still busy. Instead of gossiping I took the manuscript along the hall to David's office. David Snaith is our editor-in-chief, so he has an office that isn't a partitioned bit, but is what must have once been a morning room: a good-sized, east-facing room. Nothing could look less like a social environment than its present incarnation, however. David has kept every single piece of paper that has ever crossed his desk, and most of them are not filed, but thrown into trays, to be dealt with at some mystical "later" time. When the tray is filled, and starts to overflow, he just slings it onto a shelf where it molders gently for the next few years, with additional trays thrown on top as they fill up in turn. When they all fall over David nudges them back into a heap with his foot as he walks past, but that's the only attention they ever get. The books and spilled papers lie in heaps, and you have to walk through the snowdrifts of memos. If you stick to the little cleared pathways, and the one empty chair, you're fine. If more than one person comes in for a meeting, they are given a spare chair by David's assistant. It is much easier to carry one in than to try and excavate the ones that are already there, buried.

I tried not to get depressed when I sat down. David and I are temperamentally opposed, and it is hard for us to communicate. He has been at Timmins & Ross for nearly thirty years, ever since he left university, working his way up to editor-in-chief, which he had achieved about a decade before. He is going to stay here for the rest of his life, and they will have to carry him out feet first, probably in the same bin liners the old papers are taken away in.

I shook myself. These kind of thoughts were not helpful in getting him onside. David is so cautious, anything out of the ordinary has to be approached full-frontally, otherwise he will duck and run, pretending it isn't there.

"It's about Kit's book," I said baldly. "We are going to have to give this more than our usual once-over."

"Is it so bad?" David already looked hunted.

"It's not bad. In fact, it's terrific. It's just that all the fun stuff, the stuff everyone will want to read—and the stuff newspapers will pay big money for—is exactly what everyone concerned wants to keep hidden."

"But surely no one denies Alemán was murdered? Isn't that why we bought the book?"

"No one denies it. Except his family. Vernet. Oh, and the police. Apart from them, everyone, as you say, knows it was murder."

"Do they think it was an accident? How is that possible?"

"It isn't. They don't. They just *want* it to be one. And they think if they say so loud enough, and often enough, gradually we'll forget what really did happen."

"So what did really happen? I'm not much for fashion news. I read the proposal, but that was last year. I can't remember them all."

I tried not to look impatient. "David, this was all over the front pages for weeks. Cut down to the basics, Alemán was coming home from a club in a Paris suburb at five o'clock one morning when a car screeched out of a turning, drove up onto the pavement, hit him hard enough that his body flew over the top and bounced off the windscreen, at which point the driver backed up and ran over it again. Apparently a belt-and-braces type of killer."

"There were witnesses?"

"Five. And two were bodyguards, so they were sober. But somehow their first statements vanished, and once the Vernet lawyers got there, they saw, I believe, a little old lady who was confused about which was the brake pedal and which the accelerator. Although she was clever enough to drive a car with fake license plates, and then vanish."

"How can anyone believe that?"

"No one does. But as far as Vernet and Alemán's family is concerned, that was the inquest verdict, and the papers are too scared of being sued to print anything else."

"Why aren't we too scared, then?" David was looking at me like a puppy that's just made a mess in the house, but hopes that if he looks cute enough, it could be overlooked. David wasn't cute enough.

"Kit has done some extraordinary research: early police reports, witness statements that were suppressed, witnesses who were mysteriously never contacted by the police."

"Bottom line, what's he saying?"

"Organized crime. It's not phrased that way, naturally. He says there is a dodgy bank and companies laundering money through Vernet. Not that anyone at Vernet knew about it. Maybe Alemán didn't, either. Or didn't want to. But it's what kept the company afloat. That's how the boutiques survived without customers. Everyone knew. Only no one did."

"Does Kit have enough for us to publish safely?"

"More than enough. Names, dates, copies of invoices for goods never supplied—never even manufactured—with corresponding bank statements for cash received. *Lots* of cash received. Millions every month."

"How did Kit get it all?"

"I haven't asked and I don't intend to. He assures me he has broken no laws, and I believe him. Everything else is for him and the lawyers to sort out."

David looked pained. "Is there something about you that just magnetically attracts trouble?"

I bristled. "This isn't trouble. It just needs a legal read."

If I could go back now and erase the dumbest thing I've ever said in my whole life, it would be those two sentences.

2

By six o'clock I'd had it. Our e-mail was still down, despite everyone screaming at IT every five minutes. Possibly it was still down *because* everyone was screaming at IT every five minutes. Either way, we had been reduced to trying to read contracts and check jacket copy on our phones, and we were all fed up. There was a launch party for the newest wunderkind's novel, but I couldn't face slogging down to the Aquarium, this year's hip place for parties, to drink warm white wine and see the same people I'd just left in the office. I packed it in and headed for home.

One of the perks of my job is a car, but it's not something I take advantage of, mainly because I don't drive. I know from being driven that you don't actually get anywhere in London any faster by car. It's more pleasant, because you're insulated from people, you can have Radio 3 on instead of listening to the thirty-six different beats leaking out from the earphones of a carriage-worth of plugged-in commuters, it gives you a little bubble to decompress in at the end of the day. But you don't save time.

This, at least, is what I say when people ask. In reality, I *can* drive, I just *don't*. I am, probably, the worst driver on the planet. When I was growing up in Canada I assumed, like all North American children, that the day after I turned sixteen I would take driving lessons, and four weeks later, voilà, the driving fairy would tap me with her wand. And, up to a point, that is what happened. Well, not the fairy bit, but everything else. I took lessons, I got a license. Then my first day out, I sideswiped a parked car. Don't worry, everyone said, we all do that. So I went out again. A car hit me. That was it. I figured a third time someone would get killed, and it would probably be me. I didn't drive for years, until a holiday in the States made it a necessity. My friends took me around the first day, showing me the layout of the town. I hit a FedEx van.

My so-called friends claim that it was a truck, and that I knocked it into a ditch. This is a vicious lie. It was a van, and I only dinged it, and I shall maintain this to my dying day. But whatever it was, and whatever I did to it, that was the end of my driving career. Enough. Some things I'm good at, some things I'm not. I can live with that, and in London it isn't really crucial. I'm happy enough on public transport most days, and if I'm late or tired or fed up I get a cab. I live close enough to the center of town for it to be affordable.

It was raining when I left the office, the kind of thin, persistent drizzle that London specializes in in February, despite the fact that it had been March for several weeks. It seemed set to continue this way well into April. I turned up my collar, shifted my bookbag onto my shoulder and made a run for the Tube station.

There weren't any seats, of course. I considered myself lucky to find a square inch of space near the plexiglass divider by the door. I braced myself against it, my arms crossed tight across my body to hang on to my bag and not take up more than my fair share of space in this oversized sardine tin. There was no space to hold a book in front of me, but by craning my neck I could read over the shoulder of the woman sitting on the other side of the divider. She had that morning's *Daily Mail*, so it was a story on the idiocies of the royal family, and how to lose ten pounds in ten minutes. Then she turned the page, and a picture of a horribly mangled motorbike was spread across two pages, with a standard hyperbolic headline: THE WORST ACCIDENT BLACKSPOT IN BRITAIN? It was only when I read down the page that I realized this was the accident Inspector Field had been investigating. I turned quickly away, straight into the armpit a man bopping unselfconsciously to his earphones. Still, better than looking at the twisted metal. I resolutely stayed that way until I was finally extruded from the train at my station.

I'd moved to the flat I live in now when I first came to London, nearly twenty years ago. It was a flat share with three friends from university, the ground floor of a fairly dilapidated house in a fairly dilapidated bit of London not too far (not nearly far enough) from Camden market. Gradually the others had all moved on and out—new partners with flats of their own, marriage and children, jobs in other parts of the country—and five years ago I had bought the flat as a sitting tenant. With the others gone, over the years I'd knocked down walls, restored the floorboards, ripped out the old kitchen and bathroom, turning it from a scruffy student makeshift into a wonderfully empty, open space.

Now the flat is so much a part of me I can't imagine being any-where else. It is a quiet, white, open space, with big windows and wonderful south light pouring in for most of the day. Although I can't say that the area has improved—how can it with fifteen thousand adolescents wandering through in search of leather trousers every weekend?—it is a pleasant mix of young couples just starting out, professionals who like the slightly raffish tone, and people who were born in the area, and think gentrification is something that happens when you move to an old-age home.

Anthony and Kay Lewis, with their five-year-old son Bim, live above me, with Mr. Rudiger on the top floor. Mr. Rudiger never goes out. His daughter drops off his shopping a few times a week, and runs errands for him. In the twenty years I've lived here, I've only seen him twice: once when I needed to turn off the water in the whole building so the plumber could do some work, and I went up to warn him, the second time to discuss reroofing the house. There doesn't appear to be anything wrong with him, and he was perfectly pleasant, but he made it plain he liked being alone up there.

Anthony and Kay are different. They're both actors, and there-fore are around a lot more than most. This suits me fine, as they are happy to take parcels in for me, sort out meter readers, and water my garden when I'm away. In exchange Bim plays in my garden, and I pretend I can't hear him screaming. We enjoy each other's company without needing to be too close, which is my preference. About once every six months they come down for Sunday brunch, or to a dinner party. That's the extent of it.

I've been alone in the house for two years now. Before that Peter and I lived here together, but that had broken up messily when I got promoted. He's an academic, and he didn't like me earning more than he did. He thought I was on a glitzy media-track career—which showed how little attention he paid to what I did—and he didn't approve. At least, that was part of it. I think by the end basically we just didn't like each other very much. We didn't dislike each other. It's just that if I met him at a party and seen him the way I saw him by the end of our relationship, I wouldn't have bothered to listen to his name when he was introduced. I can't say I miss him. Sometimes on a summer Sunday I think it would be nice to have someone to go swimming with at Hampstead ponds. If that's all after a decade of living together, it's definitely time to move on. So we did.

Kay and Bim were on their way out when I arrived home. We traded smiles, and I was just putting my key in the door when she said, "You forgot to tell me about the workmen."

I turned. Bim jumped into a particularly tempting puddle and I stepped back hastily. "Workmen?"

"Yeah, you forgot to tell me. Anthony was at home this morning when they came for your key."

"Workmen? Key?"

"Bim, darling, stop that." Kay hooked her finger into Bim's hood, and looked at me doubtfully. Bim ignored her, reaching blissfully with a booted toe for the same puddle. "They said you'd told them to get the key from us. But I had it with me on my key ring and because you'd forgotten to tell me, Anthony couldn't let them in."

"What workmen?" I was sounding repetitive, but it was the only thing I could get hold of.

"I don't know what workmen—Anthony," she called upstairs

as we went into the hall, "who were the workmen?" She didn't wait for an answer, instead snapping back to me, confused. "If you don't know, who were they?"

"I don't know. But no one I know."

After dinner I tried Kit again—not work this time, just to chat. We had played telephone tag all day: He rang when I was on the phone, by the time I called him back his line was engaged again. Since he persists in refusing to learn how to use a computer, I couldn't even e-mail him, and gossip doesn't really carry via text.

Finally. "Hello!" said Kit, in a startled voice. He always answers that way—as though the phone is a wonderful toy that will bring him endless good things. As of course it will, for someone who lives on gossip.

"It's me."

"*Well*, where have you *been?*" Kit talks in italics.

I ignored this insult to my intelligence. "What's up?"

"God, I don't even know where to begin. Alemán's family have been stirring again."

"Stirring?"

"You know, not talking directly to me—they haven't done that since I started researching—but dropping hints to people: 'I hear Kit Lovell, poor thing, has signed a big contract for this book, and isn't turning anything up,' or 'Did you hear that Kit had to go dry out at that place in California?' Basically, the full range, from I've got nothing, to I'm mad, a lush, doped to the eyeballs, or possibly all four."

"What's the harm? Basically, they know you've got the goods and they're scared. But they can't do anything about it. Can they?"

"No, of course not. Vernet can refuse me access to their shows, but not having reviews in the *Sunday News* is more damaging to Alemán's replacement, and Vernet, than it is to me. In fact, having to look at that awful boy's awful stuff would damage me more. How he got through fashion college I'll never know, although I know *exactly* how he got his job, and doesn't he hate me for that."

Kit knows everything about everyone. Sometimes I'm glad my private life is so dull, because the thought of him passing on any juicy bits, making them juicier as they do the rounds, is too terrible—and he likes me. What he does to people he doesn't like doesn't bear thinking about.

"Ki-it." It's not easy to keep him focused. "They can't do anything, Vernet are doing themselves more harm than they're doing you. What's the problem?"

"Someone's been in my house."

"What? What do you mean? You were burgled?"

"No, that would be straightforward. Someone's been here, but nothing is missing. You know how when you live alone a place just has a smell, almost an aura?"

I'd have disputed this flight of fancy, if he weren't also right.

"I came in, and it was different. I thought I was being imaginative, but I looked around, and the place had been searched. Tidily, but searched all the same. A drawer I never shut entirely, because the handle is loose, was closed. The cushions were plumped up, the way I always do them, but two of them were reversed, which I wouldn't do. Things that no one who isn't tidy would notice, or no one who lives with someone else. But I'm tidy and alone."

I'm the same. When you live by yourself you have an unconscious expectation of how things will be. When that expectation is disrupted it's very noticeable.

"Did you call the police?"

"Oooh, what a *splendid* idea." He slid into a falsetto. "'Officer, someone broke into my house, leaving no visible signs, turned all my cushions over and *pouf*! Vanished.' Sam, I'm camper than a row of pink tents. How seriously do you think they'll take my cushion trauma?"

Camper than an entire Boy Scouts' jamboree, actually. "Hmm. But even if they don't take it seriously, at least there'll be a record if you are burgled later."

"Which they then won't take seriously because I'm the queen with the chintz fixation."

"All right, all right. Was anything taken?"

"No, but there's nothing here. I'm camp, not a fool. All the notes for the book are at my solicitor's."

"Any way of finding out who your sources are from a phone book? Old phone bills?"

"My phone book was with me, and you know I never keep bills."

I do. I've never met anyone like Kit. He claims never to have opened a bill since he left university. His bank pays them, and he isn't interested in finding out if he's being overcharged, or someone is racking up bills on a stolen card number. I'm fascinated, but he's not bankrupt yet, so I guess it works for him.

"I don't understand. Do you think his family did this? Would they even know how?"

"No, not the family. But don't forget that Vernet is plenty worried—money-laundering allegations will not exactly float their corporate overlords' boat. And the police who allowed themselves to agree that it was an accident aren't going to be thrilled."

"You think the *police* broke in?"

"Grow up, Sam, would you? What do you think, that the police spend their shifts saying 'Evening all' and helping old ladies across the street? The French police covered up a murder. The people involved in the cover-up probably don't even know why, but it's not the kind of thing they want the world to know. And the people actually profiting from the system won't be much happier. Even if they've lost their front man, the method was good, it worked—they don't want that exposed."

I paused.

"What are you thinking about?" he asked testily. "You know I'm right."

"I'm sure you are." I was pacific. "It's just—this sounds so melodramatic, but then so does burglary by the police, and money laundering, and—" I was babbling. I pulled myself together. "A CID inspector came to T and R this morning."

"He did? What for?"

In passing, I longed to challenge Kit's automatic assumption that the visitor had been a man, but he had been, and anyway this was not the time. "He was investigating the death of a motorcycle courier. A hit-and-run, except all of his deliveries were gone. I was on his schedule. I told him I had no way of knowing who might be sending me something, but now the hard copy of your manuscript seems a likely candidate."

There was a silence. Then, "It sounds possible, doesn't it."

"Will you ask your typist to let me have the details of what she sent, and when? I'll pass it along."

He made noises that indicated he was going through his phone book to get her number.

"In the meantime, the burglary: Where does this leave you?"

"Us, honey, us. We need to get this book out fast. Once it's published, the horse has bolted, there's no point in closing the stable door."

"Us?" I squeaked. I sounded like Kit talking to the police, but my falsetto was involuntary. "What do you mean, 'us'?"

"Whoever it is wants to stop publication. I don't think they care how. If they can find out who my sources are, and get them to recant, that will be the best way, because it will kill off the rumors. If they can't, and can just frighten me—or you—into abandoning publication, that would be fine, too."

"Kit, wait a minute. I do women's fiction. I do the occasional frock book with you, and the odd biography. This is not what I'm used to."

"Well," he said, sounding grim and not at all amusing now, "you'd better *get* used to it."

3

I was lying in wait for Miranda the next morning. I was anxious and unhappy, and I didn't see why I shouldn't spread that around. Miranda eventually came tripping in at twenty past ten, and although I try not to sound like her mother, this time I couldn't stop myself.

"Is that new?"

She smiled radiantly and flicked the fifth piercing in her ear, which had a silver skull hanging from it. "Good, isn't it?"

I moved on hastily. "Do you want to get your hands dirty with a little editorial work?"

Her radiant smile turned into a beam. Assistants spend most of their lives checking proofs and keying in schedules.

"Here's Breda's new book." I ignored her instinctive recoil. "Now, Breda hasn't been twenty in a long time. Maybe she never was. The evidence isn't in yet. I want you to go through the manuscript and suggest amendments for everything you think is inappropriate for her characters. Change the places that they go to to the kind of places girls that age would go to; fix the language to bear some resemblance to the way people that age actually talk; make the clothes right—basically, make it plausible.

"If it's at all possible, work on the title, too. We really can't publish a book called *Toujours Twenty-one*. Hell, I can't even bring myself to say it in public." I can't, either. That's why I think about it as "Breda's book." If I had to say *Toujours Twenty-one* too often, I'd come out in a rash.

Miranda was less radiant, but still hopeful. "You want me to do a serious edit?"

"Yep. Then I'll go out to Galway to see her, pass off everything you've done as my own work, while at the same time subliminally suggesting that these were all ideas she'd had and discarded. Your name won't be anywhere near this as far as she's concerned—she can't ever know that—but I'll see that you get the credit here."

She looked at the manuscript. "It might be more helpful to my career if no one knows."

"It just might at that. Do fifty pages and let's talk it through."

I left her poking at the pile of paper with a black-polished fingernail and went to call Breda. "Sorry I've been so long, but you know what it's like. . . ." She didn't, but wouldn't say so. "I've read the manuscript, and I love it." I crossed my eyes and stuck my tongue out. There's nothing like a little editorial gravitas. I went on, in my perkiest aren't-we-all-having-fun voice. "I thought, since it's a departure for both of us, maybe instead of sending you my notes, I should come out to Galway and we can go over things at a more leisurely pace."

"You think that's necessary." It wasn't a question.

I held on to the perky singsong. "Not necessary, but a nice excuse for me to get out of the office and come and see you." Breda is much too polite to say that she might not want a visit. "I've got a lot on here, and even though the manuscript won't take me any time—" well, it wouldn't take *me* any time—"I'm not going to be able to get away for about ten days. The plus is, I'll then have some jacket artwork for you to look at, too." I sounded like a kindergarten teacher promising extra biscuits if the little bastards would only lie down for nap time.

Breda was dubious but civil, as I'd known she would be, and assured me with beguiling insincerity that she'd love to have me stay for a few days. We settled on a date at the end of the following week and I hung up. Miranda didn't have much breathing space, but Breda's new book was not exactly the sort of thing you wanted to linger over. I'd try to clear some time for her, so she could get a decent run at it.

I spent the rest of the day with routine tasks—a pleasure after the last couple of days. I also e-mailed Robert Marks at Selden's, the solicitors Timmins & Ross used, to outline the questions Kit's book threw up. I explained the situation, the manuscript, and Kit's phone call last night. At least Kit was right about one thing. The phone rang almost before I'd hit SEND.

"His *cushions?*"

"Look, I know you've never looked at your sofa in your life—I'm sure you can't tell me what color it is."

There was an embarrassed silence.

"See? Your wife does that, and your children and their friends spend so much time sprawled all over it that you wouldn't know if the cushions had been plumped that morning or even that century. But it's not like that if you live alone."

Now the silence was a pitying one, thinking about sad people like me and Kit who didn't live in Virginia Water, have a wife to buy our sofas, and a large family to sit on them.

"You'll have to trust me on this, Robert, truly. Kit could tell. He wasn't imagining things."

"Even if he wasn't." He didn't want to deal with people who knew about sofa cushions. That's why he'd gone into the law, for God's sake. "Even if he wasn't, I don't understand why we're discussing this. If the book's a problem, make it go away—reject it, or whatever it is you do, for not being good enough."

"We could, of course," I said, keeping a hold on my temper, but only just. "We would then have to pay Kit the full amount of the advance—there are no contractual grounds to cancel, as he has plenty of evidence to counter any libel claims. We knew from the beginning it would present problems, and the contract reflects that. He has a good agent, so we won't get away with just saying it's bad, we'd have to say why, and we can't do that because it is every bit as good as the four books of his we have already published perfectly successfully."

"Really, who can be the judge of that?"

"His agent. Who will never sell us another book. And she and her company represent nearly ten percent of the authors on our list." I really didn't want this man's views on literature. I was beginning to think I didn't even want his views on the law. "On top of that, the newspapers are already circling, hoping for a serialization deal, which will be huge. Serial has been terrible

recently, profits are down, our standard bestseller"—Breda—
"isn't delivering this year. Do you want me to have to tell the
board we're throwing this kind of money away on your advice?"

Robert didn't. I didn't, either. Neither would David. So we were
going to be brave because we were all too cowardly to be anything else.

Kit and I were meeting for lunch to discuss marketing and publicity. Sandra, the publicist who has looked after Kit's books, had
drawn up some preliminary plans and wanted to see what he
would do and what he wouldn't. Kit wasn't difficult, it was just
that as a fashion journalist he was away an awful lot—two weeks
of prêt-à-porter and two weeks of couture shows every year in
Paris; then Milan, men's and women's, one week each; and New
York, another week.

It's hard to believe I even know about this. My interest in
clothes is so minimal I have two work skirts for everyday, two
suits I think of as my "posh" suits for author meetings, parties,
and other formalities. Shirts are tiresome, as they don't wear as
well as the skirts, which I expect to have to replace only every
three years or so. But if you keep the suits and skirts to two neutral colors (very neutral: black and dark gray), then the shirts can
all be more or less anything, and it's less of a bother. My theory
is, I'm clean, I'm tidy. Everything else is too boring to think about.

Kit claims that I am the only woman on the planet who doesn't
look in shop windows as she walks down the street. I think it's
more to do with the kind of women he knows. We once had lunch
in the Armani shop in Knightsbridge. (Surprisingly good pasta.

I'd expected three lettuce leaves, hold the dressing, and air kisses.)
He stopped in the shop on the way out and waved a white suit
in my direction.

"This is *fabulous*."

It was. I appreciate fashion in the abstract. It just has nothing to do with me.

"Try it on."

"Me? Why?"

"What do you mean, why? To buy it. You'd look great."

"I wouldn't wear white."

Now it was his turn to be confused. "Why not?"

"Too bright."

This was gibberish to Kit. "Too bright? How can white be too
bright?"

"Kit. People will look at me."

Still gibberish. "But I *love* people looking at me." Kit is tall
and extremely dark, with an elegant lion's mane of hair artfully
coiffed to give him even more height. If you didn't register his
intense Englishness, superficially you'd think he was French. He
was at his most French then, in a charcoal-gray, exquisitely cut
suit, waving his hands in the air lavishly. But I remained immune
to his projection. I don't want people to look at me. They don't,
and they probably wouldn't even if I wore white, but basically I
like being invisible.

It's something that comes with age. When you're in your teens
everyone looks at you because who knows what troublesome teen-
agers will do. When you're in your twenties, you're potential partner material, and so even someone as ordinary looking as me gets
a certain amount of attention. Once you're in your early forties,

that's it, you've vanished. You're not old enough to warrant courtesy, you're much too old to fit into the interesting category. So no one sees you anymore. At first it's a bit startling, but after a while it's very relaxing. You can do whatever you want, because no one cares. The negative part might be "because no one cares," but the positive is the "you can do whatever you want" part.

But Kit wasn't buying into this, and he didn't give up. "They do it in gray, too."

I barely glanced in the direction he was semaphoring. "Too bright."

"Gray? How can gray be too bright?"

I began to laugh helplessly. I'm not unaware of my limitations, I even know they're ludicrous. I just don't see why I should change them. "Kit, it's too bright. It's a *bright* gray. An incredibly loud, cheerful, bright gray. Practically scarlet. Now let's just go. I'm not going to buy a suit. I'm not even going to try on a suit. I *have* a suit."

The linguist Noam Chomsky once came up with a sentence to demonstrate how you could say something completely grammatical that still had no meaning at all. His was "Colorless green ideas sleep furiously." Kit obviously thought "I have a suit" was on the same level. A suit? One? And what did that one old suit have to do with this lovely new suit?

I distracted him with a discussion of his upcoming travels—I didn't know where he was going, but he was always going somewhere, so it was a safe bet—and I managed to maneuver us out of the shop. As well as the two months of the year he spends at fashion shows—or, as he so elegantly puts it, "wasting my time looking at fucking frocks"—Kit also gives a lot of lectures and acts as a consultant to a bunch of companies. He's good, and he can't say no, a lethal combination. This was why Sandra and I were having lunch with him now, nearly nine months before publication. Pinning him down for publicity was always tricky.

We went to the Groucho Club, which I loathe but Kit likes. Kit was late, of course, but I wasn't going to hang around outside for him, and one of the Groucho's less attractive aspects— one of its many unattractive aspects—is having nowhere for waiting guests to sit. The theory, I've always assumed, is that if you're not worthy of being a member, you're not worthy, full stop. Why should they make an effort—and, worse, use up space where they might otherwise be making money—for people that they'd probably rejected?

I had, however, been there enough to know that a confident exterior goes a long way. I marched up to the signing-in book and scribbled something important looking and illegible, adding Sandra as my guest. After all, what were they going to do if they caught on, force me to join?

We sat down to wait in the bar and went through the plans Sandra was going to present. It was always fun to work on things with Sandra. Publicity is a relentless business. By thirty most people are howling to get out, which means that publicists tend to be young and therefore, by definition, inexperienced. Inexperienced at best. At worst inept. Sandra was neither. She was a veteran of hundreds of campaigns, and had kept her sanity and her perspective. She had also kept her sense of humor, and it was one of the reasons she and Kit worked so well together: She was scabrously funny. For the moment, though, we were mapping out the detail, which was dull but had to be done.

"I thought you'd said there was a complete embargo," Sandra said.

"There is. I told you. Even in-house. I hope you haven't given the manuscript to anyone."

"Of course not, but if that's the case I don't understand why you said that *Vogue* could have an advance look."

"*Vogue*? I didn't. What are you talking about? Why would they want to see it anyway, apart from vulgar curiosity, that is?"

"I had a call just before we left, from a guy named Philippe Anjou, at French *Vogue*, saying you had told him to get in touch. A smoothy with a gorgeous voice."

"Me? I've never had any contacts with *Vogue*, much less French *Vogue* and their smoothies, and I wouldn't have told them to ring you—why would I? Serial is being handled by Susie. It always is."

"I wondered about that. I thought maybe you'd met him with Kit and you were playing footsie with him—or Kit was." She looked hopeful.

I hated to stamp on a perfectly good smutty rumor, but it couldn't be helped. "It's probably one of the tabloids, trying to get their hands on an advance copy."

Sandra was silent. She would have preferred me to be having a fling with a French smoothy, but had to acknowledge that a tabloid foray was more likely. A bit depressing, when I thought about it.

"Did you print out the manuscript?" I asked.

"Yes, I always do—it's easier. Why?"

"Can you lock it away? Kit had a break-in." I told her about it, but let her assume that it was the tabloid hacks. I didn't want to be overdramatic, and in the cold light of day—well, the gloomy light of the Groucho—it did seem silly.

Sandra looked bemused. "I'll try and think what to do, but I'm not sure there's anything that locks in my office."

Come to that, neither was I. My office door didn't lock. Publishers are an honest bunch—or at least we're all aware that none of us has anything worth stealing. Whatever the case, petty pilfering has never been a problem and since manuscripts are not intrinsically valuable, and we have so many, and so many copies of each one, nothing is ever locked up, or even put away. The usual filing system with manuscripts is much like David's with everything: pile them up until they topple over. They're not exactly gold bullion. Sandra's office is particularly loaded. As well as copies of each manuscript that was being published, she had proofs, presenters, or sales folders, and finished books. And, being Sandra, all of this went back for the entire time she'd been with the company. My office is much emptier, as about every six months or so the clutter and dust irritate me into getting a bin liner and throwing out everything that has already been published.

Much emptier. Much easier to find things.

I was edgy, and I was also now cross. It was one thirty, and Kit was half an hour late, which was excessive, even for him. I wanted to sort out the publicity and get back to the office for a three-thirty meeting. I tried calling him at home, but there was no answer. There was no point in trying his mobile, as although he carried it he usually forgot to turn it on, and he doesn't know how to access his voice mail. He'd asked me to answer it a couple of weeks ago when he was driving, and I discovered he had messages going back six months, none of which he even knew were there.

The waiter came over to ask what name the bill should be in. He looked at Sandra, which was understandable. She was standard publicity issue, which meant blonde, pretty, and black-lycraed. I intervened. Sandra was used to paying for all her authors. "Lovell," I said, smiling brilliantly at him, "Kit Lovell." If Kit was going to be late, he could at least pay for it.

Sandra and I went and had lunch in the Groucho's restaurant at two, also on Kit's bill. Apart from leaving increasingly irritable messages, there really wasn't any choice. By three when he hadn't still hadn't shown up, we went back to the office.

I didn't know whether to be annoyed or worried. Kit sounds flighty, but I've always found him totally professional. He'd never have got as far as he has if he was as much a butterfly as he pretended. I figure it was a persona he had assumed when he was young, as a cover for insecurity, and now it was second nature. But he'd never stood me up before. If he is going to change his plans, which he does frequently, he always rings, or gets a message to me somehow. In fact, he usually claims that it's me who does the standing up, a charge I no longer bother to deny, because it gives him such pleasure.

So where was he? I'd called Miranda, in case he'd thought we were meeting at the office, but she'd said she'd worked at her desk on Breda's book throughout lunch, and he'd neither rung nor appeared. There wasn't much I could do. I could hardly start phoning hospitals and the police because someone's missed a meeting.

Even I, with all my mothering instincts toward my authors, know that.

Mothering. Hell, I hadn't called my mother back yesterday. My parents had divorced years ago, and my father has a second family in Canada, where we'd spent part of my childhood. He and I are civil, but not close. Helena, on the other hand, lives, in mothering terms, absolutely on my doorstep, or, as she calls it "just around the corner," in St. John's Wood, and we are as close as two people who had lives that are totally incomprehensible to each other can possibly be.

I don't really understand how my mother lives her life, much less why. From time to time I consider the possibility that she is really two people, or perhaps a Martian. The Martian scenario usually wins out. My mother has been with the same City law firm forever. She made partner outrageously young, in her twenties. She had shown her fitness early: When she was twenty-two she took three days off work to have me, and has never really let me forget it, mostly by looking amazed whenever I am ill, as if to say, *You're staying home for* that? She is at the office by seven every morning, and she never leaves before seven in the evening. So what I can't work out is how she has also managed to see every play in town, go to concerts and opera regularly, have dinner with friends regularly—even worse, give her own dinner parties regularly—read all the latest novels, see all the latest films. She also walks three miles every morning before work, and has a large and close circle of friends. As I say, two people. Maybe three.

So when I say she left a message asking me to dinner, I don't want to give the impression she's some little old lady waiting only for a visit from her daughter to cast a ray of sunshine into her otherwise desolate existence.

One of her more irritating characteristics is that I always get her right away on the phone. Dammit, she's a lawyer. Why do my meetings spread over my days like ectoplasm, but not hers? "Never too busy, darling, to talk to you," she trills. I'd like to ask why not, but I know the answer. Martian.

"Sorry not to get back to you yesterday. Nightmare day at the office."

She doesn't have nightmare days, so she didn't bite. Instead, "I wanted to know, darling, if you'd like to come for dinner tomorrow. There's that nice judge I wanted you to meet, and possibly those two actors from Chichester." Mother's friends are always incredibly glamorous. "That nice judge" is never a part-time magistrate in Slough. He'll probably turn out to be a Law Lord, or the American Attorney General. The actors from Chichester won't be two struggling kids just out of drama school, but some Hollywood stars beefing up their credentials by doing a short-run stint in Britain—or, if they are just out of drama school, by the time dessert arrives they'll have had Steven Spielberg on the phone, begging them to let him direct them in his newest production.

It's not that my mother is a starfucker. Everyone genuinely likes her, she genuinely likes them. I like her, too. She's interested, interesting, good company. I'd go to her dinner parties with pleasure if she'd met me somewhere and asked me. As her daughter, though, I just feel everyone sitting there comparing us all the time. No, not comparing us. I feel them sitting there awed into silent astonishment that we could be even distantly related.

She moved on. "Have you seen the new show at the Tate? It's marvelous—do go. But go early, once the reviews come out it will get crowded."

"Mmm. I will." No I won't. The day after it finishes I'll finally find time. "And yes, thanks, I'd love to come for dinner. Eight?"

"Eight thirty. I won't get home until after eight. I haven't spoken to you in days. What's up?"

"Up? Nothing. The same. You know nothing's ever up with me."

"I do. I'm just not sure why not. You need to get out more."

"Mother. I have five manuscripts, all of which have to be read by tomorrow. I can only read after work because I've got meetings all afternoon. I'm supposed to have my detailed editorial comments to two authors about their books by tomorrow, and I'll need to do that after work, too."

Silence. She doesn't understand why I can't go to a play, then have dinner with friends, then do the work. But she doesn't want to say so, because she thinks it's so obvious that there must be something I'm not telling her.

I gave up. She gave up. We always do. Instead, I changed the subject. "Mother, if I needed to have a really good libel read done, would Selden's be enough?"

"Enough for what? Enough to prevent nuisance suits, of course. Enough to stop people who file thinking you're a big corporation and you'll give them a few thousand just to make them go away. But enough to stop a serious action? That depends on how they think they've been damaged. What's the book?"

I began to explain about Kit and Alemán. She cut in after only two sentences. "Your solicitors are a good City firm. Very prestigious. Lots of clout. Their reputation won't stop this kind of problem for twenty seconds."

"Great. I really need to hear this."

"You do need to hear it, Sam. This is precisely what you need to hear."

"Mother, we just can't find the money in the budget. It's the standard publishing story—there's never any money. We've budgeted £1,000, which is what we usually pay Selden's because we give them all our work, but I assume £1,000 is not what you're talking about."

"It most certainly is not. Being cheap now will only cost you in the end—you know what a libel action, even a small one, can cost. You're going to have to get the manuscript read by one of the heavy hitters, a firm with a powerful criminal law department as well. There's no point messing around with companies like mine. We're great for corporate work, where we are scary, but no one's going to be worried about us in a question of criminal libel."

"Criminal? Libel is a civil action. It's not criminal, for God's sake."

"It's civil here, but you've got to check the rest of Europe. Your murder victim is Spanish, the incident took place in France, and if the companies involved are Italian—"

"One is. One is French. The rest are East European."

"Well, I'm quite sure that libel is a criminal offense in Italy. And you can libel the dead there, too, so there's no loophole. I don't know about Spain and France, much less Eastern Europe, and neither will Selden's. That's my point."

"What does 'criminal' mean in this context?"

"Criminal, dear, means criminal. You understand English. It means you go to jail."

"Me?" I was saying this a lot at the moment, and always in an involuntary falsetto.

"Well, maybe not you. Maybe just Kit. Or your CEO. Or yes, maybe you as the editor. Depends how the prosecution is worded. Depends how many fish they want to catch. Depends how much trouble they want to cause. Is this something you particularly want to find out?"

"This is something I never want to find out."

"Then hire some heavy hitters. The cost is less than the cost of a jail sentence. And just because my advice is free doesn't mean it's not good. It's legal advice as well as maternal. I'd hate to have to find time to visit you in an Italian jail. I'd hate even more than that dealing with the amount of paperwork it would take to get you moved to an English jail."

She'd get me moved, I had no doubt about that. But I'd have to live with an unspoken "I told you so" for the rest of my life. That was more expensive emotionally than finding the money for a second libel read.

4

I woke up on Thursday morning with a feeling of low-level dread. It was early—the alarm hadn't gone off, and it wasn't yet light, although the dawn chorus outside my window indicated that it soon would be.

When I'd first moved to this flat the birds woke me every morning. I'd lived beside a main road at university, and cars had roared past for twenty-two and a half hours a day. If I woke in the night and there were only a few cars going past, then I knew without looking at the clock that it was between three and four thirty. That was the only quiet time there was. Silence I never heard at all.

Then I moved here, and the silence was shattering. I'd never realized how much energy we put into blocking out noise. Here I'm in a tiny dead-end street of only fourteen houses, and the street you turn off to get here is a dead end, too. So there is no through traffic. Anyone who is here is here for a purpose, which apart from the general peace it produces also means the street is, for the area, surprisingly safe. I'm becoming one of those snoopy old ladies. If I hear a car, I wonder which neighbor is coming or going, and why at such an odd hour. I've managed to control this bizarre curiosity so far, and I don't actually peer out the window, but I'm close. I figure sooner or later I'll have to get net curtains specially so that I can twitch them.

I checked the clock. Six. I didn't have to be up for an hour. I lay in the dark, contemplating going for a run, which is in theory what I do for exercise. Well, it's not exactly running. More an exhausted stagger, with periodic downshifts to a shuffle, but I tell myself it's the effort, not the style, that counts. I do a two-mile circuit, through Primrose Hill, into Regent's Park, and along the canal. There's no one around at that time except other runners, all looking irritatingly comfortable, and dog walkers. As I pass the dog walkers, puce-faced with effort, I can see their eyes flicker worriedly, wondering if they can remember what to do for a suspected heart attack. It's as vivid as if a speech bubble were over their heads.

If I made an effort, though, I could lie in bed for half an hour, debating the pros and cons of getting up, and by then it would be too late to go. I only do this about half the time, but half the time spent not running is well worth the contempt I feel for myself later. Thinking about the contempt got me up. I peered hopefully out of the window. If it was raining hard, I could go back to bed with a clear conscience. Unfortunately, it was the day that was clear. Damn. Since I've been running, I've noticed an annoying thing about the weather, which is that a day that is gray and drizzly by seven is usually bright and sunny at six. I don't know the meteorological reasons for this, but when I'm running I'm absolutely sure it is done to spite me, and I feel like hell the whole time. There are supposed to be endorphins or whatever that make you feel great when you exercise. I don't think I have any, because I only feel great when I'm lying on the sofa reading a book, possibly while simultaneously eating biscuits. That's why I work in publishing, not athletics.

I shoved in my contacts, grabbed my keys, and went. I don't do anything that they say you should, like eating or drinking something healthful and nutritious first. The idea of food on an empty stomach is nauseating. Until I've got a good layer of caffeine down, I'm not ready for health. The five minutes it takes me to get from home to Primrose Hill on the posh side of the tracks is what I call my warm-up when I feel in need of rationalization—which is when I write a check for £55 at the end of a visit to the physiotherapist to repair the damage this marvelous exercise produces.

All this is private. In public I simply say, grandly, "I run," when exercise and gyms are under discussion. I leave people to imagine that I do a brisk ten miles on Hampstead Heath every weekend after interval training all week (oh, yes, I have the vocabulary), although you only have to look at me to realize this cannot possibly be the case. However, in publishing most people's preferred sports are drinking and smoking, so by comparison my life looks healthy.

I normally try hard to think of things when I'm running, because if I allow my mind to focus on the activity itself, all I can think of is how much it hurts. If I can focus instead on a book, or a problem, or a conversation I need to have with someone, I can usually get a couple of miles under my belt without brooding on the pain. This morning, though, I was nearly through before complete paralysis of the lungs made me think how much further I had to go. The rest of the run I spent worrying about Kit.

It was absurd. The man hadn't shown up for a meeting, and he hadn't called. That was it. If it had been any other author I would have been pissed off, not worried. I wouldn't have tried to reach them endlessly. One brisk, firm message pointing out that they had missed the meeting was all they would have received—then let guilt settle in and do its job. But—and this repeated itself in time to my footsteps—Kit wasn't like that.

He was, however, an early riser, so it was possible there would be a message when I got home, or on my voice mail at the office. Our body clocks were, unusually for both our industries, set early, although mine was from necessity whereas he just liked getting up early. I hated it, but hated not having an hour or so to myself first thing even more.

I staggered home, therefore, with more than my usual speed, even finishing up with a slight flourish, as though to say to invisible watchers, *See? Easy.* Nothing on my voice mail. I showered and was out the door in half an hour, eager to get to the office. There was no real reason not to just ring through and check from home, but it seemed better to be physically there. I don't know why. I suspect it was because I wanted to postpone the moment when I found there was no message.

It wasn't even eight when I reached the office. Nothing from Kit. Nothing from his typist, either. He'd said he'd get her to send me the details of the manuscript dispatch, and it was unlike him to forget in the normal course of events. Even less likely given his burglary.

I had no idea what office hours CID officers kept. It was still early but I could always leave a voice mail: It was obviously routine. Then neither he nor I would have to think about it again. I dialed the number on the card he had given me, staring out the window—now it was raining, of course—while I tried to work out a message that didn't make it sound as if I'd given barely any thought to his visit from the moment he left my office. Normally a real live CID officer appearing in a publishing house would have been a talking point, but Kit's manuscript, and then Kit himself dropping out of sight, had sidetracked me. A man's soft "Hello?" startled me, therefore.

"Oh. I was expecting your voice mail." Waves of patience wafted down the line and I pulled myself together. I'm not nearly as foolish as I had been making myself sound for past two days. "Inspector Field, it's Samantha Clair, from Timmins and Ross. I haven't got any definitive suggestions for your missing parcel, but there is something else. I don't know, it's probably nothing, but I thought it might be worth telling you about." I trailed off.

"Anything is worth hearing. What have you got?"

"Well, it's nothing concrete. No one has rung to say, 'Didn't you get my parcel?' But I may know what it was." I told him about Kit's burglary, and how it might link to the courier. Then I went on: Kit not turning up for our meeting, the "workmen" at my flat, even the call from *Vogue*. I'd thought that when I'd said it out loud, it would dissolve, but as I put it all together, it no longer sounded nebulous.

Field didn't seem to think so, either. His voice was crisp. No fooling around now. "Will you be in your office this morning? I'll try and get to you by eleven."

He was there at ten thirty, which said either that cops had nothing to do, which I didn't think was the case, or that there was more happening in the background than I'd been told. I'd spent some time after I called making notes on everything that had happened over the past few days, so I was more coherent than I'd been on the phone.

I repeated what I'd told him on the phone, fleshing out the detail. I repeated the conversations I'd had with my mother and Selden's about libel, and highlighted Kit's findings. I also gave him Kit's contact information, which wasn't really any more than his agent's name and phone number, Kit's landline and mobile, which weren't answering, and an address. Kit and his partner of several years had split about a year before, but I passed on his ex's name. I'd only met him a few times, and had no contact information, but he worked for the EU, or had then. He should be relatively easy to find. I had no idea about Kit's family—he had a sister in Devon, but I didn't know her married name, or where exactly she lived. Inspector Field made notes, but I could see he was not really focused on this part of the story. I stopped speaking, and just waited.

He put on that face men have when they think women are making impossible demands, half-aggrieved, half-truculent. And his voice was so patient I wanted to scream as he said, "I'll pass the information on to missing persons, and they'll speak to his family. But you do realize that not much will happen, even if his family files a formal missing persons report?" He cut off my indignant reply before it had left my mouth. "He's a grown man and he didn't show up for a meeting. There are—" he looked at his notebook—"there are circumstances that mean we'll look into it, which otherwise those bare facts would not warrant, but—" hunted/aggrieved again—"but I suspect you will think it's not enough. I'll do what I can. That's all I can say."

He waited. Finally, tight-lipped, I nodded.

He did, too. "If we can go back to the manuscript."

I'd spoken to David and to Robert again at Selden's after my call once Inspector Field said he was coming to see me again, and we all agreed that while confidentiality was one thing, if our author had gone missing we had to do whatever we could. Even so, David had told me to make the police understand about serialization, and the need to keep the material under wraps. I'd agreed I would, but I was lying. I couldn't bring myself to let anyone think we were more worried about losing a serial deal than we were about losing an author.

"What I don't understand, though, is why anyone would think that a messenger would have the one and only copy of a manuscript. Before computers, before photocopiers, or typewriters even, that would make sense, but now?"

Field looked bland. "If that was what it was about. First, we have no evidence that it was anything but an accident. And then there's your hacker."

"Hacker?" I had no idea what he was talking about.

"Didn't you hear? I thought everyone in this building heard everything even before it was thought. Your IT people had to take all the e-mail servers offline. A fairly serious hacking attempt. That's why your system was down all day. There were a couple of attempts at the security code. The firewall was breached, and there was an attempt to hack several accounts, a fairly sophisticated one, apparently. Of course, that may just be a way of explaining why it was so nearly successful."

"Do we know that this is connected? Couldn't it be someone trying to get our sales figures or something?" Even as I said it, I knew how feeble it sounded.

Inspector Field thought so. "It could. But would they have the skills? And publishing doesn't seem to operate like that. Wouldn't it just be easier for one of your friends to ring you up and ask you? You people seem to spend all your time talking, and confidentiality isn't a word you use a lot." It was true, but it was clever of him to work that out after one visit. I thought we did a better imitation of appearing, if not being, professional. He went on. "How does Lovell produce his work? Longhand?"

"Yes. He doesn't use a computer. He gives a manuscript to some woman and she types it up."

He asked me for her contact details, and then added, almost as an afterthought, "What are your locks like at home?"

I had that feeling you get when you take a step in the dark and it isn't there. "Average. Enough to stop the casual thug. Nothing so complicated that a professional will get pissed off and total the whole door. If someone is searching for this manuscript, wouldn't it be better to let them burgle the place, and find out there's nothing there?" I backtracked at his quizzical look. "I'm not aiming for a break-in, but I'd rather it happened when I was out, and I'd rather they knew I had nothing there." I paused, trying to control myself. No dice. "I really, really don't like this," I snapped, as if he had tried to persuade me differently.

"You're not supposed to." If he hadn't been a cop, I'd have

assumed he was laughing at me, but looking closer I saw that he was being sympathetic. "Maybe you should go and stay with friends for a while."

I flinched, as if he'd leaned over and slapped me. This was much more real than I was prepared for. "What are you suggesting? That there's danger? Or that I should just clear out and let some stranger come and vandalize my house?" Despite my best efforts, my voice was rising to a whine. I'd suggested the very same thing only a minute before, but when he agreed, I was outraged.

Field looked gently at me, and said, "Wouldn't you rather be out of the way, if that's what's going to happen?"

"Well, stop it happening. You're a policeman. Do something."

He very kindly pretended not to hear.

By evening I had stopped feeling whiny and had moved on to mutinously aggressive. I was supposed to move myself out of my house so it could be burgled, wait for my manuscripts to be stolen, and just generally sit around while Kit was done away with? I didn't think so. I'm not particularly even-tempered at the best of times, and this was making me very, very crabby. Not adding to the general gaiety of the nation was the thought of dinner at my mother's. But if I didn't go I'd never hear the end of it, so I hauled on my good suit and stamped off to St. John's Wood, feeling martyred.

My mother looked her usual bandbox self. I always hope that, with her hectic schedule, one day I'll see her when her hair needs cutting, or with the hem on her skirt coming down, or at least, dammit, that she's sewn a button on with the wrong-colored thread. Today wasn't going to be that day. Helena's tiny, no more than five feet two inches, and a very fragile five feet two inches at that. She wears very neat, very tailored clothes, which somehow make her look irresistibly feminine, and her short, curly dark hair, still with only a few threads of gray, always looks as if she has just stepped out of the hairdresser, although I know it takes her barely five minutes in the morning.

She looked at me and carefully didn't sigh. "What's up?"

We had a few minutes before the guests came, so I filled her in on the last few days. She's good at real trouble.

"Well, you'd better come and stay for a while, hadn't you. And warn your neighbors."

"Warn them? Warn them about what? That I'm expecting burglars, and they should see that they're comfortable? Maybe make them mugs of cocoa while they're tearing my place apart?"

"Don't be silly and don't be histrionic." Maybe she's not so good if there's real trouble. She'll solve my problems, but I'd love a bit of sympathy along the way as well. She went on, disregarding my look of scorn. "The old man upstairs, he really has to be warned, and the police need to know that he's up there. Did you mention him to your inspector?"

"No, Mother, there were more important things to discuss."

"What is more important than making sure an old man isn't frightened out of his wits?"

"Making sure that I'm not! For God's sake, I'm petrified."

"Well, you're young, you're strong, and you're forewarned. He's none of those things. So do it first thing when you get home this evening. Then go through everything, make sure there's nothing locked, nothing hidden. Why deal with damage as well as trespass?"

"Why not just hang a sign outside? Come on in and take what you want."

"Sam, are you trying to miss the point? It's clear that whoever it is is not trying to steal the manuscript to prevent publication. If that were the case, they would have moved on Kit earlier, or at the typist, and dealt with it when there was only one copy. And they would be looking further afield for the notes and invoices and so on when they didn't find them at Kit's. What they want is to see the book, to see what the problem is, and how they can protect themselves."

She was right. I hadn't thought it through, just thought how silly they were being not to know that a manuscript wasn't a single thing that could be taken and destroyed. And they obviously weren't silly.

"But if it's a fishing operation, then maybe it's not the mafia." My mother raised an eyebrow at the slightly dramatic word, but what else should I call them? "I mean, Alemán's family and Vernet also want to stop publication, one for family pride, one for trade reputation. Kit thinks the French police will, too, even if they haven't been connected to the money laundering, because they won't want it coming out that the inquest was rigged, even if not by them."

"Well, the police know how to hack into a computer. Certainly a computer with as little security as most publishers have. Would Alemán's family? Who are they?"

"His father is a dentist, I think," I said, dredging up the information from Kit's manuscript. "Small town, prosperous. Not the kind to have underworld connections."

My mother was more skeptical. Being a tax lawyer makes you very cynical. "No one with a bit of cash is too far away from underworld connections."

"For goodness' sake, Mother. When was the last time you went to have a tooth filled, and while you were at it arranged a little bit of B and E?"

"That's not what I mean. All an upstanding citizen has to do is go to a detective agency, preferably one where the owner is an ex-policeman who is well below retirement age. There's usually a reason he's not in the force."

The first guest arrived, cutting short her exposition on How to Become a Criminal in Three Easy Steps. I was pleased, because by the time we spoke again, I could pretend that I'd known it all along. I was also sobered. My mother was much more devious than I'd ever imagined.

Dinner was a pleasant break. As I'd guessed, "that nice judge" was a senior high court judge. The rest of the guests were a good mix. As well as the promised actors, there was the couple who were my mother's oldest friends, a lawyer from New York who was here for a few months on a case, a medical researcher and her husband, the judge—in fact, a reasonably good sampling of professional London. By the time I headed home, refusing my mother's repeated invitation to stay, I was feeling much better.

As I came up the road, I saw a light in Mr. Rudiger's windows.

My mother was right, and I should have thought of it myself. He needed to be warned, so I continued up to his landing, noting on my way that the lightbulbs lower down had blown. The three flats together own the house, so the common parts are a joint responsibility. Since the Lewises have a small child and erratic work patterns, and Mr. Rudiger hasn't seen the common parts in years, it tends to be me who replaces bulbs, waters the horrible cheese plant an old tenant left behind and no one has the heart to murder, tidies away Bim's forgotten toys, and cleans the passageway when I do my own flat.

I tapped gently on the door. "Mr. Rudiger? It's Sam, from downstairs."

I heard him moving toward the doorway, slowly but without a pause. Good. I hadn't woken him up.

He opened the door and gestured me in without surprise, as though I were a regular caller just before midnight.

"I'm sorry to trouble you so late, but I thought perhaps this shouldn't wait until morning."

"It's no trouble." He has a faint foreign accent. I've never been sure where he's from. Central Europe, I think. I've always assumed he was a refugee before the War, but I've never asked. His formality is charming, but it sets up a barrier that is not to be breached. I like it—publishing is a tiny world, and we all know everything about everyone. It's nice to find someone who doesn't immediately want to bleed all over you.

He offered me a drink, or coffee, as though we had the night ahead of us. I was already feeling that, whatever I had to say, it could easily have waited. I didn't want to put him out further.

"No, thanks. I just wanted to tell you, there's a bit of a problem at my office that may spill over here." He listened impassively while I quickly sketched in the details, although I skipped out the money laundering and Kit's disappearance. I made it sound like a piece of industrial espionage, and left it at that. I didn't want to terrify the man, just put him on his guard about opening the door to strangers.

He nodded, as though this were the kind of thing he dealt with every week—vacuum the sitting room, prevent robbery, put the rubbish out. "Thank you, Miss Clair. It was good of you to think of me."

I blushed. I hadn't thought of him at all. "It's probably not serious, and nothing will happen, but we all ought to be alert." I wrote down Inspector Field's number. I wasn't sure if it was something I should be giving out, but it would be better than dialing 999. An old man hearing things go bump in the night might not make the emergency services leap on to their white chargers.

In passing, I also tapped at Kay and Anthony's door. No answer. I didn't want to knock more loudly, because of Bim. Anthony might be at home, even if Kay was out. When work was scarce, which it often was, she did stints as a cigarette girl for some company that arranged City functions. They always ended at about three in the morning, but the tips were good and it kept Bim in apple juice.

I would slip a note under their door before I left for work in the morning. After the "workmen" incident, they wouldn't let anyone in without my say-so. I continued downstairs, groping for the banister. How could two bulbs be out at the same time? I stopped dead halfway down the last flight. Never mind how could two bulbs be out, how could I be so stupid? Here we were, all expecting my flat to be burgled, and I was prancing about in the dark, mumbling, "Wouldn't you know it, there's never a lightbulb when you need one." I stood there, trying to figure out what to do. I could hardly ring my own phone and suggest to the burglars that they might like to leave now, as I was on my way.

I turned to go back up to Mr. Rudiger. I'd use his phone to call Inspector Field. I had a mobile but it was, naturally, in my flat—I hadn't seen any reason to take it to my mother's. I'd only gone up two steps when the hair on the back of my head lifted. Someone was standing on the landing. I couldn't see him, or hear him, but I knew he was there. He'd watched me walk up to the top, and he'd let me pass back down.

Now what?

I found out, all too soon.

I focused on the tree that grew outside my sitting room window. There was something odd about it. It had shrunk. And the window had suddenly decided it had curtains. Why was I sleeping on the sofa anyway? I heard a step behind me, and the door closed. I remembered the stairway and tried to sit up and turn quickly, but a light inside my head exploded, and I dropped back onto the cushions.

"Gently. You're fine, but you've had a knock." It was Inspector Field. How had he got into my sitting room? How had I?

Mr. Rudiger came into my line of sight with a glass of water. "Here. Just a sip."

This wasn't my sitting room, it was his, and the tree had shrunk because I was looking out from the second story. I took the water but my hand was shaking and it slopped out over what had, until the last hour, been my best suit. I pushed myself up on one elbow and looked down at myself. There was blood all over the front of my jacket, and one elbow and both knees were ripped. Damn. Now I'd have to go shopping with Kit.

Kit. Oh God.

"What happened?" I tried to stay calm, but my voice was shaking, to match my hands. I was going to cry, too, which was really embarrassing.

Mr. Rudiger sat me up and put a cushion behind me. He took away the glass, tipped out most of what I hadn't spilled into a nearby plant, and gave it back to me. "Here, sip slowly." He held a tissue in front of my nose and said, like a particularly fond mother, "Blow." His face showed no more surprise than it had when I'd first come upstairs with my news.

His impassivity and briskness, not to mention the tissue, steadied me. "I'm all right now." I think I persuaded myself. "What happened? And when? What time is it?"

Inspector Field pulled up a chair. "I've just got here. You weren't unconscious for long. You were lucky. Whoever was inside your flat must have posted a lookout. He only wanted to make sure you didn't see anybody. What I don't understand is that you were knocked on the head, and then for some reason they also pushed you down the front stairs on to the pavement as well. That seems excessive, and it reduced their chances of getting away quietly."

I was embarrassed. "Um. Well. I realized somebody was there, so as he came toward me I was ready, and I kneed him in the balls and hit him over the head with a Hornby engine Bim had left on the stairs. I'm not sure if the train connected, but my knee definitely did. That might have annoyed him enough to push me."

Inspector Field looked like he was biting the inside of his cheek. "It might be a good idea not to annoy any more people with coshes," he advised solemnly. "They get cross, you know. If I'd thought you'd get involved, I would never have—" He broke off, shaking his head, and stood up. "I'll just wait for the ambulance. Then I'll join my colleagues downstairs to see what's been going on there." He stared at me for a minute, apparently wondering what other trouble I could get up to in the ambulance.

The thought of my flat, and what it most probably looked like, made me want to cry again, and once a night was enough. So I said mutinously, "I don't need an ambulance. I'm fine." I sounded about Bim's age, but slightly less bright.

Mr. Rudiger, to my surprise, broke in. "You're very far from fine. You have to make sure you haven't got a concussion, you have to have your cuts and scrapes cleaned, and if someone can stop your nosebleed, it would make me happier about you sleeping in my spare room tonight."

My nose? I wiped my hand across my face. I was such a mess I hadn't even thought to wonder where the blood was coming from. Sure enough, my nose was bleeding, and from long experience I knew it would go on doing so until I got it cauterized. It happened often enough for no reason at all—I had to go and get it dealt with at least once every two or three years. I began to take stock. A roaring headache, but no blinding lights, no fuzzy vision. I probably wasn't concussed, but checking was reasonable enough, even though I didn't want to be reasonable. I wanted to bite somebody. That would probably be poor tactics so instead I argued, with the false civility all girls internalize before they're twelve. "I can't possibly stay here, Mr. Rudiger. Thank you, but I've caused enough trouble."

He gave me a wintry little smile, not fooled for a minute. "Trouble, yes, but not intentionally, and I don't see how you can stay downstairs."

"Why? What? What's happened downstairs?" I was agitated again.

Inspector Field returned from the phone, where he'd been having a low-voiced conversation. "Nothing much. The door's been broken open with a tire iron. It's messy, and it won't lock for the moment, but there's nothing too serious inside, mostly just things pulled out of cupboards. It looks like they were going to make it appear to be a robbery—all your electrical goods are by the door. Once you came home early, there was no point so they've left everything. Of course, we won't really know until you've been down to look, but—" He pushed me back on the sofa, disregarding my attempts to extricate myself from Mr. Rudiger's blanket. "No. We need to dust for prints, and the photographer has only just arrived, and we're going to make the place even more untidy for the moment. The ambulance is here. I'm going to take you downstairs, but you are *not* to go into your flat. Do you understand me?"

I was feeling mutinous again.

"I mean it. A constable will go with you, and bring you home if the hospital doesn't want to keep you for observation. If they release you, then you are coming straight up here. I'll bring up some clean clothes, and and then that's it. You're out of the game. Understood?"

I sighed theatrically. I was really far too knocked about to start going through a ransacked flat, but I was damned if I was going to be bossed around without some sort of protest.

Both men appeared unmoved. My drama queen routine needed work.

5

Mr. Rudiger called my mother while I was at the hospital—he and Inspector Field were plotting behind my back, and I guess they decided that Helena would be a nice old duck who could look after me. She arrived in the Casualty department, terrorized the nurse who was cauterizing my nose, reminded the registrar that his wife had appeared against her in a court action the year before, told the constable his shirt was untucked at the back, and all in all had the place whipped into shape in about thirty seconds flat. By the time the registrar agreed that no, I didn't need to stay in overnight, the entire staff had that glazed, deer-in-the-headlights look that my mother can induce at will.

Mr. Rudiger, by contrast, appeared gently amused by her and, even more oddly, she quite clearly approved of him. My mother never approves of people who don't have jobs and stay at home for what she refers to dismissively as "no reason," even if they are well past retirement age, as Mr. Rudiger plainly was, at least chronologically. It was now nearly four in the morning and I just wanted to crawl into bed and sleep for about a week. Mr. Rudiger and my mother on the other hand were both irritatingly chipper. They'd agreed, without reference to me, that it was better for me to stay at Mr. Rudiger's so I could go through my apartment with the police in the morning. I didn't care where I was, as long as people stopped talking at me and let me go to bed.

Mr. Rudiger showed me into a room that looked like a piece of Central Europe bodily transported: a gleaming wooden floor with a hook rug, white walls, dark wooden furniture, and a child's wooden bed, with a duvet with a homemade patchwork cover on it. It was like being Goldilocks in the Three Bears' house, and it was wonderfully comforting. I dozed off to the sound of adult voices murmuring down the hall. It only needed a nightlight to make my reversion to childhood complete.

In the morning the gray, watery light coming through white cotton curtains with red ducks on them woke me gently. I got out of bed, finding myself in a peculiar, crouched-over position that was all that my now-stiffened muscles would permit. In all the books I'd ever read, Our Hero is brutally assaulted, tied up for seventy-two hours, frequently being hung by his ankles in the process. When he frees himself by gnawing through the ropes, he stops only for a quick drink, and then charges straight off after the villains. Another cherished illusion gone. It was plain to me now that what Our Hero would really do was lie in bed and moan gently. That seemed sensible, so I lay down again and did that for a while. Then I shuffled off to the bathroom and soaked my muscles until they at least let me stand upright.

I'd been aware of Mr. Rudiger moving around earlier, and when I reached the kitchen he had a cup of coffee ready for me, and was placidly eating cereal and listening to the news on the radio. He nodded, and let me drink in silence, for which I was grateful. Then, "Inspector Field said he'll be here at ten to go through the flat with you. Also, will you call your mother? She's worried."

Worried? She was probably wondering why I wasn't at work. Which reminded me: If I moved quickly, I could leave a message on Miranda's voice mail at the office saying I was ill before she got in. I didn't think I could really deal with explaining what was happening just at the moment, although David and, more particularly, Selden's, were going to have to know soon that things were escalating. Robert Marks was going to be disgusted: He hadn't gone into the law to deal with criminals. David, I rather suspected, would be secretly jealous that this *Boys' Own* episode was happening to me. Whatever the case, all of publishing London would have heard the news ten minutes after I spoke to the office, and I couldn't face it right now.

Naturally my mother was already at her office, despite the fact that she couldn't have got home much before five.

"How are you feeling?" she asked, moving on before I had time to answer. "Pavel says—"

"Who?"

"Pavel Rudiger. Why didn't you tell me what a delightful man he is? Such a distinguished career." I couldn't bring myself to ask what that was. She'd spent an hour with him and had learned more than I'd found out in over fifteen years. I'd known his first name, I supposed, but I never would have thought to have used it.

"Pavel says that he's happy to have you stay with him until you get your door fixed. Do you want to, or would you rather stay with me? It will be easier for you to sort out locksmiths and so on from there." She'd already made up my mind. "Inspector Field will bring you over here at lunchtime to go through what we know." Well, that was all right, then, she had sorted out the CID, too. There was really nothing for me to do but make affirmative noises and hang up. So that is what I did.

Mr. Rudiger had watched my side of the call wearing that look I was getting to know, the one where someone was telling him slightly amusing stories just out of my earshot.

"Helena is a formidable woman," was all he said.

I didn't feel the need to answer that one.

"It's lucky she's on our side."

Our? I was oddly cheered by his assumption that he was part of whatever was going on. I smiled and rolled my eyes in a tell-me-about-it look, which he enjoyed as much as he'd enjoyed my mother.

When Inspector Field arrived Mr. Rudiger waved me out like a proud parent seeing his child off to her first day in kindergarten—he was happy to be part of the action, but not to the extent of going past his front door.

It wasn't as bad as I'd feared. Everything had been pulled out of every cupboard, and off every shelf, but I figured I could look on it as a sort of enforced spring cleaning. I said so, but only got a slightly startled look in return. I guess I did sound a bit like Pollyanna after Vesuvius erupted—"Oh goody, it's T-shirt weather!"

He contented himself with saying, "The only thing that was taken was your television. It might have been the only thing they'd got out of the house before you came home." He was choosing his words carefully, like a man inching forward in a bog.

I was firm, trying to close off this conversation. "I don't have a television."

"I'd thought of that," he said, still stepping delicately. "I couldn't see where it would have been, but I rejected the idea when we piled up some of the papers from your desk and saw a television license."

"Yes, I have a license," I said vaguely, trying to look as if I were thinking of something else.

"A license. No television. Just a license." He was determined not to phrase it as a question.

"Look, Inspector—"

"You'd better make it Jake. If I have to listen to sentences that start 'Look,' I figure we're going to be on first-name terms sooner or later."

He was laughing at me again. "Look, *Jake*," I continued, acidly. "I don't have a television because I don't watch television. But it would appear that not having a television in the twenty-first century makes you a criminal, or a psychopath, or a liar, or more likely all three. If you don't have a license in this country, the TV licensing people send men around in little vans. Then they don't believe the most obvious explanation, so I have to walk them through the house, opening all the cupboards to prove I don't have any contraband portables lurking. Then they send court summonses anyway, which I have to get my mother to deal with. So its simpler just to pay for the license. It only comes to the price of a film a month."

He didn't want to argue, but he seemed hypnotized into it. "You still have to pay for the films, though."

"No, because I don't go to them, either. I pay the fee, and then I read the books I'd read even if I had a television sitting in the corner. It saves me being harassed, and it means I'm not marked down in some file somewhere in Swansea, or wherever TV licensing heaven is."

"A file?"

I shook my head impatiently. "Data protection or no data protection, there are government and quasi-government files on all sorts of things—credit checks, professional checks, political groups, and affiliations. From the reaction I get when I say I don't have a TV, it's easier to believe that I'm a psychopath—you know, one of those kind that the neighbors say afterward, 'She was very quiet, kept herself to herself.'"

"No risk of your neighbors saying that."

I gave him what I hoped was a withering glance. He remained provokingly unwithered, so I continued, "Altogether, £145 a year is a small price to pay to not have the government drive me crazy over the fact that I don't watch television. OK?"

"It's fine by me. That's not what I'm here for."

I let a beat pass, so he could hear me thinking, *You could have fooled me.* Then, "What did you find—or not find—last night?"

"What we'd expected. A thorough search. Do you remember if your computer was switched on when you went out?"

"Yes, I was doing a backup."

"There was no sign of that, so they've been through it. My guess is they cloned your hard drive. Also, there were no memory sticks anywhere, and you must have had some?" He waited, and I nodded. "I thought so. Then they took those away and copied everything else. They probably didn't know what they were looking for. It's much more likely they were just sent in to look for manuscripts, and see what was on the computer. We heard back from the typist this morning. She had sent the manuscript from that mail shop."

"Really? Then why—" I waved my hand at the mess all around us.

"It's not just the manuscript. Our IT people think that they will have installed a keystroke recorder to keep an eye on what you've got, how much you know. Don's a nice man. Do you want me to ask if he'll sweep your system for you?"

I was amazed. I didn't really expect the police to perform personal computing services, but then I didn't really expect them to talk to me as if I were human, and Inspector Field—Jake— was treating me as a colleague rather than a member of the public crossing a police barrier.

I rescued some clean clothes from the mess on the floor, and returned to Mr. Rudiger's to try and disguise the worst of the bruising with makeup before I went out—if Bim saw me on the stairs, he'd have nightmares. It wasn't too difficult—concealer covers a multitude of sins, and all I needed to do was buy some fairly flamboyant green eye shadow for the unbruised eye, and it would look like I had a bad case of the 1960s, but nothing worse.

At my mother's office the meeting took on the aura of a case conference. The only way you could tell that Jake was the policeman and we were the civilians was that he had automatically taken charge. Then again, have you ever seen a meeting with two women and a man where that doesn't happen? Really, I suppose, the only way you could tell that Jake was a policeman was that my mother *let* him take charge.

"What have we got?" he said, leaving it up to us to decide who "we" were, and what we might have.

My mother was quite sure of both answers. "Given that Sam can't describe the man who hit her?" She raised her eyebrows at me, and I mutely shook my head. The landing was dark, and I had sensed the man, rather than seen him. "And there were no fingerprints?" She raised her eyebrows at Jake, treating him exactly as she did me.

"Nothing. Nothing, that is, that we can match at the moment—we've eliminated Sam's, and what appears to be her cleaner's, but there are stray prints that we can't source. None of them match anything we've got on file, so we're either talking about Sam's friends—most likely—or people who've never entered the system—much less likely, because they weren't very clever about it. And villains who aren't very clever we usually meet before too long. The final possibility is that they were from outside the country." He tapped off the possibilities on his palm: "There's the bank, Intinvest, and their friends; Alemán's family; Vernet; or someone we don't know about yet."

"Or the French police," I added thoughtlessly.

He acted like I hadn't spoken, with only a flattening of his look indicating that I'd gone a step too far. I moved back on to safer ground. "Is there some way of checking the prints in Europe?"

"In theory. In practice, we expect the Spanish and the French to respond in about twenty-four hours; Lithuania is anybody's guess; and the Italians may take twenty-four months. It depends on how busy they are—and if they can match the prints."

"If they can, when do you expect to hear?"

My mother looked impatiently at me. "No, dear. If they can, it's twenty-four months. It's if they can't, we'll hear back quickly."

It was lucky my mother had decided to be one of the good guys, because she'd have made a sensational baddie. But while all this was important, I couldn't really give it my full attention. I was more worried about Kit. "Surely that's more urgent? Have you heard anything?"

Jake looked gently at me. "Nothing. We've spoken to his sister, who hasn't heard from him for a few weeks, although she says that's normal. We found his ex. They'd seen each other a few months ago—he claims they're friendly." He looked over at me, to see if I knew differently, but I just shrugged. "He says he hasn't seen him since, and he was in New York when Kit missed his meeting with you." He still didn't say "disappeared," I noticed. "His passport confirms that." At least he was taking it seriously enough to check, I thought sourly. Jake continued, "His solicitor says that the papers Kit left with him have been in his safe, and there's no indication they've been disturbed. I spoke last night to the rector at the London School of Design to see if he'd heard anything."

"But Kit hasn't lectured there since—" I stopped short.

"Since he was accused of harassment by one of his students last year. It's all right, we know all about it, although you might have mentioned it to me when we spoke yesterday. It would have saved time." He saw me looking stubborn, and plowed on. "The rector didn't think that there was anything in the accusation, and an internal investigation showed that the student," he checked his notes, "Davies, was a bit of a fantasist, with a history of instability. He left the LSD soon after—" He broke off. "Can it really be called that?"

"Yes, it can. Don't bother with the jokes, they've all been made already." I refused to be distracted. "Look, Kit said Davies was really weird. And he said that before he was accused. He sort of stalked Kit. He was at all his public lectures, he followed him around the country. He must have spent a huge amount of time and money on it."

Jake wasn't interested in a dropout with a yen for fashionistas. But I was. It wasn't unusual for a student to make trouble, even if this kind of trouble was extreme, but it was very unusual for a student to put a lot of cash into something with such an unproductive end result. I thought it was worth following up. I decided I'd call the rector, who'd published a few books on design and whom I knew slightly. Nicholas Meredith was always plugged in to what was happening. If there was any gossip about Kit, he might not want to pass it on to the police, but maybe he would talk to me.

Meanwhile my mother was lining up our tasks. "I'll start to ask some questions about Intinvest and its subsidiaries. I don't think I'll get much from the East European side, but I'll see what's being said." She turned to me. "Will you get me a copy of the manuscript, please? There might be some place where I might have leverage."

I looked from her to Jake, like a puppy who isn't quite sure who it should be obeying. Jake shrugged. "Nell knows far more about corporate malfeasance than I do. The Fraud Squad is looking at the manuscript, and the papers Kit left with his solicitor, but they're more interested in the money laundering than they are in who might have arranged for his disappearance. They'll give me whatever they think is relevant, but more is always better at the beginning of an investigation."

I was momentarily sidetracked. Nell? When had Jake and Helena become so friendly? And anyway, no one ever abbreviated Helena's name. Then I heard what he'd just said. "When did you get a manuscript? And from whom?"

He looked noncommittal. "We took it off your office computer while we were looking at the hacker's attempted entry. Your IT man was very helpful."

Was he? I didn't think I liked IT going into my computer, even with the police who, presumably, had a warrant. But it probably wasn't the best time to bring that up. Jake seemed to think he was on thin ice, too, and moved on quickly. "I'll take on Diego Alemán, Alemán's brother. He's here, studying at Birkbeck, and I think it's time to talk to him."

This changed things. In some ways, everything had been comfortably distant: French police, Italian or Lithuanian thugs laundering money. But Birkbeck College wasn't distant. Most of the staff were on a different planet, it's true, but it was my kind of different—the have-no-television, "What is *The X Factor*?" kind of different.

"What is he doing at Birkbeck? Is he studying there? I might know his tutors."

Jake was playing this one close to his chest. "Let's compare notes later." "Later" was going to be sometime soon, I could see. Possibly the next millennium. I let it ride.

Jake stood. "Well, if that's all for the moment?" My mother nodded impatiently—she wanted to hit the phones and start picking up scuttlebutt. Suddenly I felt exhausted. What I really wanted to do was go home and go to bed. But I had the weekend in front of me to begin to repair the damage to my flat, and to my body. If I didn't reach Nicholas at the LSD, I wasn't going to be able to speak to him until Monday, and that was too long to put Kit's disappearance on hold. I decided to go to the office. With luck, I could skulk in while everyone was at lunch, make some calls, and leave without seeing too many people—or being seen by them.

I stopped at the chemist for some cheap eye makeup before I went into the office. The woman behind the counter tried to steer me toward neutral tones, but once I took off my sunglasses she agreed 1960s hippie green was the way to go. She even helped me match the bruises, and as she said cheerfully, "Well, honey, you look like you're really bad at makeup, but you don't look like you got beat up anymore."

Miranda didn't agree when I slunk past her desk. I'd timed my entry carefully—not that hitting lunch hour on a Friday is difficult in a publishing office. It goes on for so long, after all. Miranda was the only one there, bent over Breda's book, looking a little beat up herself. She was terrific. She didn't ask questions, didn't comment at all. She only flinched slightly, and said, "Coffee?" Even if she hadn't been able to read, I'd have kept her forever just for that.

I nodded my thanks and quickly shut myself into my office.

Lunchtime was good in that no one was around to question me, but equally, there was no one around for me to question. I left messages for Nicholas Meredith, and Chris Stanley, a friend of Peter's who taught political theory at Birkbeck. I contemplated trying to get in touch with Kit's editor on the *Sunday News,* to see if he had any ideas. I'd met him once, briefly, when Kit and I had bumped into him at the cinema. That he was terrifying was an understatement. He was a huge alpha male who was only happy when making other people cry. And if that was the read I got on him at a Rita Hayworth retrospective, imagine what he'd be like at work. I sat up straighter. *I'm not a coward,* I told myself severely. But even if I wasn't, and the statement was open to discussion, I also couldn't see how to approach him. *Hello, you won't remember me, but I'm looking for your missing journo even though I have no official reason to?* That needed work.

Instead I e-mailed Robert Marks at Selden's, and David. Then all the people in the building who had copies of the manuscript, asking them to delete them off their computers, as well as returning any printed copies to me for shredding. I worded it to imply that we had a libel problem, and therefore we couldn't afford to have stray copies lying about, but I didn't think that would hold after I'd spoken to David. I sent a list of all these people to IT, too, so they could scrub their hard drives, or whatever it was they needed to do to delete the manuscript permanently. All in all, I was a whirlwind of activity, even if none of it seemed to get me any further forward.

Miranda came in with the coffee, and stood hovering. I couldn't really blame her for wanting to know what was going on. So did I. I took a deep breath and said, "Close the door." I'd decided that, if David agreed, we'd tell the rest of the world that I'd been hurt when I came home during a burglary, and that Kit's manuscript had serious libel problems, and present them as two separate issues. But I thought it was important to tell Miranda the truth—she was in the line of fire if anyone identified her as my assistant, and anyway, I just couldn't deal with it on my own.

She tried to look professional, but she was goggling at me like a five-year-old on a school trip to the fire station. But she pulled herself together, and halfway through she began to make notes. By the time I'd finished she was acting as though I was telling her how to brief a designer for a book jacket, the most exciting thing I'd let her do so far.

"Right," she said briskly. "What story do you want me to give as your cover story, and what story should I pass as deep gossip— you know, 'I'm telling you this, but don't tell another soul'? That's the only way you'll keep a lid on this, even for a while."

It was a good plan. I couldn't stop the talk, but I could tailor it. If my colleagues thought something was being withheld from them, they'd move heaven and earth to get at the truth. If, on the other hand, they thought they had the facts, they'd be happy for days ringing each other up to say "Did you *hear* . . . ?"

I had an inspiration. "Are you still in touch with Kathleen Strong?" Kath was her ex-boss, a literary agent and a gossip to rival Kit. If you wanted a particularly vicious rumor spread, she was your girl.

Miranda grinned. "I am a bit, but not enough to call her out of the blue. She'd suspect. Can I go to the launch of that new book tonight? Kath represents the author, and she's sure to be there. I can easily drop it then."

"Yes, that's a very good idea. It's a drinks party, and no one will care how many people show up. What's our story?"

Miranda thought. Gossip was a serious business. "Well, your main idea, that you disturbed burglars, works. I think that we just need to cover it up with something else, otherwise people will link the Alemán libel problems to it. Two things happening to you on the same day is not good."

"No, heaven forbid that more than one thing should happen to me at a time."

She flashed a smile of apology, but wasn't deflected. "You got burgled, but what you're not saying is . . . How about you think it was your ex, in some sort of revenge deal?"

I hadn't laughed in days, but the thought of Peter breaking into my flat to destroy my possessions in a state of thwarted passion was irresistibly comic—and so far from anything he might actually do that it couldn't hurt. "All right, but poor Peter. Can we make it 'an' ex—suggest that I have so many that I can't be quite sure which one it was?"

I'm afraid that Miranda laughed out loud at the idea of my having legions of men lined up waiting their turn. But she had the decency to smother it quickly. "That's great. I can say that you think it wasn't Peter—a more recent acquisition who you tried out and had to let go. And I can also hint that I know more about him, and that Kath would be astonished to hear who it was. That will definitely get her attention. I can make her think it's a Timmins and Ross author, and she'll spend all her energies on that." Then she looked doubtful. "At least, it'll work if there isn't really a Timmins and Ross author . . ." She trailed off, uncertain whether asking if I had a secret lover was ruder than making the assumption that I didn't.

"No, one of our authors is fine. Make it Breda if you think that will keep Kath gossiping."

Miranda's eyes popped. Then she looked regretful. "After three days of *Toujours Twenty-one* I'd love to believe it, but I don't think Breda's ever had sex at *all*."

"You could be right—she probably found her children under a cabbage leaf. Can we bear to discuss her book? We will have to at some point—I'm due in Galway next week."

Miranda looked as though the smell of rotten eggs had just wafted through my office. "I've done about fifty pages. Do you want to look at it before I go on?"

"Want? No. Need to? I suppose so. Give it to me before I go, and I'll read it this weekend."

"Good. Do you want me to cancel your appointments for Monday? Are you going to be in? Also, you need to decide about Paris on Wednesday."

"My God, Paris. I'd completely forgotten." Kit had organized for me to go and see the couture show featuring Vernet's new designer, I think on the basis that after this book came out, he would be banned from their shows for life. I normally don't get glamorous little jaunts like this, and I'd been looking forward to it.

Miranda looked sick. If she had had an invitation to a Paris fashion show, it would take more than grievous bodily harm to make her forget about it. It had been planned as a fun day out with Kit, but now it could just be an opportunity to talk to the people at Vernet, see what they thought about Kit's disappearance.

"I'll still go to Paris. Will you get in touch with Vernet's PR? He's a ghastly man named Loïc Something-or-other—it's in the file. Make it sound like we want to make sure Vernet isn't unhappy with the book, or something. He won't have time to see me before the show, but try and book him for after. As for the rest, I'll be in on Monday, but cancel everything that isn't absolutely urgent. It's unlikely that I'll have time for anything except talking to Robert and whoever he dredges up for criminal law at Selden's—if, of course, Selden's deign to do criminal law."

I saw David go past and stuck my head out the door to stop him. Miranda was relieved we didn't have to discuss Breda anymore, so she escaped.

David looked at me warily. My eye makeup was not what he was used to. I shepherded him into his office like a particularly bossy collie dog, and shut the door.

I quickly ran through the events of the last day. David began by looking irritated, and ended by staring at me, completely speechless, mouth ajar. Crime was not something publishers ever thought would enter their lives, except as a profitable list of whodunits.

"It's as under control as it's going to be for the moment, David." I tried not to sound exasperated. "We're gathering up the manuscripts, and Miranda will shred them. The police already have their own." This did not appear to comfort him. "As far as the outside world is concerned, I had a break-in. In a totally unrelated incident, Kit's new book is having a series of libel problems, and will be delayed. End of story."

"Do you really think people are going to believe that?" David looked hopeful. He was always one to find the easiest route, even if it took him miles out of his way.

I snapped. I always find it difficult to talk to David. I constantly have to bite my lip so I won't say things like, "Stand up straight, take your hands out of your pockets, stop being so *wet*." So I was abrupt to the point of rudeness now. "No, David, I don't. But I also don't think they're going to believe that Kit has been abducted, possibly murdered, that I was beaten up by thugs trying to locate his manuscript, and that none of us know what the hell is going on." I thought and revised. "Well, they'll believe that last bit. For God's sake, we've got to leave it to the police, do some damage limitation, and move on." I had no intentions of leaving it to the police or moving on, but David wasn't going to be much use.

6

Chris Stanley was on the phone as I returned to my office, sounding a bit distant. He was a good friend of Peter's, and we hadn't kept in touch after the breakup. No animosity, but he was definitely "his" rather than "hers." I didn't bother to think of a cover story. What possible reason could I have for wanting to talk to a foreign student? Chris might not even know him. But I was in luck.

"Diego Alemán? Yes, he's one of my students, why?"

"I want to talk to him about a manuscript I'm working on. You know about his brother?"

"Of course. What's the manuscript?"

"One of my authors is writing a book on the fashion industry, and he wants to check out various things with the Alemán family." It was weak, but Chris might not think in scandalous tabloid terms about my kind of book.

He didn't. "Sure. I can get him to e-mail you. Or, I tell you what, Rosie and I are having a lunch party on Sunday—why don't you come? Diego will be there."

"That would be great." I couldn't believe it was going to be this easy. "Thanks. What time?"

"Come whenever you like after one. I can't promise you'll have much chance to talk to Diego, there'll be a lot of people, but at least you can meet."

We hung up and I tried Nicholas at the LSD again. This time he was in, and as cheerfully expansive as ever. "Sam! I haven't heard from you for ages."

"I could say the same, surely?" We'd always flirted, on the comfortable understanding that neither of us had any intention of acting on it.

He didn't bother to follow up. "What can I do for you?"

Nick hated being out of the loop, so if I dangled the bait in front of him, I knew he'd leap at it. "It's about Kit."

"Kit Lovell? We've had the *police* asking about him. Now you. For God's sake, what's going on?"

"They didn't tell you?" I murmured tantalizingly. "Just like them. Kit's vanished."

"*Vanished?* What do you mean, vanished?"

"Vanished. As in disappeared. As in, no one knows where he is." I hated saying it, and I hated even more that the police were still not treating Kit's disappearance as their priority. "Can we meet?"

Nick was really a very nice man. "My God, yes. Why didn't they say? Idiots."

"What's good for you?"

"Are you going to this party at the Tate tonight?"

I wasn't, because I wasn't nearly trendy enough to be invited. "The Tate. Sure. If I meet you there, can we go somewhere for dinner after and talk?"

Nick was nice, but he wasn't stupid. "I'll leave your name at the door and say you're my guest. It starts at six, but I won't be there until closer to eight. We can duck out after half an hour."

Three down. Only Selden's to go, and then I could go home— well, to Mr. Rudiger's—to start talking to carpenters and lock-smiths and with luck get some sleep before seeing Nick.

My conversation with Robert was easily encapsulated: (a) he was faintly revolted by the idea of crime, and, by extension, with me for bringing it to his notice; (b) he would line up some fraud and corporate law people for me to talk to on Monday; (c) would I now please go away and let him catch an early train home to his nice, orderly life. I agreed with (d) all of the above, and we hung up, mutually relieved to have postponed the problem for seventy-two hours.

I hadn't asked Nick which Tate, Modern or British, since I'd been pretending I'd been invited. Rather than call back and admit to my uncool-ness, I made a guess on Modern. I could always get a cab over to Millbank if I needed to.

One of the things that is so peculiar about London is that there are hardly any views. In most cities you stand on a long avenue, or a piazza, or a plaza, and get a dramatic sweep of the most important buildings, which have been carefully situated to say "authority," "prestige," "status," or, more simply, "money." Even New York, which is most like London in this respect, has a skyline that you could recognize anywhere. London has none of this. It's as though all the architects in the city took a course in How to Hide a Building. The best ones are tucked away down dark alleys. Even St. Paul's has to be glimpsed through a thicket of multistory car parks.

The new Tate, for all its lip service to design, is exactly the same. From the other side of the river, if you're in one of those multi-story car parks, it is probably fantastic. But approaching it from any other direction you have to wend your way through low-cost council housing and 1960s concrete bunkers cunningly disguised as pubs. But then, what do I know?

It was still raining steadily as I ducked down the appropriate underpass and there I was. I was right about the party being here. The place was ringed by warders got up to look like bodyguards in all-black uniforms: Tate Modish. None of your "accessibility" for the Tate. They pull the punters in by making it look like they aren't wanted. The thing is, it works, and people now besiege a place that shows the very same art that they avoided like the plague when the warders wore bright blue polyester.

I told one of the bodyguards that I was a guest of Nicholas Meredith. He tried not to show his disbelief openly, and after a murmured conversation into his mobile he reluctantly had to let me pass, although you could see he thought that it was a bad idea to let someone with my notions of makeup into the building.

I went down the ramp into the Turbine Hall, where Dylan Surtees's four-hundred-foot photograph, *Visitors to the Turbine Hall*, was being unveiled. It was a great piece, but I was so uncool for looking at it when I could have been looking at Lady Gaga, who was surrounded by more bodyguards than there were outside. I gave myself points for actually recognizing Lady Gaga instead, and grabbed a drink before I set off to mill around looking for Nick. It was painless, as parties go. There were plenty of journalists and authors there I knew, and by the time I arrived they were all too drunk to think my eye makeup was odd. Either that, or it was close to what I always looked like, which was not really a thought to warm the cockles of my heart. Whatever cockles were. I made a mental note to look it up when I got home. Then I made another note, to slap myself. Jesus, what a nerd I am. I got a grip and looked around.

And there, at five o'clock from where I stood, was Gerald Atworth, Kit's editor. I shifted uncomfortably. Was I really willing to barge up and talk to him? He wouldn't remember me. I wasn't someone who might one day be able to offer him a job, or access, or do him a favor. And I wasn't twenty and blonde and wearing a short skirt. Those two possibilities were the only varieties of women he'd remember. As I havered, undecided, he stepped forward, moving into the personal space of the young blonde short-skirted woman who had been cheerfully talking to him and another man. I watched as she began to drink more and talk less, taking small, unconscious steps back.

Despite this, I found that my feet had made a decision while my mind was screaming no, and I was now standing right beside them. The third in the group, the man whose back had been to me, turned. The paper's literary editor. Now it was easy, and I moved in smoothly.

"James. Good to see you." We kissed and did the how-long-it's-been-we-should-see-each-other-more-often routine, which is really just publishing-speak for "hello." I noticed out of the corner of my eye that the blonde took the pause as an opportunity to flee. I turned to Kit's editor, hand outstretched. "Sam Clair. We met with Kit Lovell."

He was bored but civil. Well, civil-ish. His eyes flickered over my shoulder to see who he could move on to as we went through the courtesies. It was obvious I didn't have long.

"Have you spoken to Kit recently? I've been trying to catch up with him, but he seems to have gone to ground."

Atworth shrugged. "I don't take attendance."

Not civil at all. I pasted my social smile on more firmly. "Of course. But an editor like you knows everything." Nothing but the best butter.

James snorted quietly into this drink. I took that to mean there wasn't enough butter in the world. And he was probably right. Atworth didn't even bother to look at me. "Maybe he just doesn't want to talk to you."

I wasn't going to get anywhere, so screw this. I widened my eyes and channeled my inner Betty Boop. "Goodness," I said with a baby lisp. "The diplomatic world must have gone into mourning when you decided to move to Madras and become a snake charmer." I shook my head admiringly, patted his arm benevolently, and stomped off.

I was standing talking to the editor of an art magazine about an author of mine who might suit one of his regular "What Do They Look At?" features when I felt two arms go around my waist in a bear hug from behind. Nick.

"Don't you look like something the cat's dragged in?" he boomed.

"Thanks, Nick. It's nice to know that not only do I feel like shit, but I look like shit, too."

He looked closer. "My God, you really do. What on earth . . . ?"

"I was burgled. I got beaten up."

He disentangled me from the art magazine editor, who was suddenly a lot more interested in our conversation, and said, "Never mind all this," his arm sweepingly dismissing the great and the good. "Is this to do with Kit?" Nick is a great big bear of a man, easily six feet two inches, and about as wide, with a reddish fuzz covering most of his face and body, as far as one could tell in public. He was now a concerned bear. Winnie-the-Pooh does worry. "When you called I thought it was serious, but I didn't realize you were personally involved. Let's get out of here and go somewhere where we can talk."

"Are you sure? You've seen everyone you need to see?" Now I knew he was hooked, I could afford to sound generous.

"Sam. Please. It's a party, for Christ's sake, not an audience with the pope." He thought about the director of the Tate for a minute and conceded, "Maybe it is an audience with the pope, but I've been and genuflected before him already. It's enough."

We left.

I'd forgotten about Nick's boy-toy mania, or I would have arranged to meet him at the restaurant. Parked just by the ramp was an enormous bike that, at a guess, I'd say was a Harley-Davidson. Nick took a second helmet off the back and handed it to me. I put it on without the protest I would have made another time. After the past two days, what did dicing with death matter?

I got on behind Nick, put my arms as far around his tree-trunk-like waist as I could manage and, clutching his leather jacket tightly, closed my eyes.

After about a thousand years, he stopped. I opened my eyes cautiously. We were at the Reform Club, of all places. Nick gave our helmets to the porter, who handled them by the extreme edges, as though they were radioactive, and pulled me up the stairs.

"The *Reform*?" I was overcome with giggles.

"It seemed like the best place. Anywhere else I know, it's either impossible to hear, and we'd have to shout at each other, which I figured you didn't want, or it's so quiet that everyone can hear every word, which I also figured you didn't want."

"And the Reform Club isn't quiet?"

"It's quiet, but that's because all the members are dead or deaf. Either suits our purposes."

He was right, so I followed him in. I knew the drill, having a couple of old crusty authors who had never discovered that there are other places to eat in London when they venture up from the country on their annual outing, so I didn't try and leave my coat with Nick's on the pegs outside the dining room. It's against the rules for women to leave their coats there. I assume that the members think these nasty girl coats will get up to something with the boy coats while we're eating, and by the time we come out there will be dozens of baby jackets, all claiming child support from the Committee. I went up the back stairs to the ladies' lav, which is where the Club has decided women are to be hidden away to do whatever it is women do, and returned to find Nick seated in a corner of the Grill room. He was right, it was a good place to talk. It was very dark, very upholstered, very hushed. If you saw it in a movie, you would think it was a parody of a gentleman's club. No one in the room had ever heard of Kit, or fashion, although from a quick guess at the price of some of their suits, quite a few knew about money laundering. But they were too far away to worry about, and anyway, they hadn't heard anything except the sounds of their own voices for decades.

We ordered and I got down to it. "What did the police say about Kit's disappearance?"

Nick looked disappointed. "I thought you were going to tell me."

"I am, but I need to know where to begin."

"Fair enough. They didn't say he had disappeared at all. Just that they were 'looking into' a few matters, and what could I tell them. I thought it was about Jonathan Davies, so I told them about our internal investigation; that Davies had left last term and we have no current address for him; that I hadn't seen Kit in months; that I would be thrilled if he came back to lecture. And then they went away."

I filled him in on Kit's book—there was nothing to lose by it, and if he could help, there was a lot to gain—and my burglary. I left out the money laundering, and most of the names outside of Vernet. Nick wasn't going to have any information about banks and investment companies. "I'm really just fishing here, but tell me about Davies. Kit said he followed him around the country."

"He did? That surprises me, because he showed no initiative in any other way. He was on the History of Fashion course—he had no practical abilities—and he rarely showed up for classes.

His grades were ordinary. Nothing to get him thrown out, but nothing to make anyone take any notice of him."

"You did. Noticed him, I mean."

"Only after he accused Kit of harassment. I've got to say, I never believed it. Davies, let's face it, was such a little twerp. There was no reason for Kit to notice him at all. If Kit tended toward students, and there was no history of that, he wouldn't have chosen Davies. He was totally null: not good, not bad; not handsome, not ugly; not interesting, not boring. Just *nothing*."

Nick was getting worked up, as though I had suggested that the harassment charge had been his fault. I tried to get him to concentrate on practical details. "When he first accused Kit, did you speak to any of his friends? Anyone I could talk to now to find out where he is?"

Nick thought for a minute. "I'm not sure. He was in his final year, so everyone who was with him will have finished their degree now. I'll check the file on Monday, and talk to a few of the lecturers. If we can come up with anyone, I'll call."

I had to leave it there—Nick was trying to be helpful. If he knew anything, I'd get it as soon as he could.

Until I saw Diego Alemán, there really wasn't much I could do. I hated the idea of sitting still when Kit might be lying dead somewhere, but the memory of my "discussion" with Kit's editor was a useful reality check. Life wasn't a novel, and I couldn't go charging about demanding that total strangers tell me all their guilty secrets. I could barely do it in real life to my friends, and they needed industrial-sized pincers to get anything out of me, so who was I kidding? The only constructive thing I could think of was sorting out my flat. So I did. I spent Saturday cajoling builders into fixing my door, locksmiths into fitting new locks, getting duplicate keys made for all the people who have keys to my place—my cleaning lady, my mother, Anthony and Kay. Mr. Rudiger got added to the list. He was always at home, and he was on "our" side—what more can a neighbor want?

I used the time waiting for the various people to arrive by spring cleaning my flat. I washed out the insides of the newly emptied cupboards, put back all the clothes that I wore, bagged up more clothes that I hadn't seen for years to take to Oxfam, went through the thousands of pages of paper now on the floor, refiling some and bagging even more for disposal. I was exhausted and covered with dust by the end, but at least I'd accomplished something, which was more than I could say of the rest of the week. I felt that I had spent all my time that week wandering around not knowing what the hell was going on, asking questions of everyone, hoping that by pure dumb luck I would hit the right person with the right question at the right time. Instead I wasn't even sure now what the questions were. I preferred to have a goal and head toward it, even if it was only the recycling center.

By evening everything was tidy, and I rang Mr. Rudiger to see if he wanted to come down for dinner. It was the least I could do after all his help. I heard the hesitation in his voice, and quickly added, "Or shall I bring it up?" He accepted with grace, as though he was pleased to have the invitation, but not as though I were humoring a disability. I still didn't know why he didn't leave his flat, but he made it appear to be a choice, not a limitation.

We had a pleasant evening, and after fifteen years I finally learnt a little about my upstairs neighbor. Pavel Rudiger had fled Czechoslovakia after the war, had become one of Britain's foremost architects (my adjective, not his), and had retired suddenly, without explanation, some forty years ago, at the height of his career. His buildings were all over the city—I walked past the Stobel House, one of his most famous private commissions, every day on my way to work. Not that he told me any of this. He just said he'd been an architect, and I found the rest in a Pevsner book on London when I came back downstairs. I'd have to tell Nick next time I saw him. From Pevsner, it was clear that Mr. Rudiger was a design legend. Or maybe I wouldn't tell Nick. Mr. Rudiger might not want to meet strangers. It had taken me fifteen years.

On Sunday, I set off for Chris and Rosie's party with a bottle of wine in one hand. Mostly because, having thrust myself on them, I had to take something, but partly, I admit, because I was nervous, and it was better than waving a rolled-up *Sunday Times* at anyone who threatened me. No one did—no one had since Thursday—but I was frightened when I was on my own all the same.

I'd never been to the Stanleys before, but it was immediately familiar. One day someone will have to write a book on why we all live in identical houses. Mine is early Victorian and theirs is later, maybe Edwardian. Apart from that, they were built to the same floor plan, and have exactly the same kind of decoration: neutral colors, bare floorboards, neutral soft furnishings. Hell, even the people were the same as my friends: well-meaning, intelligent, thoughtful people. But the last few days had made me

question my life, and the people I'd spent my life with, and I wondered what purpose we were serving by spending our time reading, writing, publishing more books, so that others could read,
write, and publish more. We were just a bunch of ants in a tiny,
if creative, rut, and when I looked at their house, so similar to
mine, so similar to everyone's that I know, our ant nests were
not much different in that respect, either.

Rosie was genuinely glad to see me. I'd always liked her, although we didn't know each other well. Peter and Chris had done
most of their socializing at work. Rosie taught French at a girls'
school nearby, and she spoke very slowly, as though constantly
trying to impose herself on girls who weren't paying any attention. If you could wait until the end of each clause, though, she
was very funny. The place was packed, with lots of adults standing with drinks, and lots of children running around at waist
level—his, hers, theirs, and probably a bunch of other people's,
too. I couldn't immediately see Chris through the crowd, so I settled down happily to talk to a couple of people I knew from my
Peter days.

After a few minutes I looked up to see where I could find a
drink, and discovered a man staring at me in horror, as though
one of the children had bitten him in the leg. I looked behind
me, but there was no one there. It was definitely me he was staring at. By the time I turned around again, he had grabbed Chris
and was talking to him urgently.

Chris looked around and, seeing me, beckoned me over. "Sam,
this is Diego Alemán."

Diego was in his late twenties. He was good-looking in a quiet
way, with lots of dark brown hair and a thin, aquiline nose.

Having seen hundreds of pictures of his brother, I could just about see the resemblance, although the fact that Diego was wearing jeans and a denim jacket made him look radically different from Rodrigo, who was usually decked out in high-camp glamour, with a shaven head, or dreadlocks, or half on each side.

In the time it had taken me to walk five feet Diego had wiped the original expression from his face. "How do you do?" was all he said. But I hadn't been mistaken. He had recognized me. And I had never seen him before in my life.

"Nice to meet you," I said, trying to give the impression that I hadn't seen what I'd seen. "Are you one of Chris's students?"

"Yes," he said, as though this were the least interesting conversation he'd had all year. Which, superficially, it probably was. "He's my Ph.D. adviser."

We began to discuss his thesis subject, which was John Wilkes and *The North Briton*. This was more interesting. In theory we were discussing his course, but given that the only thing I knew about Wilkes was that he had been an eighteenth-century MP who had been prosecuted for libel, I wondered what we were really talking about.

I moved on. "Have you been in England long?" I asked, in the way English people do, usually just as the visitor has reached the arrivals lounge at Heathrow.

"A couple of years. Before that I was in Paris. I've only recently decided to finish my degree."

"Paris, lucky you," I said, meaning *Paris? Really?*

"Yes," he said, without elaborating. Was I reading things into this, or was he just finding the conversation boring? If he was bored, he had dozens of ways of drifting away without it being rude—his glass needed refilling, he saw someone he wanted to catch before they left. It's easy to shift about at a party, but he wasn't. He was staying put. I didn't delude myself that my views on John Wilkes were what was keeping him glued to my side. And it sure as hell wasn't my snappy repartee.

"What do you do?" he said, visibly coming to a decision.

"I'm an editor at a publishing house." There was no point in pretending. He had recognized me, after all.

"What kind of books?"

"Mostly women's fiction." That was true, if not to the point.

"At least you don't get John Wilkes's kind of problem with that."

Which one of us was supposed to be fishing, for God's sake? "No, you don't. But then, criminal libel is incredibly rare. I don't think there's been a case of anything but civil libel in the courts here for nearly a century."

"No. It's different in Europe, of course."

There really wasn't anywhere to go with this. He knew, I knew, he knew I knew—but to what end?

"What are your plans? Do you think you'll stay here?" I might as well get a little practical information, if nothing else.

"Well, my thesis presentation is about a year off—I'll be here until then."

"Where are you living?"

He stared at me, as though to say, *I've got nothing to hide.* "I'm sharing with some friends in Clapham. And you?"

I stared back, as though to say, *I've got nothing to hide, either.* I didn't. Either he'd been involved in the break-in, in which case he knew where I lived, or he hadn't, in which case what did it matter. "I'm just around the corner, toward Camden."

He nodded. "I know the area."

I kept fishing. "What did you do when you were in Paris? Were you teaching?" That was, after all, the usual route for ABDs— All But Dissertation.

"No, I worked for a merchant bank."

My ears pricked up. "Really? Do they have an office here?"

"No, Intinvest only has two offices, in Paris and Rome, so I've taken temporary work with another bank. But I'll go back to work for them in the summer."

I was trying very hard not to resemble a pointer dog when it flushes a grouse, but my ears were pricked up so hard I could almost feel them quiver. Diego was nonchalant, as though we were still making idle chitchat. But Intinvest was the bank Kit had identified as the source of Vernet's funny money. Could he really be this cool? Could he really be this *dumb*?

"What were you doing for them?" This sounded a bit abrupt, so I added, "I mean, do you plan to work in banking after you've finished at Birkbeck?"

"I was in their IT department—nothing glamorous, or even well paid. Not what people expect when you say banking."

No, but exactly what you might expect when it came to hacking into a publisher's computer system; perhaps even what you would expect if a burglar wanted to install a worm on a home computer. Kit hadn't mentioned Diego at all. Did he not know that he was working at Intinvest, or had he not been there when Rodrigo was alive? Diego looked like he must have been ten years younger than Rodrigo, but he could have been there five years ago, at the time of the murder. My mind was in overdrive, and I nearly forgot to throw the conversational ball back, dull as it was. "Not what people expect, but useful. Had you been there long?" As I uttered this banality, a new thought hit me: *Who better placed to transfer dirty money around the globe than someone in IT?*

Before I could get any further Rosie came over, no doubt worrying that I was trapped by one of Chris's students, and longing to get away to play with the grown-ups. "Sam, I don't know if you saw, but lunch is ready. Do go and get something before the children take it all." I guessed that murder at a Sunday lunch was the kind of solecism people don't forgive. Otherwise I would cheerfully have wrung her neck. I smiled with shattering insincerity. "Thanks, Rosie. I'm starved. What about you, Diego?"

But she wasn't going to let me be cornered. "Don't worry. Chris asked me to introduce Diego to the Bradleys, who want someone to tutor their daughter for her Spanish A-Levels." Damn the Bradleys, and damn their daughter. I hoped vindictively that the silly moo would fail, but I knew when I was beaten. The Golden Rule of north London: A-Levels *über alles.*

I headed off, saying nonchalantly, "See you later, Diego. Nice talking to you." I thought sobbing and holding on to his leg would get me noticed.

I went into the kitchen, and swiftly decided to eat later. Lentil soufflé? If no one in France has thought of putting lentils and eggs together since the discovery of the secret of fire, I figure there must be a reason. Everything else on the table was equally nutritionally balanced, equally healthful, no doubt certified organic, and it looked like the stuff you scrape off the bottom of your shoe. I put two tiny dabs of unidentifiable brown things on my plate and pushed them around with a fork. If Rosie saw me, I could assure her it had been delicious. If Diego came into the kitchen, I could torture him into talking: "Tell me what you know, or it's a second helping of lentil soufflé for you!"

I wandered about for another half hour, chatting idly, but keeping Diego in my sights. He stayed resolutely with the Bradleys. Either he needed the cash, he was a tutoring demon, or he really, really didn't want to talk to me. I gave up and went home.

When I got in I called my mother right away and told her about Diego. Jake had designated her our corporate fraud investigator, so who was I to argue? I asked if she thought I should tell Jake, but she couldn't give it her attention. When she's working you can practically see the information clicking into place in her mental database. I could just imagine leaving a voice-mail message, faux casual: "Hi, Jake, it's Sam Clair. Just to let you know I was at lunch with friends, and met Diego Alemán. Did you know he worked for Intinvest? And that he plans to again?"

Or maybe not. Jake had more or less told me to stay away from Diego. Could I help it if my dear friends the Stanleys had invited us both for lunch, totally coincidentally? No. I didn't think I could carry it off.

I had just put out my hand to the phone, still not decided about what I was going to do, when it rang. I jumped a mile. I guess maybe I wasn't as confident about Jake's good nature as I thought.

"Sam?"

My heartbeat dropped back to something near normal. "Nick, hi."

"Are you OK? You sound strange."

"No, I'm fine." I moved on before I had to tell him that I

was so wired up even a phone call sent my pulse rocketing. "What's up?"

"I went to the College yesterday, and went through the register for last year. As I thought, almost everybody's gone, but there's one student who graduated who is now doing some tutoring here while he uses a studio to finish a big piece he started last year."

"Was he a friend of Davies?"

"No one was a friend of Davies. I told you, he wasn't part of any group. But Ian—that's Ian Childs, the sculptor—knew him as well as anyone. He will be in on Tuesday, when he's got a tutorial. It finishes at four, and I've left a message that I want to see him then. Can you come over?"

"Yes, of course. Do you think there's anyone else to talk to? I understand Davies had no mates, but there must have been someone."

"I'm not so sure about that, but I can set up a meeting with Oliver Heywood, who was his tutor, and was also part of the investigatory committee after Kit was accused."

I was dubious that someone who had found Davies to be a fantasist would have kept in touch with him, but it was better than nothing. "It's worth a shot. Thanks, Nick, I really appreciate it."

"Sam, I was really fond of Kit."

He was talking about Kit as if he were dead. I didn't think I could even bear to point it out.

7

I was glad when Monday morning rolled around. I hadn't been able to concentrate on any of my usual weekend occupations. I couldn't read, couldn't focus on the manuscripts I'd brought home. Instead I tried to think of ways to follow up on Davies. Nick would do his best, but it didn't seem enough. But what could I do? Ask Jake to find out what the police had on their files from the harassment charge? Perfect, make them think that Kit was guilty of something, anything, and then there was even less likelihood they'd take the missing persons report seriously. I googled Davies, but the millions of hits that came back with that sort of name made it useless. In fact, the only thing I could do was fret, and since I'd won Olympic medals in fretting, I did lots of that. I'd cleaned the flat to within an inch of its life on Saturday, and even I, neurotic as I am, found it hard to put much enthusiasm into tidying a flat already tidied into submission. And I stopped myself from going up to see Mr. Rudiger at least half-a-dozen times. He was interested in what was going on, but even so, I was pretending to be an adult. I couldn't stand on his doorstep and whine, "I haven't got anything to *do-o-o-o.*"

So on Monday I was at the office before eight, only to realize that there was nothing I could do there, either. No one at Selden's had ever, in the firm's two hundred years of existence, arrived at work before nine thirty, and the nine-thirty batch were only the juniors. Robert wouldn't be in before ten, and I'd bet my lunch that he'd set up an afternoon appointment with the criminal law people.

I stared at my in-tray and then, in default of anything else, plunged into Breda's manuscript, which I hadn't been able to face on the weekend. Miranda had been thorough. It almost began to read like a real novel. Maybe she was in the wrong job altogether, and should be writing the things, not editing them. After half an hour I left the manuscript on her desk with a note saying: *Great! Can you keep this up for 250 pages without losing your mind?*

That so cheered me that I roared through all the tasks I'd set to one side throughout the week: I passed proofs with reckless abandon, signed off jackets that looked like four kinds of hell, wrote stroppy notes on marketing copy. When I got to the minutes and memos I moved them straight across from IN to FILING without missing a beat. It was the most efficient solution. I would have liked to have done the same to my e-mail, which I'd also ignored all weekend, but I lost my nerve and, after I deleted the spam asking me if I wanted a mortgage, a girl, a pony, or a bigger penis, I settled down to read the rest.

One thing was quickly clear. Miranda had put the fear of God into Loïc at Vernet—or something had. There were five messages

from him. Two sent on Friday, two on Saturday, and one yesterday. All of them were attempts to set up a meeting when I arrived
in Paris. The first one offered me a drink after the show; the
second invited me to the party after the show; the third suggested dinner as well; and the fourth and fifth said whatever time
or place I chose would be fine. I figured if I left it another day
they'd send over a chauffeur-driven limousine and a dozen
couture outfits, but I wasn't cool enough to hold out. I e-mailed
back a yes to the drink, and forwarded all the messages on to Jake
with a covering note: *Why am I suddenly so desirable?*

The rest of the morning passed in the usual round of work.
We had a meeting to go through our autumn list before the sales
conference, and there were no surprises: Ben was a prat, David
a jellyfish, everyone else comatose. No one said anything particularly intelligent, but no one snored, either. Word had got around
on my burglary, and I discovered that the easiest way to deflect
questions was to let people tell me their own burglary or mug-
ging stories. It's like having a bad back. Once you have one, you
find that so does everybody you know, and they can't wait to tell
you about it. And if you let them talk, when they've finished they
think they know everything about yours.

I had asked Miranda to text me in the meeting if Selden's
wanted me before lunch, but she didn't, and I wasn't surprised.
When I got back to my office I found her in exactly the position
I'd last seen her in on Friday, hunched over Breda's manuscript,
pencil moving busily. She stopped with relief when she saw me,
and came into my office and shut the door.

"I spoke to Kath on Friday," she said, without preamble.

"Great. How did it go?"

"I was *so* fabulous. I was just glad you weren't there, because if I had seen you I would have laughed. She's called you twice already this morning. She says she has a manuscript she thinks will be up your street, and wants you to see it and meet the author. If you like it, you can have it on an exclusive. It's that new Indian novelist everyone is so crazy about—the one whose story was published in *Granta* last month?"

I recognized the author, but I was sure it would be offered to Ben. He did literary fiction, and paid much more than I did.

Miranda nodded impatiently. "Sure, but this way she can get you alone to pump you for information about your mystery man."

"Who is my man, by the way? And how many exclusives do you think I'll get out of him?"

"If you play along, I think you can build a very nice list from it—she's gagging for news. But as to who your new guy is, well, I hope you won't be angry. . . ."

"Angry? Why? We agreed you'd wing it."

"I think I might have got carried away."

"Spill." I stared at her, anxious, but also ready to laugh.

"Charles Pool."

"Charles Pool." I was mystified. "Who the hell is he?"

She wasn't sure if she was ashamed or proud. "Ben's new author."

"Ben's—? Oh my God, not the nineteen-year-old with the non-novel?"

She nodded guiltily.

"Is he even our author? Last I heard, Ben hadn't offered."

"He preempted for £150,000 on Friday."

"*One hundred fifty thousand pounds?* For three pages of nothing?

Ben's got to be out of his mind. It's not worth £5,000. It's not worth £5." I was an editor again, totally caught up in this incredibly foolish piece of publishing.

Miranda waved her hand in front of my face. I was off message. "I saw him at the launch, and he's really cute."

I remembered that he was now my new ex-lover. "Did I take up with him because he's nineteen, or because he's cute, or because he just made a lot of money?"

She shrugged. "I thought all three worked well. And everyone will be so thrilled to know that you're cradle snatching that no one will worry about Alemán, which is what you want."

She was right, but even though I knew I wasn't a cradle snatcher, it felt peculiar. "Kath must be keeping this close to her chest. Ben was still looking at me in that pitying, soon-you'll-be-in-a-nursing-home way he has in the meeting this morning. Either that, or she didn't believe you."

Miranda knew Kath better than I did. She smiled cynically. "She believed me. You wouldn't be getting this exclusive if she thought there was nothing to the story."

It was sort of insulting professionally, but also true.

I set off for Selden's at one. We were having a lunch meeting, which I'd had there before and had never wanted to repeat. A mummified secretary brought in fossil sandwiches to the boardroom, a gloomy, badly lit room lined with wooden panels from which stuffed shirts of the nineteenth century looked down at the stuffed shirts of the twenty-first. Such a treat. If I'd been Ben, they would have liked me: his flash Italian suits against my dull

English ones, his Oxford against my déclassé American university, and his naked ambition against my—what? Ambition was acceptable in a man; in a woman it was just plain vulgar. And if I didn't have any, I should just stay home and mind the children. I'm probably projecting, but it's safe to say that we don't warm to each other.

The meeting ran much as I expected. Robert came down to their reception room to collect me. If you had to paint a storybook picture of a solicitor, it would be Robert. He is, objectively, and though it hurt me to admit, good-looking, tall, with well-cut features, well-cut hair, well-cut suits. But he was also red-cheeked (red-nosed, too, if the truth be told) and so supremely satisfied with himself and his place in the world that I always thought he had to be putting it on. He shook hands with me with the air of a bishop conferring a blessing on a very humble sinner, and took me upstairs. We waited in uncomfortable silence for nearly ten minutes until their criminal law partner, Hugo Littlewood, finally appeared. Except that he was thinner, he was a mirror image of Robert: expensively groomed, expensively dressed, red-faced, red-nosed, and thrilled with himself. His first question was the one I always get from solicitors: "Any relation of Helena Clair?" When I said she was my mother, he smiled thinly. If she'd been no relation, I don't think I would have got a smile at all.

We ran through the details. I'd been through them so many times, I could decide what to keep in and what to leave out without even thinking. Basically, I gave them everything regarding the book. I left out my burglary, and my weekend sleuthing. None of their damn business. Littlewood flinched when I told him that the Fraud Squad had the manuscript, but he could hardly blame me.

This need to be fair irritated him, and he snapped at me, "Who is Lovell's solicitor? And who was Alemán's British solicitor?"

I had no idea who Kit's solicitor was, or why it was any of his business, although I only shared the first part of that thought. As to Alemán's, what did he mean? Vernet's solicitor? Alemán's personally? I assumed they'd all be different and once more, wondered not only why he thought I'd know, but why he would want to know. When I asked he shrugged, "Just wondering."

Probably fussing about whether someone he golfed with was going to get arrested. Then he threw out, as though it was loaded with meaning, "I've had a call from Kenneth Wright."

I looked blank. "Who is Kenneth Wright?"

Littlewood got that why-oh-Lord-do-I have-to-deal-with-morons? look on his face. "Wright. Kenneth Wright," he repeated, as though that explained everything.

I couldn't resist. "Of course! Kenneth *Wright*."

He nodded, pleased. I was finally there.

"I've never heard of him," I said flatly.

"You must have."

"Well, if I must, I must. But I haven't," I said, seriously pissed off now. "If you want me to talk about him, you're going to have to give me some clues. Why not start with who he is." I spoke slowly and clearly, and didn't try to hide my contempt.

Littlewood flushed angrily. This is where I always ended up with Selden's. They thought I was an idiot, I thought they were. It was not a meeting of minds.

"Wright is a solicitor in the City. He handled Vernet's UK

property deals. Surprising, for a solicitor in single practice, but he was with Cooper's before—very prestigious."

Wright must be all right. He had a pedigree: Best-in-Show at the solicitors' Kennel Club. But if this Wright looked after part of Vernet's legal work, why was Littlewood asking me about the rest? There was no point in asking. I tried a more neutral, "What did he want?"

"He didn't *want* anything," said Littlewood, stung—someone who had been at Cooper's, wanting something. What a ridiculous notion. "He offered to help us."

"Really," I said, in my most bored tone. "How was he planning to do that?"

"He offered to give us any assistance—professional courtesy." Littlewood was now so puffed up with pomposity that a single breath more would probably make him explode.

"How very civil of him. What do we think he can do for us?"

"That, surely, is for you to decide," he said in a voice dripping with contempt. "You and your *client*." He referred to Kit as though he were a derelict sleeping in a doorway.

I could feel my temper rising, which wasn't productive. I stood up, choosing the nuclear option for my exit line.

"Well, good to see you, gentlemen. Thank you for your time. If you've got anything, do give me or David Snaith a ring. Or Helena. The police have asked her to keep an eye on things."

It would have spoiled the effect to look back, so I didn't, but that didn't mean I didn't enjoy the horrified silence that followed me out the door and, I liked to imagine, all the way to the street.

I spent the rest of the afternoon in routine work, making an offer for a promising new novel, turning down half-a-dozen more, arguing about royalties with a particularly obtuse agent, and, most often, fending off Kath, who wanted to sell me this book so badly she practically crawled into my lap down the phone. Finally I went home. When I got in, there was a message on my voice mail, no name, no number. Just a man saying, "What makes you think it's sudden?"

It was definitely Jake Field, but it was hours before I remembered the e-mail I'd sent him that morning.

By the time I got to the LSD on Tuesday, I had little expectation that there would be anything to learn. Jonathan Davies had been a nuisance, and an unpleasant one at that, but I couldn't make any link between him and Alemán. Still, it was better than sitting in my office waiting for something to happen, pretending to work.

After my rip-roaring success with Atworth, I'd brooded on asking Jake if he'd give me Kit's sister's phone number. At least, I'd brooded on it until his phone message. Not now. And what would I have asked her? Atworth may have been a bully and a thug, but I couldn't really summon any enthusiasm for the idea that Kit's disappearance had anything to do with his journalistic life. I was sure plenty of people disliked him, or were jealous—he was successful, and he didn't suffer fools gladly. Although who did? Were there fool sufferers who lined up, panicked there might not be enough fools to go around? *Focus!* I shouted at myself. Kit. Professional jealousies. No, I couldn't see it. Anyone who hated him for work reasons wouldn't arrange his disappearance. They'd plant a nasty squib about him in the *Daily Mail,* or—I cast my mind about for a suitable fashionista villainy—or they'd send him Botox vouchers anonymously in the post. Maybe not, but violence seemed just as unlikely. Davies' weird behavior seemed the most important thing to follow, therefore.

I'd never been inside the LSD before. Nick and I saw each other at parties fairly often, but we had no work connection. Kit had enjoyed lecturing there, but although I went to his talks when they were related to the books we did together, the LSD was entirely off my patch. Like all schools, though, it had a sink-or-swim mentality, and there was no one to ask the way near the entrance. There were endless corridors shooting off into the distance, with nothing so designer unfriendly as a sign or a notice board. The whole place was quite un-designer-ly, in fact. It was like an overgrown primary school, filled with the sound of muffled voices, the smell of long-dead meals, and a faint but unmistakeable scent of eau-de-wet student. I chose at random, setting off down a corridor that looked as anonymous as any other, figuring I'd find someone to guide-dog me in the right direction sooner or later.

An extremely thin man in his early twenties was reading a notice board with such ferocious absorption that he jumped when I spoke to him. He looked as if he was thin from lack of food, not naturally. His clothes had a slight tang of mildew to them, his hair was unwashed, his spectacles held together with a bent paper clip. He also had some sort of skin problem, with great raw patches across one cheek and his neck. However, he knew the way to Nick's office, which was all I needed. When I didn't grasp his rather convoluted directions at once he said impatiently, "Here, I'll show you." We walked down half-a-dozen identical corridors. I asked him what he was studying, but he appeared not to know—his personality was no more prepossessing than his appearance. And apparently he thought the same about me, because he stopped dead and pointed. "Down there. First left. Third door on your right." Then he vanished.

Nick's office was a vast improvement on the dreary halls I'd just come through. It was a white cube: white floors, white walls, white wooden table acting as a desk. The four blond wood Alvar Aalto chairs were shocking in their lack of whiteness. There was nothing on display. No papers on the table, no shelves, no nothing. Instead a small drawer unit stood tidily beside the table, and white Japanese screens sheltered what I imagined to be filing cabinets and bookshelves. In the midst of this vast arctic waste Nick's big fuzzy redness was even more endearing.

Nick had rounded up both Jonathan Davies' tutor and his friend—or, as he was quick to point out—not-so-very-close friend. It was immediately obvious that they had been discussing the matter before I arrived, and had planned what they were willing to say. Ian Childs led off. He and Davies had both come down from Glasgow the same year, and for a few months at the beginning that had been enough for them to share a place to live, with two other students. "But it didn't last long. We were all involved with what we were doing, and we were also set on having a good time. Jonathan didn't like the LSD, he didn't go out, he didn't have friends back. He just didn't do anything. When we moved on, it really just never occurred to us to include him in our new plans. We moved out of that place two years ago, and I don't know where he's been living since."

Nick interrupted. "We do. At least, we have his address until last year. It's in Shepherd's Bush—Roxfield Road."

Ian said, "Number 9? That's where we were. But he left with us—he couldn't have afforded to stay on his own. We rented from Gloria Ramsay, the woman who lived downstairs. She had JESUS SAVES posters in her windows—but if Jesus saved, Gloria believed in more straightforward profit." It was a joke he must have made often, and he did it now almost automatically. "I can ring her if you like—see if she has a room for a friend of mine."

Nick said, "Great. Do it now."

While he was phoning, Oliver Heywood, Jonathan Davies' tutor, told me what he knew, which was nothing. Davies had made his accusation, Oliver and a hastily formed committee had looked into it, talking to Davies' classmates to see what they had witnessed (nothing); to the landlady to see if Kit had ever been seen at Davies' flat (he hadn't); and to Kit. Davies had said Kit kept phoning, and leaving sexually explicit messages. The calls had continued, he said, even when Kit was away, but no telephone records showed them. Kit had given the school permission to look at his mobile bills, and asked all the hotels he had stayed in to cooperate by passing their records over to the LSD. Nothing. Davies said he hadn't thought to keep the messages. No one could be found who had ever seen the two of them together, Davies couldn't produce a single witness. It boiled down to his word against Kit's, with the weight tilting toward Kit, because Davies had made accusations that records should have backed up, and they didn't. Kit's private life was as convoluted as anyone else's, but there had never been the slightest sniff of interest in a student. Davies had then upped the ante and made a formal police complaint. The police, after an agonizing wait, came to the same conclusion. So eventually Kit had said he would leave, rather than put the college in a difficult position. He'd only given a single series of lectures each year, so it didn't much matter to him.

Had it had mattered more to the LSD? Maybe that was worth thinking about. I did, for a nanosecond. Then I gave a mental *tsk*. Even if they had been distraught that Kit had created a problem and then just abandoned them, like the idea of a crazed journo wreaking vengeance, I kept coming back to People Like This Don't Do Things Like That. An academic leaves you short-staffed for a term, so you kidnap him? Come on. In the real world, no one kidnaps academics or journalists because no one wants them. It's hard enough to get rid of them after dinner. Having them around all the time, drinking you out of house and home? Please.

Leaving aside "People Like This," if I looked at what was in front of me, while Nick and his colleagues had obviously presented the story from their side, and they weren't thrilled that this whole thing was coming up again, could I see them covering up something criminal? If it had been only about Kit being a stalker, maybe, but his disappearance, maybe worse? I couldn't see it. I didn't know Nick well, but I'd known him a long time. Was the reputation of the LSD so all-encompassing for him that he'd do that? I didn't think so.

I couldn't see where to go with this. The only person I could think to speak to was his landlady, Gloria Ramsay, Ian's Jesus Saves lady. Then Ian hung up and said, "No, she hasn't seen him since we all left." So much for that.

Although, wait a minute. I turned to Oliver. "If that's the case, surely it casts doubt on the information she gave you? If she hadn't seen Davies for the past two years, it's hardly surprising if she didn't see Kit, either."

Nick interrupted. "But wait a minute. The police investigated, too. They must have known he didn't live there."

"I don't know. Maybe they did, and didn't tell you." I made a mental note to ask Jake to check. If my mother could ask him to run errands, why not me? Then I thought about his voice-mail message again. Did I want to ask him a favor? Did I want him to know I'd been talking to people on my own?

Did I know what I wanted?

I called my mother as I left the LSD. She wouldn't be able help me with the last question, even were I to lose my mind and ask her, but I thought we needed to pool our notes. She agreed, and when I got to her house at ten, she was sitting in the kitchen surrounded by papers, with a cup of coffee in her hand, as I'd seen her so often before when she was in the middle of preparing a case. This time it was my case, and Jake was sitting next to her: more papers, more coffee.

Helena's kitchen is the best room in her house. It has a red-tiled floor, bright yellow walls, a wooden table covered with a Provencal cloth. It should have been gaudy enough to need sunglasses, but it isn't—somehow it's just cheery. It always feels like the sun is shining there, even when it hadn't for days, or now, when it had been dark for five hours in the long English winter evenings. I dropped into a seat, poured some coffee for myself and nodded to both of them, pretending that I hadn't had Jake's message.

Jake had looked up only briefly anyway. He was shuffling through a pile of documents my mother had just given him. "Can you précis this for me, Nell? What have we got?"

"The manuscript makes for very interesting reading." She slanted a look at me. "Much better than I'd expected. The legal implications are fascinating."

My mother can say stuff like that with a straight face. "And for those of us who aren't interested in corporate law?"

She was serene. "You should be. Everyone should be. For one thing, Robert Marks is even thicker than I thought. This one should have sent alarm bells ringing at Selden's by page ten."

Jake looked alert. I looked confused.

"Come on, Nell," he coaxed, "let us have it."

I squinted at him. He was treating my mother like his new best friend, and leaving suggestive messages for her daughter. It was only with difficulty I dragged my attention back to what Helena was saying.

"There is the money laundering that Kit picked up, mostly involving shadow companies in Eastern Europe, and a few in the Far East, which are invoicing for nonexistent goods. That he's got, and it's all very straightforward. But he missed the money laundering at home, although he's a good enough journalist that he collected all the evidence. He just didn't recognize it for what it was."

I thought Jake was going to lunge across the table and shake the information out of her. I intervened. I'd had enough violence for a while. "What is it? Where? I didn't see anything."

"No, dear. That's because you're one of those who aren't interested in corporate law." I could see she was getting to it, so I made a shushing gesture to Jake.

She turned to him herself. "Have you spoken to NCIS?"

This was irritating. Now it was making sense to him, and I still had no idea what was going on.

"NCIS?" I asked neutrally, to the space between them.

"The National Criminal Investigation Services," he translated for me. "It's a joint investigatory body—police and Revenue and Customs—to probe anything that might involve money laundering. It gets reports from banks and lawyers on questionable transactions, which it then follows up."

I understood the bank part, but lawyers? Who turns in their own clients? If you were honest and thought a client was crooked, then you didn't act for them. If you were crooked yourself, then you weren't going to turn the client in. Either way, it didn't make any sense.

My mother picked up my unspoken question. "Solicitors are legally culpable if their clients are laundering money."

"Of course they are, if they help them. . . ." I began.

My mother smiled bitterly. "No, it's more than that. The burden of proof was shifted. Now the criteria is not if the solicitor knew, but if the solicitor *should* have known. In other words, if you're an innocent, a naïve, or just plain bad at your job, and you've been hoodwinked by a clever and unscrupulous client, it's too bad for you. You go to jail, too."

"So if you've acted for someone who has been handling dirty money—even if you didn't know where it came from—" I looked inquiringly at my mother for help.

She nodded crisply. "If you were my client, and came to me simply to buy a house, but used tainted funds, if I did the conveyancing for you on the house, then it's off to jail for me. Which means that solicitors report their clients to NCIS. Who then investigate. If there's nothing there, the client never knows. If the solicitor fails to report a dubious client, his bank probably will, and if NCIS finds evidence of money laundering, then . . ."

I was triumphant. "Then you end up with Kenneth Wright."

My mother and Jake both looked at me as if I were a toddler they had been indulging, who had suddenly started reciting Hamlet's soliloquies.

Jake spoke first. "Kenneth Wright? Who is he?"

I was proud of myself. "He does the UK property deals for Vernet."

Helena was peeved. Solicitor Land was her territory. "Where did you hear about him?"

I told them about my conversation with Selden's.

My mother looked thoughtful. "Cooper's. That does surprise me. They're extremely respectable. There's never been a hint of a problem for them. You say he's not with them now, and working on his own?"

I wasn't going to put too much faith in Selden's. "So Littlewood said. I don't know more than that."

Jake was getting impatient. "What are we saying here?"

"We're saying NCIS should be looking at Wright. Cooper's are very big, very prestigious. It's unusual that someone should leave them to set up in a small way on his own. Put that together with the fact that Vernet's property deals in this country were unnecessarily complex. . . ."

She seemed to feel she had said enough, but Jake made a rolling motion with his hand, keep going.

"It's straightforward. Kit writes that before the Regent Street shop was bought, three deals failed. It's the oldest and easiest way to launder money: make an offer on a property, put the dirty money in a solicitor's escrow account, abort the deal, and then the money comes back, fresh and clean from a reputable solicitor's bank account. And," she sat up at the thought, "*and* if it was coming from Cooper's, no one would ever think to look further—not even NCIS—you just can't get more respectable than that. Kit didn't realize what was going on, so he didn't follow it up, but Vernet was opening boutiques in ridiculous places, then discovering that the market wasn't there, and closing them again. It doesn't take a genius to know that you can't sell £4,000 dresses in places like Bradford. But if there were three or four aborted deals for every piece of property purchased, then Vernet were washing tens of millions of pounds in Britain alone every year. Multiply by all the countries they were operating in. The stuff Kit found on the false invoices was nothing—probably just a little sideline. The real money was coming from the property."

I thought I'd better add in the rest. "Did you speak to Diego Alemán?"

Jake looked at me blandly, and made a noncommittal noise. It would have been nice if information were a two-way street, but then, I didn't expect him to tell me how to edit books.

"Did he tell you he'd worked for Intinvest?"

Jake stopped looking bland.

"I met him at a party on Sunday—totally by chance, he's the student of a friend of mine who teaches at Birkbeck." I didn't expect him to believe me, but I also didn't care. "He was work-ing for Intinvest in Paris, and plans to go back to them this summer." I paused, then added, as though I was merely thinking aloud. "He said he was in IT. I have no idea what that means in his case, but I assume that that's how money gets transferred?"

Jake sat staring at the table, working the implications through.

I kept quiet and watched him. After a minute he nodded sharply once to himself, and went down the hall to make some calls privately.

I was still of two minds about nagging Jake to get the police to look at Kit's file again. Bringing the harassment to their no-tice again seemed like a bad idea, doing nothing seemed like a bad idea. Which was worse? I had no idea, and decided to hang fire for the moment. Instead I told Helena about the LSD, more to keep her amused than anything else. The Jesus Saves lady made her laugh, which I had known it would, and we sat catch-ing up on more mundane matters until Jake came back. He was pulling on his coat.

He looked at me. "I'll drive you home."

What could I say: *Look, I haven't made up my mind, and it's raining and nearly midnight, so thanks, but I'd rather walk?*

We drove the mile and a half in silence. When we got to my house Jake pulled over and cut the engine. I stared out the window.

"Whatever you want," he said.

I kept staring. This was absurd. I wasn't an adolescent, and I wasn't making a lifetime commitment. The man didn't want to marry me, he wanted to fuck me. And, despite the fact that nice men find it more comfortable to think that nice women don't jump into bed with men they've just met and don't have long-term plans for, nice women sometimes do. They definitely sometimes do.

Jake put his hand on the back of my neck and waited silently, gently rubbing behind my ear.

The car was very small suddenly, and airless.

I opened the door. "Let's go," I said.

8

Jake was up and gone by the time I woke up. Well, actually, he was up and gone by the time I stopped pretending to be asleep. I really didn't want to talk to him. I had no idea where this could go. If it had been awful, or even just dull, then it was easy—thanks a lot, it was great, but I don't think so. But it hadn't. And from what Jake had said last night, he was one of those nice men who didn't think women should be slept with and then dropped. He wasn't looking for a just a couple of fun weeks, which would also have been easy. Casual, very enjoyable sex was one thing, but could I see myself having a relationship with a policeman? I didn't think so. But how could I say that? I had no idea, so I pretended to be asleep. Which was fine for the moment, but unless I developed narcolepsy it wouldn't work for long.

I lay with my eyes firmly closed, lying still until I heard the door bang and his car start. The second it did I leaped out of bed and roared through shower, dressing, and coffee, setting the land-speed record in the process on the way to the office. The last refuge of the intelligentsia: when real life gets too difficult, go find something to read.

I was halfway there before I realized what day it was. I was supposed to be in Paris for Vernet's show that afternoon. The whole trip was ludicrous. Kit and I had planned it for fun. Now he was missing and there was no point anymore. Miranda had set up this meeting with Loïc, and I had my train tickets, but neither of those things justified five hours in a train. I stood, undecided. Then I realized that if I went, at least I'd be out of meaningful conversation distance with Jake for a bit longer. Decision made, I raced up to my office, grabbed the tickets, left a note for Miranda, and thundered back down the stairs. Hurtling through the reception area I saw the student from the LSD—the thin, not-very-clean one who had taken me to Nick's office. He was talking to Bernadette, and I had practically mown him down before I stopped.

"Hi. Are you looking for me?" I looked at my watch as I spoke. I could get to St. Pancras in half an hour—twenty minutes if I was lucky. I should make it.

He took a hurried step back, as though my momentum had unbalanced him. "No. That is—" He turned to Bernie. "Thanks very much. It's OK. I was mistaken." And he bolted.

Bernie and I stared at the door, then at each other. "Was it something I said? Or something you said?"

Bernie shrugged. "He was asking if you were in all day. He said he didn't have an appointment. I was just telling him we don't keep track of the staff." She snorted at the idea of even trying. "Then you came back and—"

"Did he leave a name?" Maybe he knew something about Davies.

Bernie shook her head.

"Well, if he comes back, nab him and get a contact number. Frisk him if you have to. I really want to talk to him."

She looked slightly sick at the idea, but I knew she'd do what she could. I didn't have time to deal with it now, anyway, and headed back out the door.

I made it with five minutes to spare, which meant that the staff at the station were giving everyone those *don't you realize how privileged you are to travel on my nice shiny train, and here you are putting me to all this trouble* looks. I ignored them. If you paid attention to all the put-upon people in England, you'd never have time to be put-upon yourself, which would take all the fun out of things.

The compartment was jammed, but once we had left the station I prowled down the corridor and found that, as usual, they'd put everyone in two carriages to minimize the work for the staff. The rest of the train was empty. I moved, ignoring the huffs of annoyance and giving my best Helena Junior stare. Then I settled down to read the morning's crop of e-mails and submissions.

It was all very straightforward, but given the tiny amount of time I'd given to anything other than worrying about Kit, there was an awful lot of it, and it filled the journey to Paris nicely. It was only as we were rumbling through the outer suburbs that I reached the e-mail from Breda, and we had arrived at the Gare du Nord before I looked up from it. It was very civil, as always from her, but she had a problem with the jacket copy that had been sent to her—the stuff that would go on the cover, to entice readers to buy the book. She wrote: *I know, Sam, that this isn't your department, but I thought I'd better discuss it with you, as it's a bit awkward. The person who wrote the blurb has missed the point of my book, and I don't know how to tell her. She hasn't realized that the book is a spoof, and has written it as though it were a chick-lit novel. What shall we do? Is it best to ask her to do it again, or, given that she has no sense of humor, is it better just to give it to someone else quietly?*

Spoof? I stared, dazed, at the passengers shrugging into their coats and collecting their bags. The *blurb writer* had no sense of humor? Where did that leave the rest of us?

As I moved through the usual rugger scrum masquerading as a taxi queue, sidestepping the thin blonde women of indefinite age with small dogs in Vuitton carry cases, I was operating entirely on automatic pilot. Every time I go through the Gare du Nord I swear I'll learn to use the Métro, but every time I get there, I can't face it and tell myself, *Just this once more*. And all the while, I turned the e-mail over and over in my mind, trying to figure out where we'd gone wrong. Breda had written a comic novel? Why had none of us laughed? Was it not funny, or had we just not expected it to be funny? Was she a bad writer or were we stupid? I had a feeling that I knew the answer to that last one. I rang Miranda once I was in a taxi and read her the e-mail. She was doubtful. "We can't all be wrong, can we?"

"Can't we." I was grim, and it wasn't a question. "Look, print out a couple of copies of the manuscript without the author's name on them and give them to your friends. Tell them it's a new comic novel that's just come in and you think it's great."

"I have to tell my *friends* that I think it's great?" Miranda saw social death looming.

"You can tell them the truth afterward if they start to treat you like a leper. None of us can read this book fresh, and we need to know if we've all had total sense of humor failure. Did we just misread it because we know Breda?"

She was un-persuaded, but it meant she could stop working on it while her friends read it. "If I pay them a reader's fee, I can ask them to do it in a couple of days."

"If there's anyone in the world who will read that stuff in forty-eight hours for £35, go for it. But find people who will give you a real response, not what they think you want to hear. Make sure you don't include the title page. I want them to read it without any preconceptions based on the author's name."

She said she'd get straight onto it, which left me free to think about the coming afternoon.

Kit had told me the drill, so I didn't worry about getting to the Palais des Sports in good time. The show was called for two thirty, and he told me it wouldn't begin before three, probably not until three thirty. So I went to find some lunch. There's a restaurant that I like, but I never take anyone I know there, because it is too ordinary. For me that's its charm. It is a neighborhood place, with a changing lunch menu of plats du jour, and a line of single tables by the door where men who eat there every day have their regular seats and napkins they fold up and leave for the following day. It serves basic food—roast chicken, stew—the kind of thing those solitary men would eat at home if only there was someone to cook it for them. The waitresses all wear white dental-nurse uniforms, and are large and forceful. If you don't eat enough of your chicken, they push the plate back to you and urge you on. It felt like a good idea to go there today and let a motherly bully tell me what to do. Pretty much like the rest of my life, now I thought about it.

I ate my chicken and sat thinking about the meeting with Loïc after the show. I wasn't quite sure why I had set it up, apart from the fact that they wanted to see me. What could I say? We know Alemán was murdered, that Intinvest has been laundering money through Vernet, now would you kindly tell us what you've done with Kit, and we'll stop publication? Apart from anything else, it probably wouldn't work. It would be good to know what they wanted, though. Vernet had been hugely obstructive, refusing throughout to talk to Kit. Now someone there was falling over themselves to talk to me. What had changed? It could only be Kit's disappearance. What I couldn't tell was whether they knew something about it, or whether they wanted to. Whichever it was, it might give me more to go on than we had now, which was zip. We knew Vernet was laundering money, which we'd known before, and we knew how, which we hadn't, but frankly I didn't care. Let them wash the entire contents of the Bank of England if it made them happy. I just wanted to know what had happened to Kit, and go back to publishing women's reads. Or, as it would now appear, comic novels.

That wasn't a route I wanted to go down, so I paid up and headed over to the Palais des Sports. I'd never been there before, but I knew that I was in the right place because it was besieged by a huge number of incredibly scruffy-looking people—much scruffier than me—all trying to push past the security guards. I held on tight to my ticket as I waved it in the air, joining in the melee. Kit had warned me about this. He said a friend of his had fainted at one of these shows, and the person who caught her as she fell stole her ticket and dumped her on the pavement. Eventually I squeezed through, and found myself in a sports stadium that had been covered with pink plush and roses to look like the Opéra. So, if they had used the Opéra, would they have ripped out all the plush and flowers to make it look like a sports stadium? I mentally shrugged. It was good to see a business that appeared to make even less sense than my own.

The bouncers inside were no less aggressive than those outside. The general feeling was, *Prove you deserve to be here.* Since I'd had a foul week, and couldn't care less about this, my basic attitude was, *Well, fuck you too sonny.* The weird thing was, it worked. I didn't even have to say it. Apparently just walking in a way that suggests *Fuck you* is the way to make people believe you're important. I wondered briefly if it would do the trick outside the fashion world, too. Something to consider.

Once inside the arena itself I was enchanted to find that the little gilt and red velvet chairs that I'd seen in movies from the 1940s were still in use. Everyone was squeezed tight, breathing in to ensure they fit. A quick look around was enough to show me that fashion people were on the whole no thinner or more stylish than the rest of the world. In fact, the bulk of the audience consisted of brisk middle-aged middle-sized women in sensible shoes, and the chairs—and the lack of space between them—were definitely not made to accommodate them.

I smiled at the woman whose lap I was about to almost sit on. It seemed rude to do so without introducing myself, so I did. She was fifty, with a wonderful quiff of gray hair, and a quizzical look for the seething, chattering masses. She told me was Mary-

Kay Montgomery, the fashion editor of the *Chicago Times*. "Do you do fashion publishing?"

"Not really. I'm working with Kit Lovell on a book on Alemán."

She was torn. The first part of the sentence had caused a pleased response—she obviously knew Kit and liked him. When I got to the bit about Alemán, she withdrew, like a snail shrinks back into its shell if you poke at it with a stick. "Yes," she said flatly, "I heard about that." There was no welcome in her voice now.

I changed the subject. "I've never been to one of these before." I waved toward the runway.

"You'd better get yourself a drink," she advised, deftly swiping a glass of champagne from a tray as it floated past. "It will be at least half an hour before we begin. The last show was nearly two hours late, and they'll wait for everyone to arrive."

She was right, it was, and we chatted idly until the lights finally went down. Mary-Kay pointed out celebrities—all of whom I had spotted by their larger-than-life behavior, and all of whom I'd misidentified. She showed me Anna Wintour, the editor of *Vogue*, sitting in what the fashion world would regard as isolated glory, although to me she just looked bored and lonely. There was Manolo Blahnik, shoemaker to the stars and permatanned to the color of a pair of brogues, manically kissing everyone on sight. The Ladies Who Lunch—the women rich enough to *buy* couture clothes—sat in a little enclave, about a dozen strong. They passed up the champagne—those calories, my dear—and looked as bored as I would have at Marks and Spencer. I was fascinated by the whole thing. It was like entering an alternate reality. The beginning of the show was signaled by a shift in the music, from thunderous to deafening, and by the photographers, penned in at the end of the runway like particularly dangerous animals, loosing off a battery of flashes that would have been bright enough to land a 747 by.

I'm not quite sure what I'd expected, maybe something that looked like MTV. The one thing I hadn't expected, though, was—well, a fashion show. Which is exactly what it was. Incredibly tall, incredibly thin women clip-clopped like ponies down the runway, opened their coats, twirled their skirts, or just flicked their hair, then walked back. They were glazed over, both mentally and physically: their makeup was an inch thick, and birds' nest wigs meant that they all looked identical. I'd also expected the kind of clothes that you see in the newspapers the next day— bare-breasted women in nothing but a pair of lavender velvet jodhpurs and a necklace of cowrie shells, say. Those were there, but there were only two of them, and they were entirely for the cameras. The rest of the clothes were totally gorgeous, totally wearable. Even a peasant like me felt the urge. There was one yellow taffeta ball dress that was larger than my entire flat, and I wanted it so badly it was like a physical need.

Then the lights came up and I shook myself. What an extraordinary thing—not theater, as I'd expected, just naked consumerism. I said so to Mary-Kay, and she nodded, "You bet. The rest—" she stuck out her chin toward the Hollywood contingent in the front row—"that's just window dressing. Completely irrelevant, except as advertising."

I'd spent so much time thinking about money laundering that I'd forgotten what big business fashion really was.

I asked Mary-Kay how I should find Loïc. She snorted, which

I had quickly discovered was most people's response to him. "Have another drink," she said. "There's no point going backstage for another half an hour at least: It'll be a zoo. After that the models will have left for the next show. Which," she added, with a look at her watch, "is what I have to do. It was nice to meet you."

I didn't have another drink, because I needed to be entirely sober for this meeting. So I wandered around, shamelessly eavesdropping. Most of it consisted of people kissing each other, then telling the next person how much they disliked the previous one. After twenty minutes I decided the hell with it, and began to search around for a way backstage. A very disgruntled bouncer finally let me through.

At best, "backstage" was a polite lie for a corridor. It actually wasn't quite as nice as that makes it sound—it was a gray, concrete area smelling of dead cigarettes and spilled alcohol. The clothes were gone, as were the models. All that was left was the Vernet office staff, standing around looking as gray as the walls, completely exhausted, while their friends stood beside them, telling them how fabulous it had been.

Loïc was in a corner making appointments for journalists to view the collection quietly the next day. He saw me, but felt that he couldn't maintain his status if he acknowledged me right away. He was right. If he'd behaved civilly I would have had to revise my opinion that he was a poisonous little runt. After waiting for ten minutes while he pretended I was invisible I grabbed a chair and pulled out a book. That got him—there is no fun in ignoring someone who is happy to be ignored. He slouched over. "Well," he demanded.

"Very well, thank you for asking," I said. The single glass of champagne that I'd had before the show had given me a head-ache, and I was cranky and back in fuck-you mode. He'd asked for—begged for—this meeting, not me. He could tell me what he wanted or I was going home. I stared, stony-faced, at him.

He was a small man—delicately built, and probably only about five foot five without the lifts, with dark skin, dark eyes, and plat-inum hair, razored in the center like a crop circle. His shirt was open to the waist, which was a deeply unappetizing sight, and his trousers rode low on what in a normal-sized person would have been his hips. You knew he'd spent an hour getting them to hang in the right place. He made me tired just to look at him, and I let my face reflect this. As with the bouncers, it was the right approach, and he suddenly became ingratiating.

"Monsieur Conway is looking forward to meeting you," he said, although the words must have pained him. I made sure I showed no surprise, but I was astonished. Patrick Conway was the CEO of Lambert-Lorraine, the conglomerate that owned Vernet, among a huge portfolio of companies. Vernet turned over tens of millions, while Lambert-Lorraine probably saw that daily. What was he bothering with me for?

I nodded, and said, as though still exhausted, "I want to make some calls first. Is there somewhere quiet?"

He said, "The car's waiting, you can call from there."

Sure, I was going to make my calls in front of him and the driver. I walked out to the car with him and gestured him ahead of me. Then I said, "I won't be a moment," and slammed the door on him.

It was now raining, but I felt more comfortable calling from the open air. It felt absurdly like a Sherlock Holmes story—take neither the first hansom cab, nor the second, which may present itself—but I wanted to talk to Jake, and I wanted him to know where I was. I just hoped I could reach him.

He answered his mobile on the first ring. He was intimidatingly like my mother. Didn't either of them ever have meetings?

"Good morning," he said.

"Yeah, sure." I realized how bitchy I sounded, and where we'd last seen each other. I backed up and started again. "Sorry, Jake, I didn't mean it like that, but we'll have to do that later. I'm standing in a car park in Paris, and they're about to take me to meet Patrick Conway. One, should I go? Two, is there anything you want me to ask him? Have you spoken to him yourself?"

"*What?*"

"What do you mean, *what?* They're taking me—"

He cut in, clearly furious. "I mean, what the fuck are you doing in Paris, and what the fuck do you think you're doing interfering in a police investigation?"

At that volume, he didn't really need the phone. I don't respond well to being shouted at. "Interfering in a police investigation? Excuse me, but who sat down with Helena and me and agreed who would check out what?"

"That was Helena, not you, and she is doing paperwork, not running around like an overgrown Girl Guide trying to get her merit badge in mixing in."

It was lucky we were three hundred miles apart, and with the Channel in-between, because if we had been on the same landmass, Jake's murder would have been the CID's next investigation. Unfortunately, anger was making me speechless, which in turn infuriated me further.

Jake made the mistake of continuing. "I want you to leave *now*. It's very simple. Just say you've had a call from London and have to go back right away."

It was very simple, I agreed. The man was toast. "What a pity for you, *Inspector*," I said, my voice dripping acid, "that I don't work for the police. But since I don't, stuff your orders. I am in Paris doing my job, which is what I will continue to do until I have finished it to my own satisfaction. Why don't you go and bully some poor little WPC who can't answer back instead? I'm sure you'd be more comfortable with that. And, in case we don't speak again, which I very much hope we won't, go fuck yourself." I disconnected. All right, not mature—not even witty—but I was boiling.

I got back in the car and snapped to Loïc: "Let's go."

He started to stay something but I glared at him with a look so filled with venom that he shrank back in his seat. Good. I had enough assholes in my life already.

We had just left the car park when my phone rang. I stabbed at it. "*What?*" I snarled.

Jake had calmed down, and was back to his normal even keel. That made one of us, then.

"I'm sorry." He really sounded very contrite.

"You should be." Sorry wasn't going to do it.

"Sam, please. If you want to have a fight, can we postpone it till you're home? It'll be more fun then anyway."

I narrowed my eyes. "Not for you it won't. You'll be dead." Despite my best efforts I wanted to laugh. His reasonable behavior was turning my fury into a comedy routine.

He could smell a weakness at twenty paces. "Fine. I'll give you a list of relatives to invite to the funeral. Now listen, how much do you know about Patrick Conway?"

I gave up. "Not much. What you read in the papers." I glanced over at Loïc. "I'm being taken there now by a PR."

"Can you talk?"

"No, of course not. You missed that chance."

He ignored the dig. "It doesn't matter. No one from here has spoken to him. The Fraud Squad has been putting out feelers, but there's nothing there yet that would warrant more than us talking to the French police. Since you're not coming home—" he paused. I let him wait. "Fine, all right, I give up. Just go easy, listen, don't talk, and keep your phone on. I'll call if there's anything. What train are you supposed to catch home?"

"The seven-oh-seven."

"Call me once you're on it. I'll meet you at St. Pancras. If you need me, call me before, my phone will be on."

I had hoped he'd tell me what to do, which I could then have resented. Now I felt as if a support I'd counted on had been removed without warning.

I was still peeved. "Don't trouble yourself. I'll get the Tube."

He wasn't going to be needled into quarreling again. "I'll be there." This time he hung up first.

I don't know Paris well—not well enough to be able to tell where I was being driven in the dark, so I decided not to worry about it. After about fifteen minutes, during which Loïc maintained his disgruntled silence, we drew up outside a building on one of the streets that I thought must be near the Avenue Montaigne, and I was escorted through the courtyard of an imposing *hôtel particulier*, straight up to a sitting room. It would be rude to call it an office—there was a desk in the corner, but it had nothing remotely signifying office work on it. Impressionist paintings hung on the wall, and the ceiling was covered with what looked like an Angelica Kaufmann. I was left to kick my heels for nearly half an hour, so I returned to my book, and looked up only when the door closed and steps approached the sofa I was on, my finger marking the page.

Patrick Conway stood before me without any expression on his face; his assistant was a few steps behind, horrified by my *lèse-majesté*. Between Jake, Loïc, the wait, and my champagne-induced headache, I was now in a complete snit. I nodded coolly and waited for him to speak.

"Miss Clair?"

"Ms." I might as well stick with bad-tempered. It had worked so far.

"Sure, and of course," he said, in an accent that you could cut out and keep.

I sniffed. "That's a fairly impressive accent for someone who left Ireland at the age of three."

The assistant actually took a step back at this. Conway swelled up. He was going to explode. Then he laughed, and said in a completely neutral accent, "It works. It makes the English feel superior, and Europeans are comfortable with it."

I held out my hand and smiled. "How do you do?"

He sat down. "A drink?"

"Coffee, please. Black, no sugar."

Conway nodded at the assistant without turning around, and she scuttled out before I could tell her that the Emperor wore no clothes. She didn't want to hear about it.

He looked at me closely. "We need to talk, don't we?"

"Go ahead," I said, although less aggressively than I would have two minutes before.

"We've got a problem, and you've got a problem. Two problems. If we merge them together, we might have only one."

I waited for him to continue.

"We have been trying to reach Kit Lovell for the last week, to discuss this book with him. He doesn't return calls. What's-his-name—Vernet's PR, the boy who brought you here—says he wasn't at the show this afternoon, and thinks he hasn't been at any of the others."

This was the one thing I was not prepared for. Did Conway really not know Kit had disappeared? We hadn't put ads in the newspapers—LOST, ONE FASHION JOURNALIST, RETURN TO PUB-LISHER FOR REWARD—but it had never crossed my mind that the news wasn't everywhere. I thought about it. Who knew? Kit's family, his solicitor, the police. And if, as Jake said, the police gave low priority to missing people without signs of criminality around the disappearance, maybe they hadn't spoken to anyone at his office. Atwood after all had appeared to have no idea when I'd seen him at the Tate. I pressed my lips together in fury at the thought, then pushed it back, concentrating on what was in front of me: that there actually was no reason why anyone connected with Alemán should know. That is, they wouldn't know unless they had arranged his disappearance in the first place. It was a big "unless." I contemplated Conway, who was fiddling with his coffee cup. Was this some sort of sophisticated double bluff? Had Lambert-Lorraine "disappeared" him, as they say in South America, and was this recent desire to talk to us just an act they were staging for our benefit? I couldn't see why they would bother. With the underworld connections that went with drugs and arms dealing, Kit would never reappear, and that was that. On the other hand, if they truly didn't know Kit was gone, then this meeting began to make more sense.

Conway seemed to think I was being inscrutable, rather than just thinking, and he went on. "As we can't get hold of Lovell, I thought I ought to have the conversation with you that I would otherwise have had with him."

I waited again. Silence had worked so far, so I stuck with it.

Conway continued, staring down at the coffee table. "The rumor mill is in overdrive that Lovell has come up with evidence of malfeasance." He paused. When nothing came back he said, "This is not something we like to hear, but we are concerned that if there is any truth in these rumors, that the people involved are dealt with by the police, and not tipped off by a book, or rumors of a book, so that they can cover up their activities and continue them in a different time and a different place." He looked up at me from under his eyelashes. "I know you are not in a position to respond, but I would be grateful if you would carry this message back."

That was that then. I stood up. "Thank you for your time, Mr. Conway. If there is anything I can do, I'll come back to you."

He stood as well. "I'd like to see the manuscript."

"I'm sure you would. While it was a publishing matter, I wouldn't have shown the book to you on principle. Now that it's a police matter, I can't."

He had known I would say that. It was more a matter of putting the request on the table. He didn't expect a return immediately. Conway was someone who played for long-term advantage, and he was looking several moves ahead.

He scribbled down a number on the back of a card. "That's my assistant's direct line. He'll find me."

On the whole I believed what he had said. I wasn't sure if that was smart or not, but he seemed on the level. I didn't for a moment think he was acting from altruism, or from notions of upright citizenship, or even from the goodness of his heart, but I did believe he wanted his company to be run for his benefit, not for the benefit of unknown and unnamed others.

I was taken back to the Gare du Nord in the car that had brought me from the Palais des Sports, but Loïc had vanished. I was pleased on a personal level, and because it gave me time to think, but I felt badly that I couldn't pass on the good news that his boss didn't know his name. Big business is big business, but it's important not to lose sight of the small pleasures of life.

9

When I got on the train I texted Jake to say I'd get home on my own, but he was waiting for me on the platform all the same. He must have used his police credentials to get past the barrier. I wondered whether that meant I was police business, or if it was just a perk of the job.

I kissed him decorously on the cheek. It was the kind of kiss that in publishing you give someone you've never met before. When he jerked his head back as if he'd been burned, I deduced that the CID didn't have the same social customs.

I curled my lip. "Yeah, you don't want to get caught kissing strange women in public, do you?" I might not be angry anymore, but that didn't mean I wasn't going to give him a hard time.

He put his hand on the back of my neck, then quickly took it away again and instead held me by the elbow, like a felon. "I always kiss my colleagues when I start a shift," he said through gritted teeth. "I'm only worried about being seen kissing you because you are *so* strange."

I looked away. Bored. "So leave. I told you I'd take the Tube."

He snapped me around and held me by both shoulders. I thought he was going to shout at me again, but instead he reached out and with careful concentration buttoned my coat. "It's cold out," was all he said. He put his hand in my pocket together with mine, and, fingers enlaced, we walked out to his car.

We didn't speak again until we were in the car and had navigated the one-way system outside the station. Then he took a deep breath and said, "How did it go?"

I repeated the message from Conway very precisely. I had jotted down an outline of the meeting as soon as I'd left, and I put the notes on the dashboard.

He didn't comment, just reached out and picked them up, putting them in his jacket pocket. Then he said, "I called Nell after I spoke to you. She'd already started to look into Vernet, and she's got some interesting stuff. She thinks Conway is straight. It may be useful to talk to him again. If he liked you—?"

I bit back a remark about Girl Guides and merit badges. Instead I shrugged. "Who knows? He was extremely charming, but that's second nature. It didn't have anything to do with me. For what it's worth, I think he genuinely does not know Kit is missing. And if he doesn't know that, then surely the rest of the structure we've been building falls to the ground. Which means we're back to where we started, and no closer to knowing what's happened to Kit." I stared blankly out the window. It was raining again, that dank, depressing rain that you can't see, but which covers everything with a fine, dismal mist.

The car went through the underpass behind the station. In its sodium glare Jake was visibly not at all depressed. "We're not back where we were. Not remotely. If we believe Conway, then we're quite substantially further on. He didn't have Kit abducted, and that's a help, because with his resources that would mean Kit could be anywhere. If we believe that Conway equally didn't know about the money laundering, we're looking for someone lower down the ladder, and that's a help, too, because it focuses our search. Even better, Conway will let his people help us, and we can't begin to match his resources, or his knowledge of the territory." Us. Apparently now I was back in London, and under his eye, I was allowed to be part of the investigation again. There was no mileage in pointing this out. Jake drummed a cheerful tattoo against the steering wheel. "Today may not have seemed like much, but the picture is radically altered—and in our favor."

"Altered about Lambert-Lorraine, and your courier. Not about Kit, though. If we believe Conway, he knows nothing about Kit's disappearance." I bit my tongue. For the first time, I'd almost used a much more final word about Kit. I realized, suddenly, that he wasn't coming back. I turned my head and stared out the window again.

Jake was smart enough not to try and soothe me with false hope. He drove without speaking, and after a few minutes I pulled myself together. Weeping wasn't going to help. Instead I ran over the possibilities, more as a way of clarifying the situation for myself than anything else. "We have someone who is washing money in two ways: through Eastern European companies, and through property here in the UK. Those may be two separate groups of people, or maybe just one. We don't know who either is—that is, how high up the chain it goes, or how institutionalized. Is it a rogue employee, or employees, or does it come from the top, run by the companies themselves?" I stopped to think about that for a moment. "Are those the only possibilities? Could it be at a local level?"

"I don't see why not, for the property at any rate. The person dealing with the UK market, whether here or in France, could easily arrange for the deals to fall through, whether it's because the survey shows flaws, or the contract's not right. According to Nell, that's all it takes. Whether the invoicing for goods through dummy companies can be done locally depends on whether the buying for Vernet is centralized or not. If every country does its own buying, then that could be a local scam, too. If every store does its own buying, or the complete opposite, if all the buying is centralized in Paris, then things probably become less straight-forward."

"Which means we don't know whether we're looking for people based in Paris or here. Speaking of which, did you ever get any responses to your request for the fingerprints in my flat?"

"We got responses. France, Spain, and Italy all came through. No matches. Which means either the prints belonged to your friends, or they're people we haven't come across before. As you know, I think it's the former."

A thought struck me. "Do you know where in my flat the prints came from?"

"I don't, but they will have been logged. Why?"

"If it's a door, or the loo, or the kitchen, then it could be any-one. But if it was my desk, or the computer keyboard, then it was me or the burglars. No one except me goes into my office at all. Well, my cleaning lady. But you took her prints, didn't you?"

He nodded. "Not standard procedure in the case of burglaries, but it wasn't a standard burglary. It's a good point. I'll get it checked." We'd reached the flat, and he waited until we were inside before phoning his office. "They'll dig out the notes, and I'll have it in the morning."

"I'm glad to know you have colleagues." He raised his eyebrows in query. "Well, except the night I was burgled, I've never seen anyone else on this case, and you're always at the end of the phone. I was beginning to wonder if you were the only officer the CID had."

He reached out and tucked a piece of hair behind my ear. "I thought it was a good idea for me to focus on you."

"Oh." I tried not to look shifty. "Are you staying tonight?"

"I hoped I'd be asked."

"I'd love you to, but . . ." I tried to look fragile and wan. Not my most successful look. "I know we need to talk, but can it wait until the morning? I'm exhausted."

"The talking part can wait. As long as you don't pretend to be asleep tomorrow, too."

My eyes widened.

He smiled. "I'm a detective, remember?"

If he winked at me, I was going to thump him one.

I slipped out of bed early and went for a run—the first time I'd been out in the morning since my break-in. My running was even less accomplished than usual, but it gave me time to prepare what I wanted to say.

As I came in the door, Jake was going down the hall to the kitchen. He looked at my red face and said, "My God."

"It's what I look like in the morning." My tone said, *Back off the jokes, buster.* I slipped past him to the shower.

By the time I was out he had the coffee made, and I was as ready as I was ever going to be.

He said, mildly, "It's not a firing squad, you know."

I concentrated on finding a banana of just the right level of ripeness. "Are you sure?"

He sighed. "I suppose we have to do this?"

"If you can see a way for us to continue for any length of time without ever having talked to each other, I'd be interested to hear."

He was silent.

"Me neither. So let's get this over with. From my side, the situation is like this: I like you, or, at least what I know of you so far. It's just that I hate your job." There. It was out.

He nodded. "Of course you do."

"What? You knew?"

"Sure. Everyone like you does. You want your crimes solved, your cities kept safe, you just don't want us cluttering up your sitting rooms."

"No, wait, that's unfair. That's not what I mean. It's just that the police . . ." I trailed off. I couldn't really bring myself to say it.

He finished for me: ". . . are corrupt, and violent, and fit up innocent people. Have I left anything out?"

I was apologetic, but I couldn't leave it alone. "Apart from the odd death from using illegal choke holds, and shooting people taking their tables to be repaired, and some all-around general brutality, no, I think you've covered just about everything."

He flushed, but didn't lose his temper. "And do you think any of these things refer to me?" he asked levelly.

I didn't need to hesitate about that. "No. Absolutely not."

"So, you think you might not want to have a relationship with me—you might not want to even think of *perhaps* having a relationship with me—because of the way some, and I emphasize, *some,* of my colleagues operate?" He paused to let me think about that, and then went on. "I don't deny that these things happen. I would be an idiot, and I would be complicit, if I did. But power corrupts, and opportunity is a very seductive thing. The people I work with have power, and they have opportunity. If you and your colleagues had this kind of power, how would you all behave?"

I opened my mouth to reject the idea that a gaggle of editors would ever want to baton charge protest marchers, but he stopped me. "I'm not suggesting violence, because that doesn't crop up much in your line of work. But if your colleagues were offered bribes, would they all refuse them?"

I reviewed the people I worked with. He watched me run through the list in my head and nodded. "Yet you work with them. They aren't necessarily decent because they're decent people; they're decent because the opportunity to behave otherwise hasn't cropped up in their lives. Those opportunities have been presented to some—" he slapped his hand on the table, the only sign he'd given of how angry he was—"to *some* of my colleagues, and they have succumbed. Are you to blame if one of the editors in your office takes a bribe to publish a bad book?"

"No, but I am to blame if I don't do anything about it."

"And what does that consist of? Reporting it? That happens. Physically preventing officers you are with from violence? That happens, too. What doesn't happen is that I leap into a phone booth and rush out in my red underpants to prevent all corruption, all racism, all brutality, everywhere in the force. Is that something you can't live with?"

I sat staring at the table. What I wasn't sure I could live with was that Jake was a reasonable man, with thoughtful, measured responses, and that I would lose most of our arguments. Wild exaggeration and sarcasm, my weapons of choice, weren't going to be much use.

I relaxed back in my chair for the first time since I'd come into the kitchen. "I really hate it when you're right." I smiled tentatively.

I hadn't realized how tense he'd been until he smiled, too. "I see your problem, but you'll have to learn to live with it. I'm right a lot."

"That's really come-hitherish."

"You want come-hitherish?" He reached across the table.

"No. Absolutely not. At least, not now." I jumped up and put the chair between us. "I'm late for work already. OK, what's the deal? I'm happy to see where things go, but a few details would be good. Boring stuff, like where do you live? Oh, and are you married? We women like to have that kind of information about the men we fall into bed with."

"You're a fussy lot, aren't you? I live in Hammersmith, and I've been there since my divorce ten years ago." He answered the next question before I had a chance to ask. "One child. My son, Tonio—Antonio. He's fourteen. He lives with his mother in Lisbon. She's Portuguese and she went back after we divorced."

I made a meaningless motion with my hand. "I'm sorry."

He looked away. "I see him once a year. Twice if we can work it out. It's not what I want, but it's what I've got." He changed the subject. "I don't need to ask all this stuff about you, because I know already: single, no children, ex who is an academic, childhood in Canada. You've been at Timmins and Ross five years, at Tetrarch before that."

I stared at him, outraged. "How many fillings have I got in my teeth?"

"None."

"*What?* You unmitigated creep! Who have you been talking to?"

"Who else? Helena. She saw all this—" he waved his arm around, taking in the intangible domesticity of early-morning coffee together—"when she brought you back from the hospital after the break-in."

"So she gave you my dental records? What's the matter with you—what's the matter with both of you?"

Jake smothered a laugh. "No, sweetheart, funnily enough we didn't discuss your teeth at all. That was a guess, that and a knowledge of North American dentistry. Nell just said you used to live with an academic, and she told me about her job in Canada when you were a child. The rest, including the dental work, I figured out for myself."

"I'm getting less and less sure about the benefits of being with someone who makes deductions for a living."

"Look on the bright side. With most men, you can be in a white rage with them for days, and they don't even notice."

I rolled my eyes, he grinned, and we both went to work.

* * *

I had made a lunch date with Kath. If I was going to be known for sleeping with Hot Young Authors, I figured I'd better get as many books as I could before the news got back to the Hot Young Etcs. and my cover was blown. I took her to a very new, very trendy place in Notting Hill called Les Deux. It was so trendy it felt no need to tell us Les Deux What. It wasn't convenient for her or for me, but we trendy people are willing to be inconvenienced for fashion. I also figured it would be noisy enough that any evasions about my (non-)relationship with Charles Pool could be put down to not wanting to be overheard.

I'd reread the story in *Granta,* which had triggered off all the interest in Shapurji Mehta, Kath's author. It was very good, even better than I'd remembered. The first three chapters of his novel, which Kath had e-mailed over while I was in Paris, were really exciting. Whoever got this book would be lucky, and I was prepared to barter my supposed private life for a chance at it.

I knocked on David's door before I left. He was on his way out, too, so I suggested we share a cab. Once in it, I told him that I was meeting Kath to discuss Mehta's book. He looked amazed, which was downright rude. "I think Ben was expecting to be offered that," he said.

"Was he?" I tried not to appear too pleased with myself. "She sent it to me exclusively. If we want it, we need to discuss our offer. I know she'll want something definite today."

David looked hangdog, one of his favorite modes. "Well, Ben . . ."

What, I was suddenly in a meeting with an editorial board? With editors who weren't present, and hadn't been offered the book? I briefly wondered what you called a group of editors—a chatter of editors? I thought about Ben and revised: a pompous of publishers, definitely.

"Ben what? Ben hasn't been offered this book. I have. So let's forget Ben, because for whatever reason, Kath didn't think it was right for him." All my submerged irritation with Ben was in my tone, and David backed off.

Apart from the interoffice relationships, David knew perfectly well that if I passed on the book it wouldn't necessarily go to Ben. It would most likely go to another publisher entirely, so he accepted the inevitable. He had read the *Granta* story as well, and knew how good Mehta was. I had run some figures on projected sales, I'd talked to marketing and publicity, and I knew they thought they could do a lot with it. It could, as Ben would have said if only he'd had the chance, be mega. So David and I discussed how far he thought I should go on my offer. It was big money, much bigger than I paid for anyone except Breda, and with her we knew to the last copy exactly how much each book would sell. Mehta's was a first novel. It could, we thought, be huge, but it could also fail. In my new guise as literary hotshot I harped on the "huge" side, and steered away from the "fail" part. David and I agreed a sum, and I walked into lunch looking, I hoped, confident and ready to buy.

First I had to parry Kath's seemingly idle chat about T&R's new literary fiction, all designed to let her head oh-so-casually to questions about Charles Pool. Whom I had still never seen. Looking shifty was fine—she thought I was avoiding the subject because I was embarrassed, whereas I was really avoiding it because I hadn't made up the answers yet. We ordered and then I said, "Let's get the business out of the way. Then we can have a nice long gossip." After that she would have sold me her sister.

I didn't want her sister, but I did want Mehta. In ten minutes the thing was tied up. There were formalities—she needed to put my offer to Mehta for his agreement, we had to meet, but I could see that the money was what she had been expecting, and she thought the book was mine. Not only that, but we ran through a couple of other things she was going to offer in the next few months, and I got a chance to tell her what I was interested in. Usually with Kath I got the stuff that the bigger spenders had already rejected. It was fun being a big spender myself. Even if it was because I was a baby snatcher.

Eventually we had to discuss my new tendencies toward adolescents. Fair was fair after all. Kath was direct. She put down her coffee cup and said, "Have you known Charles for long?"

I looked as shocked as I could manage. "Who told you?" I lowered my voice. "We don't really want to talk about it yet."

Kath was prim. "I won't say a word. Promise." Yeah, right. She wouldn't say a word, she'd say about a million. She egged me on: "I heard Peter was very upset."

I tried not to look puzzled. Peter? What the hell had he got to do with it? Then I remembered that in the Gospel According to Miranda he'd broken into my flat in a state of thwarted rage. I tried to sound like I was lying, which was easy, because I was. "Well, we don't *know* that it was Peter."

Kath was skeptical, so I moved on quickly. "At least, it might have been, but it might have been . . . Well, it's just that after Peter I'd been seeing two other guys. One after the other," I added virtuously. I didn't want her to think I was a total slut.

Kath's eyes bulged. If I didn't control myself, I'd be telling her that the All Blacks stopped by regularly whenever they played Twickenham, forming an orderly queue down the garden path. I looked at my watch. I really did have to get back to the office, and anyway, I couldn't keep this up for much longer. Kath had enough to keep the phone lines white-hot for weeks, and I might even get a couple more books out of her. It had been a worthwhile lunch all around.

As we got our coats she said, "Is the one keeping tabs on you now one of them?"

"Keeping tabs? What do you mean?"

She thought I was trying to bluff her. "Come on, the guy near the door, sitting at the bar. The one who arrived just after you did, who has been looking over here the whole meal, and who asked for his bill as we stood up."

I whipped around. It was the thin boy from the LSD. I pulled Kath around so she was between him and me. "Can you just stand there, as if we're talking, so he can't see me for a minute?"

I was going to get books from Kath for life. If she'd had doubts about the Pool thing before, she didn't now. Here was another man barely into his twenties following me around. Granted, he wasn't particularly attractive, but no one was following her around. I was a little more concerned.

I rang Jake, and as usual he answered on the first ring. "Me. Hi."

"What's wrong?" he said immediately. He was right, there were pluses to seeing a detective.

"I'm in Les Deux in Notting Hill. That guy from the LSD, the one who was in Timmins and Ross yesterday, has followed me to lunch. The friend I'm with spotted him. What shall I do?"

"Does he know you've seen him?"

"I don't think so. I'm phoning out of his sight."

"I'm in the middle of something and I can't get away. Go back to your office, by bus if you can so he can follow you easily. Wait there."

"I really want to talk to him."

"Me, too, but you're not—*not*—to approach him on your own. Do you hear?"

I disconnected.

I hooked my arm through Kath's, who was enthralled. I said, "As you can see, there's a bit of a situation. I don't think he'll do anything, but can we just walk past chatting about publishing? I don't want him to know I've seen him."

"Sure, absolutely. Is he one of the ones who . . . ?"

I shook my head impatiently. "No, he's just trouble. My problem is, I don't know what kind."

Kath had no idea what I was talking about, but she didn't care. Who would have thought having lunch with Sam Clair would produce this much gossip?

As Kath and I drew level with the Thin Boy, as I now thought of him, he turned his head away, which was good because Kath was ogling him unashamedly. I'd contemplated trying to corner him, whatever Jake said, but he was in the middle of the bar, with empty seats on either side. Whichever way I approached, he could cut and run. So instead I asked Kath about a launch party that she had been at the night before. She was immediately diverted by the thrill of being the first to tell me all about the scandalous behavior of an agent and the husband of one of her authors. I knew them, and I figured they'd got involved because no one else would even talk to them, much less sleep with them. I managed not to share this view with Kath.

We air-kissed on the pavement after I told her I was taking the bus, which rocked her view of me as Hot. Well, at least I was a Public Transport Princess with four lovers, all insanely jealous.

After all that, my return to the office was anticlimactic. The Thin Boy made no effort to follow me outside, much less get on the bus. The stop was visible from the restaurant, so maybe he just figured I was going back to work? I contemplated waiting for him to come out to see where he went. *I* could follow *him*, I thought, patting myself on the back. Then I realized I'd just invented a street version of French farce: I'd follow a man who was following me so that I could . . . Either we'd chase each other around the block, or we'd both stubbornly sit at the bus stop till we grew old and forgot what we were doing. Instead I got on the bus and tried not to think about him anymore. I was having enough trouble working out what I was doing these days, without wondering what strangers were doing.

As I walked down the hall, Miranda was finishing a phone conversation. She held up a finger to delay me, and when she put down the receiver she followed me into my office looking confused and worried. I sighed. I wasn't sure I could deal with any more. Maybe I should go into craft books: *How to Knit a Chicken*, with diagrams. No one worried about those. I pulled myself together.

"What's the problem?"

"There isn't one. That's the problem."

She didn't appear to be drunk, or high. Just worried. "Start at the beginning," I said gently. "First tell me what we're talking about."

"Breda."

"Go on," I said, still trying to encourage her. It wasn't like Miranda to be incoherent. "What about Breda?"

"They love it."

Maybe it was me. Maybe I just attracted nutters. "Miranda, stop. Who loves what? What are you talking about?"

She laughed, which was a small improvement. "Sorry. I've just got the third call, and it threw me." She saw me looking patient again. "Sorry, sorry, sorry. It's about Breda's book. I gave the manuscript to a bunch of people yesterday, when you told me to." I nodded encouragingly, trying not to let hope blossom. "Not just my friends—two friends, and also my sister, who is two years younger than I am. I offered them a double fee if they read it overnight. And I sent it to Nadila from WHSmith. Do you know her? She does their author events. We met when you did Breda's last book, and we're quite friendly, so I sent it as a 'favor.' You know, letting her get a sneak preview."

I nodded again, hoping that if I didn't talk, what she seemed to be saying would indeed be true.

"Well, I've had three calls so far—three out of the four—and they all love it. They think it's the funniest thing they've read in years." She stared at me with a *now what?* look. "That last call was from Nadila, who said she'd sat up all night reading it, then she'd given it to her colleagues this morning, and two read it over lunchtime, and, well, the result is, they want it for the September Book of the Month, to lead off the main push before Christmas. Her only concern was that we hadn't highlighted it in our presentation, so did that mean that we were giving the other chains preference?"

I argued, just because none of this could possibly be real, "They've settled the September book already. It's one of Ben's."

"I know." Miranda sounded incredibly smug. "They said they've never changed one before, but they hope that since it's in-house it won't cause problems."

"Yeah, right. Out-of-house, it wouldn't have caused problems. In-house it's going to be blood on the carpet tiles. Especially since I think I've just bought the Mehta from Kath."

Miranda was jubilant. "*Yesss!*" She sobered up. "How are you going to tell Ben?"

"Wearing a flak jacket." She laughed and I tried to think. "Not today. I want to get the trip to Galway over with first. And get David on side. In the Tuesday meeting, I guess."

Miranda put her hand up, stopping me in my tracks. "The meeting has been moved to Monday, because of all the foreign publishers coming through for the Book Fair next week."

I closed my eyes. The London Book Fair. Maybe it wasn't too late to run away and join the circus. I pushed away the alluring thoughts of having spangly tights and no authors and concentrated on breathing deeply. "Fine." It wasn't, but what could I do? "I'll tell him then. In the meantime, ring Breda and let her know I won't be staying for the weekend. Since there's suddenly no editorial work to do, I can go, present the marketing and publicity plans, show her the jacket, and get back tomorrow night. She'll be thrilled. Once you've spoken to her, will you make me a reservation home on the seven-thirty-five?" She made a note. "Now, about the book itself. How stupid do we want to appear?" Miranda looked blank. "Did you tell everyone you'd read it and it was awful?"

"God, no, I never mentioned it at all if I could help it. It was too embarrassing."

"Me too. I gave it to everyone else to read, and didn't argue when they made sick noises, but I didn't actually say I thought it stank, because those things have a way of getting back to authors. So. Neither you nor I have said anything. Given that we have been telling lies like sociopaths for the last week, do you think we can carry off the impression that we knew all along that *Toujours Twenty-one* was a comic novel?"

For the first time, Miranda looked at me with real respect. "Can we?"

"Get me the cover brief, and let's see what I told the designer." I looked at it, and said, "It doesn't actually say what the book is about at all, mostly because I was too ashamed to write it down. It suggests that the jacket should be a send-up, and asks for a kitsch look. I was trying to disguise the contents, but I don't see why we can't claim we knew it was the very send-up and kitsch comedy that I asked for on the cover."

I thought through the people I'd talked to. "I'll have to tell Sandra. We talked about it at length. But she's not going to want anyone to think she hasn't got her finger on the pulse, and didn't recognize a comic masterpiece when she read it."

Miranda was awed. "It's Stalinist. Airbrushing history. Can you get away with it?"

"Watch me."

* * *

My mother rang me while Sandra and I were finalizing our plans. "Do you want to be my date tonight? It's the dinner for the Anglo-American Bar Association."

"Jesus Christ, Mother, what a totally awful idea."

"You do, you know."

"No, Mother, I don't." My mind was still on marketing and publicity budgets.

"Cooper's are this year's hosts, and they'll have at least twenty of their partners there. Kenneth Wright will be there. But if you're too busy . . ."

"Right, I'm with you now. What time, where?"

"The Dorchester, drinks at six thirty. I'll see you then. And wear a dress, for goodness' sake."

At six forty-five I was pushing my way through a be-suited throng. The Dorchester has always struck me as a really strange place, and having a posse of solicitors collected in one of its function rooms wasn't making it any less strange. The outside of the building is a rather severe gray Art Deco monolith, sort of attractive if you like that kind of thing. But waltz through the revolving door and you're in kitsch 1950s stage-design land, full of rococo twirls and cream-and-gilt flourishes. I always expect a line of chorus girls to appear, and the foyer really needs them. It's too silly to contain nothing but a bunch of people in business suits checking in and out, with suitcases creating an obstacle path at the entrance, just like in any downmarket motel.

Once directed upstairs to the room where the drinks party was being held—excuse me, the "Messel Suite"—the Dorchester had no truck with mere "rooms," it was Suites for the Suits—

the same feeling of dislocation persisted. The place was jammed with people talking and drinking, like any publishing party, but these people looked different to the ones I worked with. They spent more time and money on presentation. They also sounded different. They spoke more assertively, laughed much less. Helena, as always, was the diminutive center of an appreciative crowd. At least these ones were laughing. I joined them, first stopping one of the waiters passing trays of drinks. Another difference. At publishers' parties it's hard to find a non-alcoholic drink. Here three-quarters of the glasses were filled with water. I took wine. Me and six hundred lawyers. It was going to be a long night.

Helena introduced me to Derek Gascoigne, Cooper's senior partner. "This is my daughter, Samantha."

He looked at me with some interest, which surprised me. I'm not usually a magnet for the City crowd. Then he said, "Pat Conway told me about you."

I blinked. How did that man end up everywhere? My confusion must have showed, and he filled me in. "Cooper's are Lambert-Lorraine's solicitors."

"Ah," I said, neutrally. Lambert-Lorraine's solicitors were the same people who had employed the man who now looked after Vernet's property deals? He had probably looked after Vernet at Cooper's, and they went with him when he set up on his own. It made sense, I supposed. But none of this was a reason for Conway to be discussing me with his solicitor. I didn't know how to phrase that without sounding as though I were accusing them of something, so I said nothing.

Gascoigne was extremely tall—probably over six foot three, a blond elegantly turning silver, in a suit that must have cost two months' salary. Even I, with no eye at all, could tell that. He nodded now, as if my response had been what he was expecting. "He said you listened more than you talked. He was impressed."

There was no point in pretending to be what I wasn't. "I didn't have anything to say."

Gascoigne took my arm and drew me apart from the rest of the group, stooping over me like a distinguished stork. "That doesn't usually stop people." I took a sip of my drink. "He was right. You're not saying anything now."

I shrugged again. "I'm not fencing. I'm just not sure what we should be talking about. When I spoke to Mr. Conway he had a message for me to deliver. I delivered it. Where we go from here is up to him, surely."

"We want the same thing. Pat wants to find out what has been going on in his company; you want to find out who has been doing it so you can publish your book without fear of libel. It's in both our interests to work together."

I waited.

"We're happy to cooperate with the police—of course," he added hastily.

"Of course," I echoed, trying not to sound bitchy.

He looked at me as if I'd said something clever. "But they may be forced to act before it suits us to do so. There's no mileage for us in simply exposing the operation without ensuring that all of those who have been running it are eliminated. If that happens, we will get the drones, but not necessarily the queen bee. In fact, almost assuredly not the queen bee. That is not what we want at all."

"I don't see how I can help."

Either Gascoigne was tired of bending down to my level so he could talk without shouting, or he was getting to the point. He steered me into the ballroom where the dinner would be held later. More gilt, more flourishes, more rococo swirls. I was mildly surprised not to find a stray cherub tootling a horn from the ceiling. The room appeared bare without. Instead, sixty round white tables, with sixty round white flower arrangements tortured into low-key fashionability dotted the floor. Gascoigne pulled out a chair at the nearest table and held it for me. We looked like two black-cloaked co-conspirators planning a raid in the vast white-on-white elegance.

"Diego Alemán came to see me yesterday." That made me sit up. "He said he'd had an interesting conversation with you, that you thought he was involved."

"Interesting. How did he know about you? How did he know there was something to be involved in?"

Gascoigne nodded. "I wondered, too. What did you talk about?"

I looked bland. "Seditious libel."

"*Seditious* libel? Is there such a thing anymore? I do corporate law, but I would have thought . . ." His voice trailed away.

I waved it away. "It's not important. It was a way of talking about what we didn't want to talk about openly." I stared at the tablecloth, thinking. "What I'm saying is that we were talking about this book I'm publishing—about a dead fashion designer and his company, not about, shall we say, creative accounting methods. Diego worked for Intinvest, which we both know—" I slid my eyes to him, and when he nodded, I continued—"which we both know may or may not have had some involvement with" and now I mimicked his phrase, "with what has been going on in *one* of Lambert-Lorraine's companies. Vernet is high profile, but if Diego Alemán is clean, how did he know to come to you? And about what? As far as I can see, as a member of the Alemán family, he's concerned about his brother's death, about his brother's memory, and therefore me, as the publisher of a book that may damage that. But Vernet's business practices? He should know nothing about them."

"We don't know that he does."

"He knows that there's something to know. Otherwise why come to you? If there's a problem, he should be going to his boss at Intinvest. Unless he can't."

I sat and watched Gascoigne process the information. He came to a decision. "Pat will be here in the morning. Can you come to a meeting at seven?"

Seven. Jesus. "I can. But what for?"

"I think we'll have Alemán back. We're liaising with NCIS and Revenue and Customs, and they'll give us some rope, but not much. What we need is to pool everything we've got and make some decisions."

"Yes, I understand why you're going ahead. But what do you want me for? I'm a publisher. I know about books. I don't know about corporate fraud—" he winced at the word—"and I don't know about the business world. I don't see what I can bring to this."

"You've read the manuscript. You know the players."

I shrugged. Whatever Conway had said, I didn't believe they

couldn't get their hands on a manuscript if they wanted one. According to Helena, Kit had only spelled out one aspect of the fraud—they would have to do their own digging for the rest, although that shouldn't be difficult. Once you know what you are looking for, and where, it is never hard to find. They wanted me for something else, and I couldn't figure out what. But as long as they wanted me, I could make my own demands.

"I need to catch a ten-fifteen flight to Galway. I'm due there for a lunch meeting. Will the meeting be finished for me to get to Gatwick in time?"

Gascoigne looked dubious. "It would be better if we didn't have to rush. Let me speak to the office." He pulled out his phone and moved away from the table.

While I had no idea why they wanted me there, I wanted to be there. Maybe some information about Kit might surface. Even so, I couldn't cancel Breda—playing Nancy Drew was a pastime, but I had to earn a living, and too much hung on what now looked to be a bestseller. Yet I wanted to use Lambert-Lorraine as much as they wanted to use me. My concern was still Kit, and it looked like finding the route for the money meant finding out what had happened to him.

I sat quietly, staring into space, pleased to have a breathing space. Between the office, a potential new relationship, and Kit's disappearance, I was just reeling from crisis to crisis without any fixed purpose. I allowed my thoughts to drift, and jumped when Gascoigne touched me on the shoulder. He looked pleased with himself. "It's not a problem. Pat is flying in tomorrow morning. His plane will wait for you and take you to Galway. I've arranged a car to drive you to Luton after our meeting. That way we can talk as long as we want, and you'll still get to your appointment by lunchtime."

I tried to look as if I was offered the use of private jets every day, sometimes twice a day before breakfast. I obviously failed, because Gascoigne touched me on the shoulder again, and said, "I told you you'd impressed him."

If not talking had got me this far, it would be a shame to blow it, so I just smiled, hooked my arm through his, and drew him back toward the party.

As we walked back into the heaving mass of solicitors enjoying themselves, my mother wormed her way through to me and said crossly, "What did you say to him?"

I was startled. "Gascoigne? Nothing, we just—"

"Not Gascoigne." Helena was impatient. "Wright."

Wright? I craned my neck to scan the crowd. Not really very intelligent, since I didn't know what he looked like. Helena realized I was clueless. Again. Or maybe still. "Over there," she said, jutting her chin. "Medium height, brown hair, five o'clock shadow."

I looked where she was looking. "Red tie with horses? Got him."

He'd got me, too. He saw me watching him, and nodded and smiled as if we were old acquaintances. "Shit," I muttered. "Heading this way."

My mother was dismissive. "A horrible man with sweaty palms. Came up and introduced himself. He said he thought we should talk. I suggested that a dinner was neither the time nor the place." The look she gave me at this point froze my blood. I hated to think what it would do to a stranger. "He melted away again, but if you haven't spoken to him, it's odd that he came to me, not you." She was curiously cheered by this.

Before she could say more, Wright had made his way over. "Miss Clair," he announced, in case I hadn't been sure. "And the lovely Mrs. Clair once more." Not the way to my mother's heart, being patronized. Or mine, come to that.

We made noises that an optimist might have interpreted as welcoming. Any sane person would have turned tail and fled.

That clarified Wright's status. He beamed at both of us impartially. "I hear," he announced portentously to me, "that you had a useful meeting with my friend Hugo."

I stared blankly, not able to summon the social skills to pretend I knew what, or rather, who he was talking about.

"Hugo," he repeated, a testy edge entering his voice. "Hugo Littlewood, at Selden's."

So much had happened, and my life was suddenly teeming with law firms, that I'd forgotten all about Selden's original gambit.

I tried to look as though it had never been far from my thoughts, but the most I could manage, after an embarrassing pause, was, "I'm pleased he thought so."

"Always good to get these things out on the table."

Was the man an idiot? He was mixing in to an affair he should, by right, have no interest in. I couldn't imagine what possessed him, what he thought he could get from us that would be more valuable than keeping a low profile and staying away from the whole thing.

"Isn't it." I said, with no attempt at charm.

Wright acted as if this was the most delightful sentiment he'd heard all week. "We should get together and discuss this. I might be able to help you."

Helena muttered an excuse and slipped away. I didn't turn, but I marked it down on the slate. She owed me for leaving me like this.

"You may be able to help me," I repeated woodenly. Again, I was careful to phrase it as a statement.

"With my time at Cooper's . . ." he said, in a manner that might have been enticing if I had been a solicitor, but I wasn't. His smile began to falter. He'd given me opening after opening, and I wasn't biting. He hadn't planned on being direct, but now didn't have any choice. "As Vernet's UK solicitor, I feel we should discuss the possibilities of publishing your book."

"Possibilities? There are no possibilities." He smiled. "It's a certainty." It wasn't, anymore, but it was fun lying to this man. Now Wright was beginning to sweat, and in a pulling-the-wings-off-flies kind of way I was enjoying myself.

Wright began to bluster. "Young lady, I don't think you understand the legal situation."

One of the things that most endears people to me is being called "young lady"; second is trying to frighten me with the law. I smiled my best middle-class well-brought-up-girl smile. I may even have fluttered my eyelashes at him. I'm not prepared to swear that I didn't. "Thank you so much, Mr. Wright. It would never have occurred to me that there were legal problems. *So* good of you to point it out. Is there anything else you feel the need to instruct me in?"

Wright's bonhomous, man-of-the-people beam, which hadn't dipped below 100 watts for our entire conversation, was by now entirely extinguished. "Your solicitors will hear from me."

I smiled even more sweetly. "I'm sure they will be looking forward to it."

10

I staggered out of bed the next morning at five thirty and stared at my sleep-sodden face in the mirror. My mother did this every day of her life. Was she crazy? It was still dark when I set off for Cooper's offices in the City. Public transport at that hour was eerie: a scattering of people going home from night shifts, another scattering who cleaned the offices and shops of those thousands who would follow in a couple of hours. And a third group, the City workers, who got to work by seven to deal with the Japanese market, and stayed until late to deal with San Francisco. Everyone sat silently, huddled in their own little worlds. It wasn't particularly cold for March, but it felt cold all the same. The day hadn't really started yet, and the dream of warm beds hovered over us all.

By the time I reached Fenchurch Street, the coffee shops were beginning to open. The dead-eyed people I had watched on the Tube joined their dead-eyed colleagues in the queues, hoping to inject enough caffeine into their systems to get them through the day. I followed their example, more so that I could have a quiet place to call Jake than because I wanted the foul Starbucks coffee. I bought the smallest cup possible, refusing to use those ridiculous fake Italian sizes the minimum-wage employees from Eastern Europe were supposed to find second nature. What a protest. I'm sure it made the folks in Seattle quake in their eco-friendly sandals.

"Hey," I said into the phone. "Me."

"Good morning. Do you always start this early?"

"Nope. But I'm a City type now, and I'm off to bond with other City types."

Jake was smarter than that. He just waited.

"I met Derek Gascoigne from Cooper's at my mother's Bar Association knees-up last night. Patrick Conway is flying in for a meeting this morning, and for reasons I can't fathom, they think I should be there." I filled him in quickly on Alemán's visit to Gascoigne. "What do you think he's playing at?"

Jake ignored the question. "What do they want *you* for?"

It wouldn't have been a rude question—it was one I'd been asking myself—if it hadn't been for the stress on the "you." I bit back a smart-ass remark, but filed it away in the grievance drawer. Later. Instead I said, "Just what I was wondering. Gascoigne said that they had NCIS and the Revenue and Customs rounded up. What a publisher can bring to the table is anyone's guess, but it seemed worth following up."

"Let's talk when you're through."

"I'll call. Changing the subject, what should I do if I see that guy from the LSD? When I got back to the office yesterday he'd vanished."

This was not high on Jake's list just at the moment. "Have you seen him today?"

"No, but on the other hand, it is only six thirty in the morning."

"Stalkers aren't usually worried about the time," he said dryly.

"A *stalker*? Is that what you think he is?" I wasn't quite sure how I felt about that.

"I don't know what he is, but if he's not following you, I'm not sure what I can do about it. I'm not sure what I can do about it even if he is following you. There's no manpower to get someone to follow you to see who is following you, if you see what I mean. Even if there were, it's not my department. Are you frightened?"

"No more than I have been for the last week. I think I might be too stupid to be afraid."

Jake ignored that. Sensible. "Keep an eye out for him when you leave Cooper's, and let me know."

"I will. Just one thing I don't understand."

"If you've got it narrowed down to one, you're way ahead of me."

Jake was sounding bleak, and I didn't waste time laughing politely. "It's about the police investigation at the LSD. They decided that there were no grounds for a prosecution in part because Davies' landlady said that she had never seen Kit, and Davies had claimed he was hanging around outside the flat."

"So?"

"Well, according to the landlady this week, Davies had moved two years before the harassment charge was made. She wouldn't have seen Kit even if Kit was in fact harassing him, for the simple reason that Davies wasn't living there."

"Are you trying to make a case for the prosecution?"

"Of course not. Don't go official on me. It's odd, and it doesn't fit, and that makes me wonder."

"If we investigated everything that was odd and didn't fit, you'd never see me at all. Look, don't worry about Davies. Just call me when you leave Cooper's."

Maybe he was right, and I was fixating. Maybe I just wanted it to mean something because that would give us something to go on. The way it was, we had nothing at all. "Yes, I will, but don't forget I'm going straight to Galway."

"When will you be home?" He paused. "I would rather have told you this face-to-face but . . ." He hesitated again.

"What?" I demanded. "Just tell me. You being mysterious is much worse than whatever it is."

"I don't think so." He paused, thinking about his words. "A floater was pulled out of the Thames late last night. We think it might be Kit."

I made an involuntary small noise, the kind you do when someone knocks you flying from behind. I pushed away what he was saying, and tried to grasp at whatever hope there was. "You *think?*"

"It's the right age, sex, height, weight, hair color. From the location the body was found, the river police estimate it went into the river at Chelsea Embankment. Kit was last seen at the Chelsea Arts Club."

"What does his sister say? Has she identified him?"

"There's nothing for her to identify."

I understood. "If she doesn't want to—if she—that is, I will, if you want." I didn't want to, but Kit's sister must be in her seventies. A formal identification of a body that had been in the river for a week might be too much for her.

Jake's voice was harsh. "No. Not that we don't want her to do it. That there's nothing for her to see. The body was caught in the propeller of a boat." He repeated it, as if I might have failed to understand. "There's nothing to identify."

I was frozen. Human kind cannot bear very much reality.

Jake was worried. I am rarely silent. "Sam. Are you there?"

I pulled my coat tighter around me, as if that would keep the demons at bay. "Yes. Yes, I'm here. What happens now?"

"We're getting a DNA sample from his sister sent up from Devon. It will take three or four days before we know whether we have a match. In any case, we have a murder investigation, whoever this turns out to be."

"Murder? He didn't drown?"

"No. A preliminary look says he was knocked out, then strangled. It'll be a while before we get the full picture."

I waited for him to go on. I was numb.

"If the identification is confirmed, I'll need to talk to you in more detail about Kit's private life: friends, lovers, whatever names you know."

I stiffened. Turn Kit's private life into newspaper fodder? I calmed myself. Jake was now doing what I'd been furious he'd failed to do when Kit first vanished. "I'll tell you what I can, but I don't know a lot. For such a public man he was very private."

"I'm sorry. Sorry to tell you like this, too." Jake turned his head to speak to someone. A muffled voice replied, and there was laughter. He came back on the line. "We don't need to do this yet, not until we get a positive ID. Just think about it. Make a list. I have to go. We'll talk tonight. Do you want to call when you arrive at Gatwick? If I can get away, I'll come and collect you."

I pulled myself together. I was out of my depth, but even so, I didn't expect him to take time out from a murder investigation to chauffeur me about. "No need. Why don't you come back to the flat when—if—you can? I'll cook something that will keep if you don't get there."

"It's my job. It's always going to be like this, you know."

"I'll worry about how I feel about that later. Right now, I'd much rather you find out what happened to Kit than that you take me out to dinner."

I disconnected from him, and disconnected my emotions. I slid down off the stool. Time to face the suits.

I arrived at Cooper's bang on seven o'clock. There had apparently been a pre-meeting meeting, because everyone at the table had a well-worn look. Jesus. Didn't these people ever sleep? I swiftly compared a prestige City firm's meeting room to Timmins & Ross's grubby version. No chipped melamine table here, no catering-sized coffee machine with burned-smelling coffee belching uncomfortably on a rickety side table. Cooper's didn't go for Selden's attempt at Victorian grandeur, either, settling instead for high-powered ultramodern. Good for them. Black Eames chairs were drawn up to a vast, smoked-glass and chrome table. Glass? My mind, glad of the distraction, skittered away to wonder who cleaned off the smears and marks that glass collects every time you walk past it. Then I looked again at the smooth, sleek creatures sitting there, and decided they didn't make smears. They were a special kind of gleaming super race. Tradition was nodded to with a beautiful Rosenthal coffee set, laid out beside two chrome-plated thermos jugs. Elegance and functionality. They'd got it down pat.

As well as Derek Gascoigne there was a woman introduced as Dara Janes, his assistant, and Michael Eliot, also from Cooper's. You could spot them by their expensive suits, their all-around polish. They were easily separated from two men from NCIS, who were not introduced, and a man who only said he was an observer from Revenue and Customs. They had Marks and Spencer linen suits that hadn't been ironed this side of the millennium, with polyester ties yanked down into tiny crumpled knots to reveal unbuttoned collar buttons. And at the head of the table, looking as elegant as if he had just stepped out of an advertisement in a men's magazine, was Patrick Conway.

He and Gascoigne stood up when I was shown in. Eliot hadn't planned to, but when he saw the way Conway greeted me, he leaped to his feet as though it were natural to him. The NCIS and Revenue men looked up from their files and one acknowledged my entrance by tugging his tie further down his neck.

Conway took my proffered hand in both of his, and made a great fuss of setting out a chair next to his at the end of the table. The NCIS men looked sourly at me, and I couldn't really blame them. If I were them, I would have looked sourly at me, too. I was feeling rather oppressed by Conway's charm. It was too thick, and too overwhelming. Yet he was a clever man, and must know that it—and the small matter of the use of a private jet— would make me wonder what I had that he wanted.

Conway turned to the table. "Well, let's sum up what we've got. You," he spoke to NCIS, "will hold off taking any further action until we have conducted our own inquiries. If we don't have anything concrete within the next two weeks, then we will turn everything over to you. If what we have we can act upon, we will let you know in advance what it is, and what we plan to do. You can then deal with whatever falls outside our remit."

The NCIS men conferred briefly, and not too happily.

"Agreed?" prodded Conway, sharply.

"We'd still like to put our own people in," said the man I'd decided was in charge. It was very obviously an argument that had been going on for some time.

"I've said it over and over"—Conway's accent was thickening, which I assumed meant he wasn't nearly as upset as he wanted to appear—"you can put in your own men in this country, which will immediately become apparent to the entire company, whatever you think. You will then lose us whatever leverage we have, and probably the big fish, while you net the small fry. If that's what you want. . . ." He threw up his hands, in a highly dramatic picture of a man pushed beyond his patience. I didn't think he was at all. He talked of big fish, but he was the angler, and he was playing his catch very cleverly. I particularly liked the way he'd slipped in the phrase "in this country." He knew perfectly well that the bulk of his corporation was out of reach of UK law, and he was dangling in front of NCIS the possibility that everything would be snatched from them if they were too precipitate. But he did it elegantly, so they could all pretend that it was not happening.

The NCIS men and their colleagues nodded sourly. They had

known that this was where they would end up, but they had wanted their protest on the record. Conway stood again. "Thank you for coming, gentlemen. I appreciate it, and we'll be keeping you up-to-date."

They were astonished: They had expected to stay. Conway was shepherding them toward the door with a double dose of charm. They didn't like it, but hadn't any option. Interesting. I was supposed to see them, but not know what they had discussed. They were supposed to see me, but not know what Conway was going to talk to me about. I wondered if he knew about me and Jake, whom I assumed was sending any information he thought important back to his colleagues at NCIS. Were we all being played by Conway?

He sat down again, looking pleased with himself. "Well," he said, "that's the bureaucracy out of the way. Now let's roll up our sleeves and see what we've got." Conway's tailor would faint at the idea of him rolling up his sleeves: £3,000 suits are not to be fooled with. He turned to me. "We have Diego Alemán coming in shortly, but in the first instance can you run through your conversation with him? It would be helpful to know what triggered his visit."

I didn't see why not. He'd had the bulk of it already from Gascoigne. "It's not that straightforward. We didn't actually discuss the book, or his brother, or anything to do with Vernet. The name never even cropped up."

Michael Eliot blurted, "Then what did you talk about?" and looked horrified when Gascoigne and Conway turned to him.

"John Wilkes, mostly."

The others looked blank, while Conway burst out laughing. "Wilkes the MP?"

I nodded. The others continued to look blank.

"Ms. Clair," he said, "it's a joy working with you." The others now looked blank and annoyed. "For those who have never heard of him, John Wilkes was an eighteenth-century MP who was accused of libel. He was even found guilty, was he not?"

"Yes. I looked him up afterward. I can't say I knew a lot about him before. He was charged with seditious libel, stripped of his parliamentary privilege, outlawed, imprisoned, then his 'outlawry' was reversed—I have absolutely no idea what that means—and he was, eventually, reelected to parliament."

Conway considered. "A libel, found guilty, the result overturned. Is there anything there?"

"If there is, I'm not smart enough to work it out. If Diego Alemán was trying to tell me more than the fact that the book I am hoping to publish is defamatory of his brother in countries where you can libel the dead, then it went over my head. But the conversation, apart from eighteenth-century history, only brought up the fact that he'd worked in the IT department of Intinvest in Paris, and planned to go back there this summer. And that you must have known as soon as he came to see you." I turned toward Gascoigne. "What exactly did he say to you?"

Gascoigne looked toward Conway, as if for permission. I saw no signal, but Gascoigne must have, because he sat back, put the tips of his fingers together and, staring at them, began. "He rang up to make an appointment. Normally I wouldn't see someone I don't know out of the blue, but his name made him interesting.

Even if there hadn't been rumors swirling about this book, I would have made time for Rodrigo Alemán's brother. When he arrived, he asked me if I knew you." He shot me a puzzled look, and then returned to contemplating his fingers. "I asked in connection with what, and he said that he had met you at the weekend, that you were suspicious of him, thought that he was involved somehow."

"Involved," I repeated. "Involved in what? Did he say?"

Gascoigne thought. "He said, as near as I can remember, 'She thinks I'm involved with Intinvest.'"

"That's an interesting way of putting it. He *told* me he was involved with them, that is, that he worked for them. I never brought up the subject, because until then it wouldn't have occurred to me. 'Involved' implies more. We know from the work Kit Lovell has done that Intinvest may be laundering money. It sounds like Diego Alemán thinks so, too. And that either he isn't part of the money laundering, or he would like us to think he isn't."

Gascoigne nodded. "But if he is, and he would like us to think he isn't, he's been very foolish to bring himself to our attention in this way."

Conway put in: "Is he foolish?"

Gascoigne considered. "I wouldn't have thought so, no. He struck me as clever. And more than clever, as thoughtful."

"And," said Conway, thinking aloud, "thoughtful people don't make those kinds of mistakes. So for the moment we assume that he isn't involved himself, but is aware of what's going on." He raised his eyebrows at me, and I made a what-do-I-know? gesture in response. "We need to talk to him. We can deal with him on that level. If he isn't straight, it can do no harm now for him to know we're investigating." He turned to me. "What are we going to tell him about Lovell's plans?"

A lightbulb went on over my head. *This* was what they wanted me for. I could have wept with frustration. Kit's disappearance was so much on my mind that I hadn't remembered Conway's original approach.

I cleared my throat. "The police haven't spoken to any of you about Kit?"

Gascoigne and Conway stiffened in their seats. The other two just looked curious. Gascoigne spoke first: "What about Lovell?"

I saw no point in hiding the news. It was a murder investigation now, and the papers would get wind of it soon enough. I was surprised they hadn't already. "Kit's disappeared. Vanished. No one knows where. He's been gone for over a week, and the police are assuming it's murder." I hated even saying the word. I couldn't bring myself to tell them about the body in the river. Saying it out loud might mean I had to believe it.

Conway sat back in his chair as if I'd hit him. "Vanished? What do you mean, vanished?"

Unhappiness was making me angry. "I've just told you. I don't know. No one knows." I clenched my teeth so I wouldn't scream at him.

"Jesus, Mary, and Joseph." He thought about it for a moment. "You knew this when I saw you two days ago?"

"I was astonished that you didn't. It hadn't occurred to me that it wasn't public knowledge."

"Why didn't you say so then?"

"Because I didn't know what you wanted. I still don't, for that matter." I ran my hands through my hair in frustration. "How is it relevant, anyway? If you didn't arrange to have him, well, 'disappeared,' shall we say, and if you don't know who did, then your not knowing two days ago doesn't change things."

Conway stood up so abruptly his chair fell over and banged back against the wall. He put his hands, curled into fists, on the table and leaned across at me. "If I didn't *what*? Just what the hell do you think I am? I ought to—" He shook off Gascoigne, who had quickly stood to put a restraining hand on his shoulder. "Am I some sort of godfather who goes around rubbing out anyone who gets in my path? Is that it?" He was purple with rage, and his accent had totally vanished.

I felt curiously detached. I was sure his anger was real, and if I worked for him, I would have been afraid, but what did it matter to me? What did any of this matter? It was a shame that these people were having business problems, but they weren't my problems. I said wearily, "How should I know what you are, or what you do? I first laid eyes on you forty-eight hours ago. I know nothing about your ethics, and couldn't care less. I'm concerned that my author—that my *friend*—has gone missing and is probably dead. The police are assuming a body pulled out of the Thames yesterday is Kit. If it is, then I have no further interest in any of this." I waved my arm tiredly toward the meeting room's luxurious austerity. "If it isn't, then I'll go on looking for him. If, in passing, I can help with your business problems, well and good, but that's not what I'm here for. I want to find out what happened to Kit Lovell. That's it. Beginning, middle, and end. Now why don't you stop shouting, sit down, and we can try and do something useful."

I sounded like his nanny, and the others looked like they were going to go and find the nearest nuclear fallout shelter to hide in, but it worked. Conway took a deep breath and sat down. The man had style. He didn't even look behind him to see if the chair had been picked up—he just assumed it had and sat.

He didn't look at anyone else. "I'm sorry," he said, holding out his hand.

I put mine in his. "So am I." I was, too. I had thought he was straight when I'd met him. To accuse him in passing of murder was plain stupid and, worse than stupid, not helpful. "Let's start again. Kit vanished, probably last Wednesday. No one has seen him or heard from him since; according to the police his bank accounts and credit cards have not been used; no telephone calls have been made on any of his numbers; there has been no sign of him at all." I took a breath. "He may be this body from the river. It's not—" I boggled. "It's not identifiable."

Conway had stopped being angry, and was thinking constructively again. "When we spoke in Paris, you said I couldn't see the manuscript, and Lovell's sources, because it was a police matter. I thought you were referring to the money laundering. Instead, you were thinking about his disappearance."

Conway and Gascoigne quickly looked at each other and away. I wondered if they would have called this meeting, and decided to share their information on money laundering with me, much less invite NCIS and the Revenue in, if they had known that the police weren't looking for corporate fraud, but for a fashion journalist. How much had they been pushed into their Good Citizen number by anxiety about what would be found out, and how much because they *knew* what would be found out?

To give Conway and Gascoigne needed time to digest the

information about Kit, I recapped on the highlights of the last week, including my break-in.

There was a gleam of a smile on Conway's face. "Ah," he said, tapping the corner of his own eye.

I didn't want to discuss it, so I ignored him and carried on. "Do you have any sense of where this, um, problem is coming from inside your company?" All four faces looked studiedly blank. I wasn't going to get anything there. I continued on to a more comfortable subject. "What can you ask Alemán that won't tell him more than he gives in return?"

"Let's have him in, and we'll see." Conway was back to his urbane self, that out-of-control moment over as if it had never been. For now.

Dara ushered Alemán in. I was unreasonably touched to see that he wore what was plainly his "interview" suit. He looked much more vulnerable than he had when I'd seen him at the Stanleys. He was surprised to see me with the Lambert-Lorraine people, but he immediately wiped his face of all emotions.

"Sit down, sit down," said Conway, at his most stage Irish.

Diego Alemán sat on the very edge of his chair and refused coffee.

Conway flicked a look at Gascoigne, who began the interview. "We're grateful to you for coming, Mr. Alemán."

Diego cleared his throat nervously.

"We've been discussing your suggestions to me last week, and we thought it would be helpful if we could talk it through with you."

Diego nodded. The only way he was going to say anything was by direct questioning.

Gascoigne recognized that. "You said last week that you feared that Ms. Clair thought you were 'involved' with Intinvest. Would you like to elaborate?"

Diego slid a glance toward me, and then looked away quickly when our eyes met. He cleared his throat again. "I don't really know what more to say. It's just that she—you—were so obviously suspicious."

Gascoigne was silky. "Suspicious of what, Mr. Alemán? What is there to be suspicious of?"

"Of? Of my brother's death, of course. I knew about the book she was publishing, and I wanted to know more. My family is very unhappy."

"I understand." Gascoigne's voice sharpened. "But family unhappiness about a book produced by an independent publisher is hardly likely to bring you to the office of Lambert-Lorraine's solicitors. Let's get to the point. What information, exactly, did you think Ms. Clair had, and what information do you want us to have?"

Diego thought for a moment. "I don't know what Ms. Clair had. That is a family matter, and not one I'm happy with, but it's separate. What I wanted to talk to you about was Intinvest. You know I worked in the IT department?" He looked around for confirmation and got a series of nods. "I regulated the system, made sure that the international units were coordinated." Here he lapsed into technicalities that entirely passed me by, but I saw Michael Eliot start to scribble furiously. The others looked almost as glazed as I was. The two men began to talk exclusively to each other, jargon and abbreviations spilling out.

After ten minutes, Eliot stopped and turned to Conway. "Shall I sum up, sir?"

"I think you'd better."

"What it boils down to is that there are two laundering systems running simultaneously, one working with the high-end items. The top-end is done through shell companies and false invoicing, the low-end through the usual route—understating cash sales."

Everyone nodded. They all knew what was going on, and were not really surprised. Gascoigne must have seen that I had no idea what Eliot was talking about. "As well as the legitimate goods and services, phantom deliveries are being made, goods and services that are never supplied, things like software or consultancy services. Vernet is invoiced, and the money goes through as a legitimate payment for legitimate goods. That's the first route. The second is where inexpensive items, like makeup, which are often paid for in cash, are targeted. Vernet ships two million lipsticks retailing at £10 apiece to a Vernet subsidiary, but only invoices for one million at £5. The subsidiary pays £5 million on the books, and banks the difference offshore."

Now I nodded, too, and Eliot continued. "Ordinarily, domestic and offshore are run through two separate systems, but a server failure meant that the disaster recovery plan ran all the data through a single person: Diego."

Diego interposed. "At first I thought it was a blip, but as I recovered terabytes of data the pattern was clear. I was afraid to raise it internally, because I couldn't see who had been doing this, only that it had been done. So I created a snapshot covering all transactions over the past year and rsynced it to an encrypted cloud storage facility. It was all I could do without setting off alarm bells."

Conway snapped, "And what are you expecting out of this?"

Diego flushed, and looked very young and vulnerable. He was hurt. "Nothing. Intinvest are selling armaments to both the governments and the insurgents in Chechnya, in South Sudan—anywhere civil war is a business opportunity. I've only had proof for a couple of months. It has taken me longer than it should to come to you, but I wasn't sure that anyone would listen."

I believed him, but this was the material Kit had found, and for which he had evidence. What about the property deals? They had vanished into thin air.

Conway turned to me. "Have you anything to ask?"

I shook my head. I needed to talk to Helena.

At nine thirty I whispered to Gascoigne that I really had to go. The meeting was dragging on and on, and while I recognized that this was important to Lambert-Lorraine, I had nothing to contribute. After an effusive good-bye and elaborate thanks—*for what?*—from Conway, Gascoigne took me down to a car, and I set off for Luton.

I had never realized before that the great quality of money is not convenience, but insulation. Had I followed my humble little Ryanair pattern, I would have had to take the Tube, then the train, then gone through the check-in and security rigmarole at the airport, before I was surrounded by screaming babies and cabin attendants attempting to sell me duty free. Now a car drove me to the airport and drew up at a small building by a runway. I was escorted from the car directly to the plane, and ten minutes after I arrived we took off. A cabin attendant (who knew private planes had them?) said, "I'll be sitting up there. If you want anything, ring," and then I was left entirely alone.

The quiet was in some ways unwelcome. Yes, it was wonderful luxury, but if I'd had to fight my way through commuter hell, I wouldn't have had time to think about the morning's events. Now I circled endlessly around the few details Jake had given me. I didn't want to think about it, but I couldn't stop. I tried to focus on what the meeting had thrown up, but it was the same circular pattern. I decided to treat it like an editorial problem, as though the plot in a novel needed sorting out. I pulled out a pad and began to make notes. We had three separate issues: Kit's disappearance; the money laundering through false invoicing; and now, it appeared, a property scam that Helena had picked up right away but no one else was mentioning.

That was worth considering. If that had been part of Intinvest's fraud, then surely Diego would have mentioned it. If Diego was telling the truth. If he wasn't, then the property scam might be part of Intinvest's laundering program, but one they thought they could still keep hidden, as no one had apparently noticed it. And Kit's—Kit's murder. I wrote the word down, so I'd believe it. I presumed, or at least I presumed the police presumed, that his death was the result of his uncovering Intinvest's money laundering. After all, he hadn't known about the money laundering via the property. Or had he? And where did the Thin

Boy fit in? Who was he, and why was he following me? I couldn't see how that was linked to anything else. By the end of the trip, my pad was filled with names and arrows pointing wildly in all directions, but I wasn't any more sure of what I was looking at than when I'd set off.

We landed, and I tried to put everything except Breda out of my mind. The last week's happenings had made me feel that publishing wasn't important, and I really couldn't risk communicating this to any author, much less my star author.

Breda's husband, Austin, was at the airport to meet me, which he always did. They were good, kind people, and the fact that Breda hadn't wanted me to visit, and thought my trip a waste of my time and hers, would never have stopped her from making sure that I was not inconvenienced in any way. I liked Austin, who taught physics at the university in Galway, and we chatted amicably. He looked exactly like the cartoon image of the absent-minded professor: he was short, and stooped, and had flyaway white hair in a crescent around a bald crown. He was thin because when he was working he forgot to eat, and his clothes looked like they'd been bought in the local Oxfam shop, which I suspected they had. Breda had made a fortune, but apart from their large, extremely pretty house, they weren't interested in spending their money. Most of it went to their children, and to dozens of charities.

Austin was absent-minded, but he was very astute and, when he wasn't working, very observant of the world around him. After

a few miles, he said, "Are you all right?"—making the same gesture to his eye that Conway had done that morning. My makeup
skills were plainly lacking at six in the morning.

For no reason at all, I found myself confiding in him. I started
by telling him about the break-in, as I had to so many people
already, but before I knew it I had told him about Kit, and the
manuscript, and Vernet. I stopped short at the money laundering. I didn't really care about it, only about Kit.

Austin was a love. He pulled over to the side of the road, and
sat staring through the windscreen while it all came pouring out,
without interrupting me or making those noises of gratified horror people make when they are listening to gossip that doesn't
touch them. After I finished he continued to sit for several
minutes, turning it over in his mind. Then he said the last thing
I'd expected. "What do you know about Rudiger?"

"What? What do you mean? He's been my neighbor for nearly
twenty years."

"Yes. But Jack the Ripper was somebody's neighbor, too." He
held up his hand to stop my reaction. "I didn't mean it quite like
that. But everybody is somebody's neighbor, unless they live in
a hut in the woods. I'm intrigued by the fact that he suddenly
made overtures of friendship after so long. From what you say, it
was entirely out of character."

I wanted to protest, but he was right. I'd spoken to the man
twice: ten minutes' conversation in fifteen-plus years, then out
of nowhere he was offering me the use of his spare room. Mr.
Rudiger had been, so we believed, a distinguished architect. That
in itself was a passport in my kind of world, and the respect it
generated meant we didn't ask too many questions. I thought

about him. He had helped me when I was burgled, and Jake had trusted him. Hadn't he? Was I simply reading that into the situation because *I* had trusted him? I'd kept him up-to-date over the last week, frequently dropping in on my way home from work, and he had been interested, pleased to hear what was happening, and pleased, I flattered myself, to see me. But the alternatives were worth considering.

Austin waited, to see if I wanted to say anything else. When it was clear that I didn't, he put the car in gear, and we traveled the last few miles to the house in silence. Just before we turned into the drive he said, "Would you prefer for me not to discuss this with Breda?" I hesitated. Breda wrote about teachers having midlife crises. What could she say that would be helpful? As if reading my mind Austin said, "Don't forget she worked for a solicitor for nearly twenty years. She hasn't had a sheltered life. Even more, she understands people, and motive. It's what makes her a good writer."

He was right. I said, weakly, "Let's see how it goes."

Breda was at the door to welcome me. I felt a rush of affection for her as we drove up. The horrors of the past week—and the different sort of horror on receiving her book—had made me forget the genuine fondness I felt for her. She had turned sixty the year before, and had greeted that milestone with a generosity of spirit that I admired. She had a big party, but she announced that she couldn't bear to receive presents: She was a wealthy woman, and if she didn't have a whatever-it-was, it was because she didn't want one. So would we all please donate whatever we planned to give her to our own favorite charities. She, in turn, gave the same amount as the party cost her to a charity that worked to drill wells in Third World countries. She told me that she couldn't drink champagne comfortably in Galway if she thought children in Africa couldn't even drink water. But this wasn't some big announcement, she hadn't made a deal out of it. She only told me because I'd asked. She had done it, and was pleased to have done it, but she didn't need the approval and acknowledgment of her friends in order to make it happen.

I kissed her more warmly than usual, out of relief at seeing someone who was genuinely good—something that had been in small supply over the last week. I was so relieved to be able to say honestly how thrilled everyone was with her book that I was more effusive than usual. "I was saving the best news until I got here," I said, smiling. "W H Smith's have chosen *Toujours Twenty-one* for their September Book of the Month. They love it."

Breda was pleased, but not as overwhelmed as I'd expected. I kept forgetting that she'd known all along she was the goose that had laid yet another golden egg, in a long line of golden eggs. It was only Timmins & Ross that had thought she had transformed herself into a turkey.

"The satisfying thing for us has been how many young people—both at the publisher, and at Smith's—have taken to it. We're really going to extend your readership with this one."

She nodded. That's what she'd been expecting. Only her publisher had been too dim to see it. She took me straight into the kitchen, where she had set out a late lunch. The house was Georgian, and it was large, but any ideas of palatial rock-star piles behind electronic gates were very far from the mark. The house had probably belonged to a land agent who looked after an es-

tate for an aristocratic landlord. It was compact, and manage-
able, and Breda fit into it as neatly as any nineteenth-century
land agent's wife would have, making sure her guests were comfortable. I watched her with affection as she went over to the
cooker and turned on the gas under the soup. She looked much
younger than sixty. Her hair was tucked up into a neat chignon
that from pictures I knew she had always worn. She was trim and
efficient in corduroys and a blue-flannel shirt, and her movements
were swift and neat.

While we waited for the soup to heat we began to discuss the
plans Sandra and I had made for publicity, the marketing and
promotion plans, where we would like her to appear, what kind
of publicity she'd be willing to undertake. All the basic appara-
tus of a Breda McManus bestseller. I showed her the artwork for
the jacket, which she liked with reservations—reservations that
were hardly surprising, since it was a hastily toned-down version
of the camp send-up I'd originally asked for—and in general got
the schedule in order.

Then there was nothing to do except relax and chat about
mutual acquaintances over the lunch table until it was time for
me to go back to the airport. Breda was still puzzled about why
I'd bothered to make the trip, but I had no intention of enlight-
ening her. Finally one silence got too long for comfort, and I
looked at Austin. He nodded, and said, "Sam's found herself in
a bit of trouble recently."

Breda looked interested. I waited, and Austin set out the story,
putting it far more concisely than I'd managed to in my notes
on the plane. When he got to the question of Mr. Rudiger, Breda

put her head on one side and looked at me sharply, like a robin outside the kitchen window that thinks your reason for existence is keeping the bird table topped up with bacon scraps.

"What was your impression?"

"I liked him. I *like* him," I corrected, defiantly. "It's so melodramatic to think of him sitting upstairs, an agoraphobic criminal mastermind."

"Melodrama is popular because it's very often true," she said, absently. "Still, your judgment of him is not valueless."

"Thank you," I said, aiming for pleasant rather than sarcastic.

I failed, and she laughed. "I didn't mean it that way. People don't wear masks, and even when they do, their real features come through. If you like him, it's because there is something likable there. Yet it doesn't necessarily mean that he is a good person—there are plenty of charming rogues in the world. Austin is right. It's worth considering why he surfaced just now. It may be that you were never in need of help before in a way that came to his attention. It may be something else."

By the time I was on my way home, this time in the noisy confusion that was commercial air travel, I had again mentally deposited publishing into a file marked NOT IMPORTANT. I would have to face Ben on Monday with the news about Smith's change of heart, and I needed to focus on that, but at the speed things were happening, forty-eight hours was a lifetime. Instead I called Helena as soon as we landed.

She was still at the office. I filled her in briefly on my meeting in the morning. "I think we need to sit down and see where we've got to, don't you?"

"Absolutely. It's worrying that the property problems have just vanished. What did you think of Conway? Does he not know about it, or does he not want you to?"

I shrugged, always useful when talking on the phone. "Your guess is as good as mine. He strikes me as on the level, but then again he runs a company valued at a couple of billion dollars. Who knows what is legitimate to people like that?"

My mother was used to dealing with mega-wealthy corporations, and was not swayed. "Avoidance of tax is one thing, evasion and corruption are another. If he's honest, he knows that. Is he?" My mother can sum up a person at fifty paces and she can never understand why I'm not even willing to try.

"At a guess I'd say yes, but it's only a guess. He's charming, and clever, and I'd guess unscrupulous. Whether that unscrupulousness extends to outright illegality, I don't know. What worries me, though, is why? Why would he bother with something as small as this? It's tens of millions, I understand, but why would a man earning the same tens of millions every year—"

Helena interrupted, "Tens of millions in a month."

"In a month," I agreed. "Why would he bother? It would be like you or me stealing a couple of years' salary. That kind of money would be nice, but it simply wouldn't outweigh the risk. Proportionately, that's all we're talking about here."

"Then he's honest. Or at least, we work on the assumption that in this particular instance he is. Lambert-Lorraine has the reputation for being clean, and it seems to be so in fact as well. I know where to look, and if there was anything, I would have found it."

"So we're back at square one."

"Maybe. Let's sit down tomorrow and talk. Shall I come to you at eight?"

"Mother, it's the weekend. Could you make it nine?"

A sigh of wonderment drifted down the line.

I sighed in response. A good person to have on your side, but still a Martian.

11

I am not a late-night person at the best of times, and it had been a long week. When the phone rang at eleven thirty, I was just falling asleep. Jake.

"Is it too late?"

"Depends for what." I reached for the light.

"Me."

"Still depends for what," I said, waking up properly. "If you mean dinner, yes, it's too late unless you want to heat it up and eat by yourself. If you mean to sleep with me, no, not too late at all."

"I'll take what I can get."

I affected mock outrage. "Are you suggesting that you'd prefer dinner, but you'll settle for sex?"

"I'll be there in twenty minutes." Not disregarding me, just focused.

I got up and went into the kitchen. I talk a better game than I play, I know. I really couldn't sit by while a guest—and the relationship was tenuous, he was still a guest—opened a tin of soup in my kitchen. Anyway, I didn't have a tin of soup. I like cooking, and I don't do tins.

When Jake rang the bell he stood slumped against the wall by the front door for a minute. Then he yanked off his jacket and said, "I really need a drink."

I kissed him sedately. "I hate to be the one to tell you this, but you need a shower even more. I'd offer to come and wash your back but, quite frankly, you don't look up to it. Go and shower, and I'll open some wine."

He went without protest, which was a sign of how low he really was. By the time he was back, wearing my toweling robe, and carrying it off as though fuchsia was just the color he would have chosen for himself if he'd been asked, I had opened a bottle and had some soup warmed up.

"My God, is this the kind of service you always provide?"

"Pretty much."

He sat down without a further word, and didn't look up again until he'd finished two bowls of soup and half a loaf of bread.

"Have you eaten at all today?" I demanded.

He shook his head, revived a bit by the food but still tired. "Could we try to manage without your famous imitation of my mother, just for tonight, please?"

"Not a problem. I really only do tea, the sympathy you have to get somewhere else."

He spoke to an empty chair. "Now she tells me."

I ignored that. "What now? Bed, or do you want to talk about what's been going on?"

"You're such a romantic."

"You bet. If you know anything more important, then you're with the wrong woman."

"Unfortunately, most of today was more important, even if a lot less fun."

So we were going to talk about it. I supposed that I wanted to know, although pulling the duvet up over my head and pretending that none of it was happening for the next eight hours was awfully enticing.

"You first."

Jake slumped back in his chair. "There's not much to tell in that sense. Most of the day was spent setting up an incident room, putting in motion all the routine of a murder investigation. It's depressing and you don't want the details. We had a press conference. Appeals for witnesses. That kind of thing. There was a bulletin on the news, and it will be in tomorrow's papers." I wrapped my arms around myself, cold suddenly. "It's the best way of getting information. By morning there will be a hundred reported sightings." He stared ahead cheerlessly at the thought of what tomorrow would bring.

"It makes it real. I hate it." I took a deep breath. "Particularly as what I was doing this morning was so unreal. These people are talking about Monopoly money. None of it means anything. I know it's important, but I can't feel it. I can't feel any of it matters."

"Tell me anyway."

I reported the meeting with Conway and his merry men. I didn't see any reason not to. Jake didn't look surprised. His NCIS buddies must have reported back, at least for as much as they'd been allowed to sit in on. "The thing I don't understand is that the property deals have never been mentioned. I know that for a huge corporation it's not a fortune, but it's still millions of pounds. Someone, somewhere is making a lot of money off their backs.

"The other thing is that the more I think about it, the more convinced I am that they didn't know Kit had vanished. Conway was really angry." I shivered. In retrospect I found him frightening in a way I hadn't at the time. "He could have been that angry because I'd suggested something true that he thought was hidden, but it didn't have that smell. He was . . ." I paused to consider. "He was insulted, I'd say. Enraged that anyone would think that of him. It was vanity, but not the kind of vanity where a man thinks he can do anything because he's powerful enough." I trailed away. "I don't know. This is all guesswork."

Jake was listening carefully. "Guesswork is usually all we have. You've spent nearly three hours with the man now. If there were inconsistencies, you didn't see them, and that's important. I'd like to know what NCIS has turned up, but while they tell us they're giving us everything, they never are." He thought for a minute about that, and then, moving on, said, "I forgot to tell you yesterday, I checked where the fingerprints were found here." He waved around the kitchen.

"Useful?" I was so tired I was practically telegraphing.

"Not very. As you'd guessed, everything was in the 'public' part of the flat—bathroom, kitchen, sitting room. In the office there were smudges, meaning gloves, but that's all, apart from you and your cleaning lady."

I nodded wearily. "So now all you have to do is find a burglar who knows about fingerprints, and how to avoid making them."

Jake was almost as tired. "Yeah. Cuts the possibilities right down." We were both slumped at the table, barely awake. "Have you spoken to your mother?"

"She's coming in the morning."

"Great." He stood up. "Am I staying until then?"

I looked at him appraisingly. Even in fuchsia, he was very nice-looking. Not devastatingly handsome, not the kind of man you'd turn and look at on the street. But attractive. Sure of himself, and sure of what he wanted. And I wanted it, too. I smiled as I stood up. "Now you've showered you are."

Helena was merciful. She didn't arrive until nine thirty, and when she came she was bearing fresh croissants. You can forgive a lot for that. I made coffee and we sat down at the table. It looked like one of those meetings you see in films about Wall Street: coffee, papers, stacks of files. The only thing missing was the fluorescent light making everyone look slightly green.

Jake was, as I suspected was his habit, in charge. He looked at my mother. "Why don't you go through what you've got first."

My mother had her reading glasses perched on the end of her nose. She looked like a very severe elf. "There's not much, or not much that's useful. It's really a long list of negatives. Lambert-Lorraine seems to be clean. At least, as clean as any company of that size can be."

"Meaning?"

"Meaning that money is being ping-ponged through a host of companies in Panama, the Bahamas, and the Cayman Islands. But it's all normal creative accountancy, well within the law. They take advantage of every possible loophole, but never stray near, much less over the line. I've gone through a list of their company officers, and none of them has any history of involvement with any financial impropriety. I'm not saying there isn't any. Without an inside contact, and without wanting them to know I'm looking, that's not possible to say. What is possible to say is that it looks unlikely in that environment."

"What about Cooper's? Can anything be coming from there?"

She looked wistful for a moment. "I wish I could say yes. It would give me enormous pleasure to think such monuments of rectitude had a secret life. But if they do, it's covered up better than Queen Victoria's underwear. Not a glimpse of anything showing. The one I'm really interested in, and the only one that I think is worth following up, is Kenneth Wright. Sam and I spoke to him briefly on Thursday, and there's definitely something to be uncovered there."

Jake turned to me. "Anything on him from your end?"

"No. Selden's have gone to ground. They're horrified to be caught up in something as undignified as this, and the only word we've had from them is a prissy little e-mail more or less saying they don't know anything, and if we could keep our problems to ourselves, they'd be grateful."

Helena snorted. Now she looked like an elf who had just discovered that Santa wasn't going to give her a Christmas bonus. "I always said they were about as useful as a wet Kleenex. Honestly—"

I broke in. I'd heard Helena's Selden's rant before. "I know, I know. What I don't know is if they think there's something to cover up, or just don't want to be mixed up in anything as icky as crime."

"I would have said the latter if they hadn't been the ones to bring up Wright's name. Can we focus on him for a minute?"

Jake and I looked at each other like schoolchildren brought to order. Another second and we'd be passing notes. "Absolutely, Helena," he said, chastened. "Go on."

I was intrigued by the "Helena." She'd been Nell the day after they'd met. Had he reverted to Helena because he was sleeping with me? Did that mean if we became a couple he'd move on to "Mrs. Clair"?

Helena wasn't wasting her time on such fripperies. I dragged my attention back to what she was saying. "He's a tricky customer. Something is going on, because no one at Cooper's will talk. I have a lot of friends there, and I shouldn't have any problems getting information about an ex-employee. But I am, and that's puzzling. This is not normal discretion. At a guess I would say an order has come down from the partners that no one is to talk."

"But don't you know any of the partners well enough to ask off the record?" I was amazed. Helena knows everybody.

"Of course I do." She looked at me as if I were an idiot. "But they're not talking, either. I let it be understood he'd approached us for a job, and that should have loosened tongues, but it hasn't. Several of them are old friends, and if he had been sacked, they would have told me, and they would have told me why. I'm not getting either of those responses."

"Which means?" Jake encouraged.

"Which means that whatever it was he did or didn't do, he's

either got the goods on someone there, or he involved the firm in something illegal. The former is unlikely. I've known most of the senior partners forever, and I doubt they have done anything worse than anyone else, which means there are no goods to be had. So it's the latter. If he was laundering money, say . . ." She paused, thinking it through. "If he had been laundering money for Vernet, or an employee of Vernet, and Cooper's got wind of it, then they'd sack him, but they would keep the lid on it, because it would have been Cooper's escrow accounts that had been used."

"But wouldn't they have reported it to NCIS?" said Jake. "It would look bad for them if anyone else reported it, and they hadn't. They don't strike me as the type to take a risk like that."

"That's what's odd. You're not getting any reports of this back from NCIS?" Jake shook his head. "Would you? I know there are interdepartmental problems, and you don't always hear everything."

Jake looked uncomfortable, but said, "I think once the missing persons report was elevated to a murder inquiry NCIS would have sent me everything."

"You 'think'?" Helena looked at her papers, allowing Jake to be embarrassed on his own. I got up to make more coffee.

But Jake wasn't embarrassed, he was angry. "*I think.* That's all I can say. It's all I know."

"Fine." Helena wasn't going to waste time on office politics. "Let's work on the assumption that Cooper's did report to NCIS, and for whatever reason NCIS hasn't sent the report on. Can you get it? Although we should consider whether actually having the report will do us any good. Will it be any more useful to thinking about Wright than just making the assumption that it happened? It's Wright we're interested in, after all." She thought for a moment. "The other possibility is that Cooper's became suspicious, but there was no evidence. Wright was only a salaried partner, and so they could just let him go, and clamp down on the reason. They were worried enough to get rid of him, but without even enough to go to NCIS with." She considered it again. "Maybe." She wasn't happy.

I put in, "What can you find out—" I thought about Helena's usual methods, and changed the question—"What have you already found out about him?"

She looked at me approvingly. "He does well for himself: big office, expensive location. But there's no corresponding client list. Apart from Vernet's property portfolio, Wright has only a handful of clients he brought with him from Cooper's, and that is all I can find. It might be an idea to get a full list." She turned to Jake. "Can you do that? I've done a fair amount of digging, and I'm fairly sure my list is complete, but it would be nice to know for certain." Jake made a note. "If those are his only clients, he's not generating enough income to support his office, much less his family." She turned over a couple of pages: "Big flat in Kensington, house in Gloucestershire, no mortgage on either; son at Winchester, daughter at Bedales. *Very* expensive wife. He's sleeping with his secretary. Also expensive." I peeked at Jake, who was staring openmouthed at Helena. Good. He'd finally discovered she was a Martian, too. "He'd need half a million after taxes to stay even modestly afloat, and he's doing better than that. There's no family money." Jake made another note. "You don't have to check. There isn't."

Jake said mildly, "I'm sure there isn't if you say so. Anything else?"

"I talked to his secretary yesterday. Tiffanie Harris. Tiffanie with an 'ie.'" She sniffed.

I blinked at her priorities. "And she probably dots the 'i' with a smiley. But this isn't the time. What did she say?" I prompted.

"Nothing. I offered her a job, said I'd heard about her from Cooper's, and she turned it down."

"So she likes working for Wright. It's unimaginable to us, but there you go. She is sleeping with the man. It's not surprising that she doesn't want to move."

"Yes it is." Helena was dogged. "I offered her double what she's earning now, in a company where she'd have a chance to climb the ladder, instead of a dead-end job in a one-man office."

"But she's having an affair with Wright. I can quite see—" Jake tried to mediate.

Helena flattened him. "I didn't tell her there was a no-shagging policy. She could have had double the money and still gone on sleeping him." She shuddered delicately.

Jake backed down, dubious, but he was on rocky ground on the shagging front. I tried not to smirk. He saw it, though, and pushed me into the firing line. "What have you got?" He smiled meanly.

I would have made a devastatingly crushing remark, if only I could have thought of one. In addition, I had nothing that I hadn't already passed on already. So I shared with them the Mc-Manuses' question about Mr. Rudiger. To my amazement both Jake and Helena agreed.

"You think that? But he's been so kind."

Now they teamed up, wondering how to try to convey information to someone as mentally deficient as me. My mother, naturally, volunteered. "Sam, really. He's a very pleasant man, and because he's famous in his field we think we know everything there is to know about him. But what do we know in fact? Do we even know that he *is* Pavel Rudiger?"

I don't like being taken for an idiot. "Well, he has been calling himself that for the past fifteen odd years. I think it's unlikely he would have taken on an alias all that time ago, just in case one day his downstairs neighbor decided to commission a book on a company with which he was illegally involved, don't you?"

Jake intervened, before Helena and I had a mother-daughter moment. "I don't think that's what Helena meant, Sam. His name *is* Rudiger, because as you say he's been using it for a long time. Do we know his first name is Pavel? I imagine you do—you all must see each other's post when it arrives?" I nodded. "But even with that information, do we know he is the Pavel Rudiger who was an architect?" I started to protest, but he went on. "And even then if that is confirmed, and we are sure he is the Pavel Rudiger who was an architect, that still doesn't tell us anything useful. That man was last heard of forty-two years ago, when he retired for reasons no one knows. Who can say what happened then, or even what has happened between now and then? What's his source of income? He's worth looking into."

"Have you mistrusted him from the beginning?" I demanded. Jake shrugged. "But you let me stay with him—you left me there to sleep in his flat." I sounded like a child abandoned at boarding school for the first time.

Jake was patient. "He knew that both the police and Helena

knew you were there. You weren't going to come to any harm, and you had to sleep somewhere. But that doesn't give him a past. We're not saying anything against him. Just that he's an unknown, and it's important not to dismiss people we know nothing about simply because they have an attractive manner."

I felt as I had at the very beginning, when Kit told me about his burglary. I was walking in the dark. If I couldn't trust my own impressions, what was there to trust?

Jake had learned all he could from us, and as usual he wasn't giving anything away. "Thanks. That's useful. If you need me, I'll be at the office all day. We should have a flood of information to go through by now." And with that he was gone. Helena tidied away her papers and followed shortly, leaving me to stare at the walls. They had jobs to do, things to follow up. What about me?

I sat at the table for a while, and eventually got up to do my usual Saturday chores: laundry, tidying, the weekly shop. By lunchtime I admitted to myself that the big children had left me behind. They weren't going to let poor Rudolph join in the other reindeers' games. I got out some manuscripts—I was desperately behind in my reading—and settled down for the afternoon.

I'd spent a couple of hours catching up on work when I heard someone thundering down the stairs and a barrage of knocks at the door. I knew before I opened it that it was Kay. Kay is tall and thin—she's a head taller than me, and probably weighs half of what I do, and even so she makes more noise than all the rest of the inhabitants of the house put together. She thuds up and down the stairs; she can't see a table without knocking it over;

or lift a bag of groceries without dropping it. When I opened the door she bounded in, long blonde hair flying, glitter sparkle on her cheeks, bright-pink flip-flops with yet more sparkles, this time flowers, on her feet, matching her bright-pink toenails.

"Hi! I thought I'd better warn and invite you!" Shorthand is one of her specialities. "We're having one of those parties—I think everyone's arriving this afternoon, but I'm not sure." She sat down, knocking over a pile of manuscripts that I could have sworn was at least five feet off her course between the door and the chair. Her swirly, 1950s retro skirt belled out as she sat down and caught the lamp. It was touch and go, but the fabric was, luckily for me, thin, and only a pad and pencil went flying.

Anthony and Kay have a party about once a year. They usually start by inviting a few friends around for lunch, and then they both get carried away and invite everyone they know, and lots of people they don't. Showing up at the Lewises' annual bash without clutching a stranger by the hand is almost as rude as showing up at a normal dinner party without clutching a bottle of wine. Somehow everyone is sandwiched into their flat—friends, strangers, friends' and strangers' children, children who appear to have no adult in tow at all—and the party goes on until all the food and drink are gone, usually well into the next day. I tend to go for an hour or so—their friends are a lot younger than me, and very quickly a lot drunker. It isn't really my sort of thing, but it feels un-neighborly not to appear for a while. So I thanked her and promised to come up later.

"Do you want some wine?" I asked.

"That would be fantastic, thanks."

We went into the kitchen, and I put a couple of bottles into a supermarket carrier bag. At the door the handle snapped and the bottles rolled down the hall. I didn't even flinch. I'd known it would happen, but you can't tell a grown woman that she's not capable of carrying a bag up a flight of stairs. The corridor was carpeted, and nothing had broken. I walked down toward the front door to pick up the second bottle where it had rolled, and I noticed that the letter box was open, as though someone had put a letter through and forgotten to put the flap down. But there was no letter, nor the usual tidal wave of pizza delivery fliers. I opened the door, but there was no one there. Kay was looking at me oddly, so I took the bottles up for her, to get them safely to her front door. Anthony could take over from there, I figured.

By three o'clock the reverberations through the ceiling, and the shrill of voices, indicated the party was in full swing. If I went up now, I could chat for a bit and then escape before it got too loud. By the time I left no one would remember who was where, or for how long. I went up and edged into a room that was only fractionally less crowded than the Tokyo subway at rush hour. All that was missing were the men with white gloves at the door, pushing everyone in. Maybe I'd suggest it for next year.

Bim was the first person I recognized, and he shrieked, "Come and see the fort we've built!" That's me, big with the five-year-old set. I went. Bim was in his element. He was a sturdy little blond boy in a pair of dungarees with a bright yellow shirt and yellow socks, one of which was coming off his foot and trailing behind him like a small rudder. He was directing children twice his age like a seasoned traffic cop, and they obeyed him happily. The kids had taken all the chairs Kay and Anthony had moved out of the sitting room, put them into a wagon-train circle and covered them with the guests' coats, a squashed tepee with dozens of giggling bodies stuffed inside. It looked cozy: back to the womb. I mentally shook myself. Really? A children's tent looks good because it's safe? *Time to get a grip*, I told myself sternly. Then I told Bim sincerely that it was the best fort I'd ever seen, and I'd be back in a bit, and headed down the hall for the grown-up end of things.

And there, squashed in a corner of the sofa, between four men having a furious argument about who should or should not have been chosen to play for England (I think), was the guy from the LSD: the Thin Boy who had walked me to Nick's office. He was no cleaner than he had been then. Still lank, still greasy, he looked very out of place among Anthony and Kay's actor friends, who were always pleased to have an opportunity to dress up and show off their party plumage.

He hadn't seen me yet, and I didn't think he could escape from the sofa quickly, so I grabbed Kay as she went past with a bottle, refilling glasses. "Who's that?" I said, pointing with my chin.

Kay dropped the bottle. We both bent down to pick it up and knocked our heads together. Really, being with Kay was like being in a Laurel and Hardy film. By the time we'd untangled ourselves, I'd been spotted.

"Quick," I said, grabbing Kay by the arm. "I really want to talk to him."

"Who? Him? I don't know him. Someone brought him. I think. I don't know." Kay was disconcerted by my sudden anxiety. I herded her over toward the sofa. "Talk to him," I said quietly. "Find out who he is."

Kay looked at me like I'd sprouted horns, but headed off the Thin Boy before he could go further. She gestured with her rescued bottle. "Refill?"

He leaped back to avoid the spurt of wine, and was engulfed in the football group again. "No. No, thanks. I have to be going. . . ."

Kay wasn't going to do anything to stop him, so as he emerged from the football huddle I grabbed him by the arm and smiled. "Hi! Great to see you again. We met at the LSD, didn't we?" He tried to pull away without showing it, but I was terrier-like. "Do you know Kay? This is her party." That would be harder to escape from.

"Hi," he smiled weakly. "I came with . . ." He pointed back into the crowd vaguely.

"Let's go talk in the kitchen," I said.

"I was just going."

"Sure. But you've got time. It's early." I held on with an iron grip, smiling all the while. Sam Clair: everybody's pal.

We pushed through. The kitchen was heaving, but not quite as bad as the rest of the flat. I found a quiet corner and pushed him into it. "So. What's your name?"

This appeared to be a harder question than it looked. He looked around for an escape route. I was standing in front of the only door, and I must have looked as peeved as I felt. He shrugged. "David."

"Good to meet you, David. David what?"

A bit of fight returned. "Nathanson. Now, I really need to go. I don't know who you are or what you want. Yes, I remember you from the LSD. I showed the way. Where I come from, that doesn't make us friends for life."

Not where I come from, either. But, "I've seen you since then, too."

He wasn't going to crumple. "Have you? I haven't seen you."

"How about in Les Deux?"

"How about what? I've eaten there, yes. It's a public place."

I knew he'd been following me. He knew I knew. And we both knew there was nothing I could do about it. One last try. "Who are the people who brought you here? Maybe we have friends in common."

He stared at me in contempt. "I don't think so. John Smith." He crossed his arms and stared.

I wasn't going to get anything more from him, so I walked away.

John Smith didn't mean anything to me, but then, I didn't think it would mean anything to anyone. He had obviously made it up on the spot, and intended that I know it. But you couldn't arrest someone for being unpleasant at a party. I was quite sure of that, because if you could, I would have been jailed long ago.

I had a drink and thought about the conversation. It didn't get me anywhere. I assumed he'd been following me, or knew where I lived, and when he realized there was a party going on, he just walked in. It wouldn't have been difficult. In fact, nothing could have been easier. It was creepy, but what could I do? I had his name, maybe, if it was his, but nothing else was different. I'd been followed by an unknown man. Now I was being followed by someone whose name I knew. The only step forward was that he knew I was aware of him. If he had any malign intent, it would make him a bit warier, but that was it.

I waved good-bye to Anthony, who was ten or twelve layers of people away, and started off down the stairs. As I got to the first landing, the door above me opened. A voice floated out. "Ms. Clair. Sam."

Mr. Rudiger.

"Hi, how are you?" I called up.

"Very well. Would you like to come in and have some coffee? If you're not too busy."

What could I say? He knew that with that din going on, no one could be doing anything else in the house. "Thanks," I called back. "I'd love to. I'm just going to—to change my sweater. The smoke in there," I added, feebly. "I'll be up in ten minutes." I couldn't refuse, but I could let Jake know where I was, and let him know about the Thin Boy—or David, as I suppose he probably was really called. Maybe.

I made the call, and when it went straight to voice mail I left a message. Then I headed back up the stairs. Mr. Rudiger was waiting by the door, and he looked so pleased to see me I felt like a shit for suspecting him. His daughter had just made her biweekly visit, and he had little Viennese pastries and fresh coffee all set out. I knew that the McManuses had a point. But it was almost repellent to distrust this courtly old man. Like kicking one of those white-whiskered, stately dogs that spend their days sunning themselves, but still feel obliged to creak to their feet to greet a newcomer.

His walls were shaking with the noise from downstairs. I nodded toward them. "Does it bother you?"

He smiled and spread his hands: "They're young, they're

having a good time. What harm can it do?" He was so benevolent. "Have you been at the party? You're young, too—you should go out and enjoy yourself more."

"I do enjoy myself." Why was I defending my social life to a man who never left his flat? "I just don't like shouting. Also—" I broke off.

If Mr. Rudiger had pushed me, I would have probably shut up. As it was he busied himself with coffee, getting me a napkin, making sure the pastries were within easy reach.

"There was someone there who I'd seen at the London School of Design last week. It was just a coincidence. . . ." I trailed away. Mr. Rudiger looked pleasantly interested, but not curious, and that impelled me to go on. "I'm getting crazed now. I keep thinking he's following me." I gave a short laugh, encouraging him to agree with me on how silly I'd been. He didn't, which made me determined to convince him, and me, that this had been nothing but a chance meeting. "I'd gone for a meeting with the rector. It had nothing to do with this boy, who I only met in the corridor for a minute. I'm spooked, but it's nothing."

To change the subject, I filled him in on my trip to Ireland. It was a good neutral topic, and he didn't seem to mind my change of subject, which relieved my mind. He quizzed me on Breda's books, and I confessed to our sense of humor failure over her newest, which made him laugh delightedly. "That's the problem with professionals. They never see what's under their feet."

I wasn't sure if that was a comment on publishers, or on architects. Or whether it was something else entirely. What were we supposed to be seeing, did he think? Was he seeing a bigger picture, and if so, how? More importantly, why? The comfortable mood that had overtaken me evaporated instantly. Mr. Rudiger looked concerned, like a worried uncle, and said, "I've seen the papers."

I'd refused to look at them that morning, or put on the radio. I didn't want to know what they were saying about Kit. On Monday it would be all over the office, and that was soon enough. I didn't reply, and he went on hesitantly, in formal, old-fashioned phrases. "I know he was a good friend to you. You must feel his loss."

The finality of his words washed over me, and I burst into tears. I managed to gulp, "Excuse me," before I ran back down the stairs.

12

I closed the front door behind me and sank down on the floor and cried. After ten minutes I had to stop. No one can cry wholeheartedly for longer. It's just too tiring. I went into the bathroom and ran a basin of cold water. My face was swollen and pale, and my eyes and nose were red. I looked like the White Rabbit.

After I splashed water on my face for a few minutes I was more in control of myself, and I stared at my reflection in the mirror, wondering what to do next. How could this be happening to me? I'd always been conservative, cautious. When I was young everything had frightened me. I'd felt as if life was like a play, and I'd come in at the interval. The rest of the audience knew what was going on, while I was the only one who was mystified by the dialogue. As I got older I worked out that that's what everyone thought. We were all watching the second act of a play, usually one performed in a foreign language. Knowing that made me more confident, but I never became particularly adventurous. I had a quiet, placid life, and I'd enjoyed it that way. Now I was mixed up with organized crime, money laundering, and murder. The reflection that stared back at me was the same ordinary, forty-year-old face. It didn't look like it had anything more on its mind than work, home, and family—the average cares of average people.

Maybe that was an advantage. No one had talked to Jonathan Davies' landlady—or ex-landlady, depending on whose story you believed—since the harassment case a year ago. If she had anything to hide, she wasn't going to share it with the police investigating an accusation against her ex-lodger. But if an ordinary middle-aged woman arrived, would she let slip something? It would at least be interesting to meet her, and talk to her about Davies. If she truly hadn't seen him for years, maybe she'd have some ideas.

I thought about calling Jake, but dismissed it. He'd just sound patient, that would make me cross, and he had enough to worry about at the moment. I googled the address and printed out the map, grabbed my jacket, and headed out for the Tube before I changed my mind.

Getting from Camden to Shepherd's Bush by public transport takes determination and ingenuity. It's almost as if the two Tube lines were designed by sworn enemies, who built the system with the express intention of staying as far away from each other as possible. But then, that holds true for most of public transport in London, and I've just learned to go with it. Normally I have a book—a long book—to cover the endless delays, but today I'd forgotten, so unwillingly I bought a paper at the station. I told myself I didn't have to read it, but when I got to the platform and saw that there were no trains for another twenty minutes,

I didn't really have a choice. I couldn't stare endlessly at a poster advertising a radio station I wasn't going to listen to, fronted by a celebrity I had never heard of, parodying a program I had never seen.

I turned to the front page, and there it was, a picture of Kit taken after a show, chatting to a couple of barely clothed models, and looking like he was having a wonderful time. It was one of the nicest things about Kit—whatever he was doing, he was always sure that at that moment it was the most fun anyone could possibly have. I quickly scanned the story, but there wasn't anything I didn't know—police would be grateful for any information leading to etc. etc., and then a rundown of Kit's career. Nothing about the LSD, nothing about the sexual harassment charge. I didn't think that would last another day. Blaming the victim, insinuating that he was responsible for everything that had happened to him, always makes a journalist's day. I folded the page back, and tucked the section under my arm. It was too distressing to read, and I turned to the book reviews so I could get irritated over other people's authors getting more coverage than mine. I'm better equipped to deal with that kind of thing.

As we approached Shepherd's Bush I took out the printout. The entire area is lined with red-brick terraced houses, all built at the same time, to more or less the same plan, row after row, reaching, it sometimes feels, to the end of the world. Roxfield Road was a mirror image of the street before and the street after it. I didn't see how I was going to find out anything here in this endless procession of anonymity. I couldn't remember what street number Ian Childs had said the day we met at the LSD, but if there were still JESUS SAVES posters in the window, that would narrow down the possibilities. I walked the length of the street, which was fairly short, and there was just the one house with any posters at all in the window, much less JESUS SAVES: number 9.

I hadn't yet thought of an approach when the front window opened and a woman leaned out and said, aggressively, "Yes?"

I had, I realized, seen her in the window as I'd walked up the other side of the road, so she'd watched me pass by twice. I couldn't pretend to be lost. I smiled, as though I were pleased to see her, and said, "Are you Gloria Ramsay?"

She stiffened. She hadn't liked a stranger looking at the house. She liked someone knowing her name even less. "Who are you? What do you want?"

She was probably in her late fifties or early sixties. She was top-heavy, solid, and packed into a matching Argyll polyester skirt and waistcoat, with a white, high-necked polyester blouse underneath. I was quite certain there was not a single natural fiber in her entire wardrobe. Her graying hair was cut in a 1950s bubble cut, which she had carefully blow-dried that morning. She looked like a librarian from a movie. A bad movie. No one dressed like that.

I pretended not to notice her hostility. I looked at my watch. "Gosh, isn't Ian here yet? Ian Childs," I added helpfully, looking around vaguely, as though I expected to see him nestled under the sad little excuse for a lavender bush she had outside her front door.

It's hard to say what she did, but she relaxed slightly, as if she'd taken off a mental girdle. "Are you a friend of Ian's?"

"Yes." I held out my hand. "I'm—" Damn. I should have thought about this. Who the hell was I? "I'm Miranda Nicholls."

Miranda wouldn't mind. She'd think it was a great joke. I hoped. "I was telling Ian yesterday that I'd suddenly had to move—a flood from upstairs, you know—" I had no idea what that meant, but figured neither would she—"and he said that he'd loved living with you. He said he'd spoken to you recently, and you didn't have a lodger at the moment, so I decided not to waste any time, but to rush right over." I smiled as winningly as I knew how.

She was cross, but not worried anymore. I wondered what I'd said that had relieved her mind. "He shouldn't have given out my name and address without speaking to me first," she said, grudgingly.

"Of course he shouldn't." I looked righteously indignant, on her behalf. "He said he was going to ring you, but I guess he forgot—and it looks like he forgot our appointment. He was going to introduce us."

"I don't have a room, so it doesn't matter. It's let."

"What a pity. I was walking up and down the street while I waited for Ian, and I was just thinking what a nice neighborhood this is. I don't suppose your lodger would mind if I saw the room? It would give me an idea of what was around in this neighborhood. And then if he left, maybe you could call me."

She was on guard again. I'd said something that disturbed her. Asking to see the room? Was Jonathan Davies living there after all?

She didn't bother to deal with the details of my request. "It's let, I said," she said, and shut the window smartly in my face, leaving me to stare at the blank face of the curtains.

Now what?

There was a small, gloomy, gray stone church at the corner,

with a bench behind a hedge, overlooking a tiny patch where once local residents had been buried, and that now served as a repository for the remains of fast-food meals. I didn't think that anyone in the house could see me if I sat there. I didn't know what I could learn by watching, but it was better than going back to Camden with nothing. I tucked myself into the corner, almost sure I was invisible from the road. And then I sat. And nothing happened. Being a detective was fantastically boring, I discovered. I read the newspaper from cover to cover, from the story about Kit, through the competition to win a Blu-ray player, to the ads for denture fixative. Then I stared into space. Nothing happened. I stared some more. I'd been there about an hour and a half, and it was cold. No one had come in or gone out of number 9; hardly anyone had walked along Roxfield Road, and none had stopped; no cars had stopped there, either. In fact, so little had happened that I was beginning to think that was suspicious, too. Slowly, lights were going on along the street, and I could see through the windows of the houses on either side of Gloria Ramsay's, to families that were eating dinner, watching television, talking on the phone. No lights went on in number 9. If Gloria was sitting in a backroom, I'd expect to see some reflected light spilling out into the hall and through the fanlight above the door. There was none. The house looked empty. Interesting. If you stretched the meaning of interesting. A lot.

I tilted my wrist toward the streetlight to check the time for the tenth time in ten minutes. I weighed up staying out in the cold and watching a dark house where nothing was happening and which had no known connection with any part of the problems facing me, or going home and having something hot to eat. It began to drizzle. Tough call.

By the time I got home it was pelting down, and I switched on all the lights and closed the shutters against the dull misery outside before I listened to my messages. There was one from Helena, saying that she'd set up an appointment for us in the morning, and would I please be ready at seven. Irritatingly, she didn't say what it was. With her, it might be the unmasking of a murderer, or it might be a visit to an art gallery. If I thought she'd be home on a Saturday night, I would have phoned her and yelled. Instead I deleted the message with a particularly vicious jab of my finger. That would show her.

There was also a message from Jake, saying that he was working that night, and if I had expected him, I should stop; if I hadn't expected him, he was sorry for presuming. I resolved never to start a relationship during a murder investigation again. It was too complicated.

It was still raining the next morning, in that deadly London way, solidly, unremittingly. There was no sign of letup, and the sky was a flat, low gray. I was looking out the front window, waiting for Helena when she drove up a quarter of an hour early. Luckily, I inherited her time-keeping genes, and I had been ready twenty minutes early myself, so I ran out of the house before she began looking at her watch and drumming her fingers on the steering wheel.

I kissed her cheek and said, "I hope this is good."

"Me, too," she said, as sourly as I'd ever heard her. "Otherwise I'm going to be struck off."

I stared at her with my mouth open. My mother puts being a solicitor—being a good solicitor—before almost everything.

"Don't look at me like that," she said irritably.

"How else can I look at you? What do you mean, you're going to be struck off?"

"Breaking and entering is generally frowned upon in the profession."

"*Breaking and entering?* You're going to burgle someone? What are you talking about?"

"Well," she modified absently, as she backed down my one-way street the wrong way, "you're actually going to be the one doing the breaking. I'm only going to enter. As an accessory I might get away with a reprimand."

"And I get to go to jail? Excuse me, but what are we talking about?"

"You won't go to jail, because I'll make sure you don't. We're talking about looking at Kenneth Wright's offices."

I didn't say anything because I couldn't. I was speechless. My mother scribbles over stamps that the post office has forgotten to cancel. She returns 10p to the bank if they balance her account in her favor. She pays back to her firm a percentage for any office supplies she might have used for personal business. Now she was setting out to burgle someone's office. One of us had lost her mind. "Mother, please. From the beginning, slowly."

"It's very simple," she said, suspiciously bright and cheery. "I can't get anything more on Kenneth Wright, and the only way to do so is to have a quick look at his office and his computer.

If there's nothing there, I know enough about computer systems that I can put a cookie in place to track his e-mail and Internet use."

I was momentarily diverted. "You do? Where did you learn that?"

She looked inscrutable. "So we'll just slip into his office— Philip Mount has an office on the same floor, and I've told him I'm dropping by this morning—and see what we need to see."

"While your friend Philip Mount holds the door for us?"

"Darling, don't be silly." *Silly.* I bit my lip. "I told him I'd be there at ten, so you can talk to him about doing freelance libel reading for Timmins and Ross. He's just starting out, and can use the money. By nine thirty we'll be standing outside his door, waiting."

"And if he's there already?" I didn't really care, I just wanted to argue. Burgling someone's office? What was she thinking?

"He won't be. He was at a dinner party last night, and it didn't break up until after two."

Her intelligence was usually good, but this was ridiculous. "How do you know?"

She looked luminous, as though she'd had at least eight hours' sleep every night for a year. "Because I was there, too, of course."

Of course. I sat back. I was going to burgle someone's office because my mother told me to. I wondered if the judge would consider that a mitigating circumstance.

When we got to the office building, Helena signed in, her usually precise handwriting becoming a little untidy when it came to the time. She smiled at the elderly security guard, addressed him by name, and asked him about his children—remembering their names, too, their school histories, and the sporting prowess of the youngest. Normally I would have begun to wonder about aliens again, but I was numb. With a final, "Good to see you again, Arnie," she broke away and we rode up in the lift in silence and dropped our wet coats and umbrellas by Philip Mount's door. Helena thought for a moment and slipped off her shoes, and I followed. If Mount arrived early, he was in for a surprise.

As we walked down the corridor, I said, "Isn't Wright going to be suspicious when he sees a broken lock? If he's as dishonest as we think, won't that make him check his computer and files?"

Helena looked at me as if I were mad. "Why would the lock be broken?" She opened her bag and pulled out two pairs of latex gloves and a ring of keys. "One of these should fit. I checked the lock the other day. Put the gloves on first." My mother could not only recognize different makes of lock, but knew where to get skeleton keys to open them. I didn't want to know any more. She handed them to me, and repeated, "One of these will fit."

I put on the gloves and did as I was told. She was right. The third one opened the door and we went in, Helena locking up behind us, flicking the snib up. "We don't want any nasty surprises."

I couldn't resist. "Don't you have Wright's schedule for the day?"

She looked at me pityingly. She knew it was an attempt at sarcasm, so she said very gently, "He's supposed to be going to his son's sports day. But plans change." She didn't wait for a response, and went over to the computer in the inner office. "Try the filing cabinets," she said. "Look for ones that are locked. Anything in the open is probably not interesting. One of the smaller keys will work. Filing cabinet locks are not very sophisticated."

None of the cabinets was locked. Everything inside looked like client files, dated, cross-referenced, open and aboveboard, a model of what a solicitor's files should look like. I flicked through the drawer given over to Vernet. There was a lot, but he was their solicitor. There should be a lot. I decided to snoop around first. If I didn't find anything else, I'd go back and photocopy what was there. I sighed at the thought. Nothing in Wright's desk drawers. Nothing on his shelves except law books, and behind one a bottle of whiskey. So he drank. A quick look at his complexion would have told me the same thing without a breaking-and-entering charge.

I went back into the outer office. More files, all innocent looking. I opened a coat cupboard. Big surprise. Coats. There was a briefcase at the bottom that I tried. Locked. I thought for a moment and went and got the keys Helena had given me. All were too big. I put my head around Wright's door. "Mother, do you have a briefcase key on your ring?"

She didn't look up. "In my bag," she said, in the same tone of voice she used to use when I was at school and couldn't find a clean shirt.

I got her bag and found the keys. At first I thought it wasn't going to work, but I jiggled the lock while I turned it gently, and it gave with a snap. Bingo. In the front flap was an address book, with numbers and initials. In the case itself were three files, all unlabeled. "I'm going to photocopy this," I said.

"Mmm," replied Helena. She had lines of code scrolling across the screen, and was intent.

I photocopied the pages, and returned them carefully to the files in the same order. Then I refilled the paper tray of the photocopier from a stash I found behind the machine, so no one would think anything was different from the way it was left on Friday. I was quite proud of thinking of that, which was worrying. Becoming a good burglar hadn't been part of my life plan.

Helena was still engrossed, so I looked around the outer office, idly snooping. She was right, Kenneth Wright appeared to be doing extremely well for himself. All the chairs were leather, upholstered to within an inch of their lives; the two desks were solid mahogany. They were all reproduction, but reproduction didn't mean cheap. New got up to look like old costs just as much as old. I sat in the secretary's typing chair, swinging myself back and forth, opening and shutting her desk drawers. The top one held office supplies. In the next were personal bits and pieces—stray items of makeup, ibuprofen, contact lens fluid—and at the bottom old steno pads, and an engagement diary for 2007, discarded and buried under a spare pair of tights that had come unrolled and were wrapped in close embrace with a chocolate bar that had turned white with age. I closed the drawer. The remaining drawers were what you would expect. Everything labeled, everything in apple-pie order.

Helena pulled a memory stick out of the computer and put it in her bag. She switched off the power and said, "That's everything. Let's go."

We were halfway down the hall when I said, "Hang on. Wait." I ran back to Wright's office and rebroke and reentered. I opened Tiffanie Harris's bottom desk drawer and grabbed the diary. Plenty of people keep old diaries, but either you keep them all, or you keep only last year's. Why keep one five-year-old diary? I shoved it in my bag, relocked, pushed the gloves and keys on top of the diary, and was standing on Philip Mount's doormat, all in less than a minute. "Tell you later," I said. I was out of breath, not with rushing but with excitement, even if I wasn't sure what I was excited about.

An hour later, as Helena and I idly played "Great books you've never read," Philip Mount arrived, looking much worse for the wear after his late night. He was a tall and pale, still boyish-looking, with excessive care paid to his floppy mouse-brown hair. He wore studiedly "dress-down" weekend clothes, but the ironed crease down the front of his corduroys indicated his soul wasn't really into casual. Twenty minutes later we all left together, me with my booty, and with a new libel lawyer. I wasn't quite sure how I was going to get that one past Selden's.

We took the copied files back to Helena's. She suggested that we didn't want Jake arriving unexpectedly at my flat, and having to explain how we'd got hold of the files.

"I don't think he'd arrive without ringing first," I said. "It's not like that."

"That's a shame. You could do a lot worse." She thought about it. "You have done a lot worse."

"Thanks, Mother. Your vote of confidence is always welcome."

"It's not a vote of confidence you need, it's a long, hard look at your life. You've cocooned yourself in your little publishing en-clave: you see the same half-dozen people endlessly, you never step outside into the real world. The worst is, you're happy that way."

She had blindsided me again. I hadn't seen this coming. "What is this—Pick on Sam Week?"

Helena was unruffled. "You're fine now, but how are you going to be in twenty years? I'm not, as you know, someone who thinks any man is better than no man, but you've just shut down the emotional side of your life, and it's not healthy."

"And you're such an expert," I retaliated feebly.

"Yes, I am. I'm an expert in living with an emotional life, and in living without one, and I know which is better."

I turned to stare at her. We'd never discussed her break with my father, and we'd definitely never discussed her private life after the divorce. I wasn't sure that I wanted to now. In fact, I was absolutely certain I didn't. She sensed my withdrawal and put her hand briefly on mine. "Don't worry. I'm not going to 'share'—I haven't taken to watching *Oprah* in secret. It's just that you should think about where you're going.

"Now." Her voice returned to its usual briskness. "What I'd like to do is set up the computer, so that everything Wright does gets backed up. On the first run through of the files it would be useful to separate out everything mentioning Vernet; everything mentioning property transactions; and then anything that doesn't indicate clearly what it is: files that have no client names, documents without subject lines or reference numbers. Will you do that?"

I nodded dumbly. I thought I could probably be trusted to shuffle papers. Everything else in my life was open to question.

Helena left me with the paperwork spread out at the kitchen table while she went to set up whatever illegal surveillance operations she had learned God knows where. I switched on the radio. The coffee was dripping slowly through on the hob and the smell filled the warm room. The rain beat against the windowpanes. If only I were reading the newspaper, instead of criminally acquired legal documents, it might even have been a pleasant way to spend a Sunday morning.

We sat at the table for the next six hours, slowly going through everything. Helena was the legal mind, but my editorial training was helpful, too. Papers that were not obviously linked I could see, by style, by approach, by the way they were worded, actually belonged together. Gradually we put things in order, and the story was easy to read. This was where the money laundering on all the UK property deals—deals that were processing up to £100 million a year—was coming from. Kenneth Wright was the source.

I got up and stretched. Helena looked as fresh as when we'd started. "The computer will be useful, but it's really not necessary. I'm going to summarize all of this, and write a précis, and then we can hand it all over."

"To whom?"

"To the police. NCIS, I imagine. But we'll go through Jake. He might as well get the credit, and anyway, he can organize a warrant and the documents can be reacquired legally. What we have here is information, but it's not evidence because it's not admissible."

"What about Conway?"

"I'd thought of that. I think you should ring him. I don't want to trigger any warning bells around Wright—he can't be allowed to slip through the net—but at the same time, it would be no bad thing for Conway to know that Cooper's aren't the only solicitors in the City."

I squinted at her in disbelief. "You robbed an office—"

"Burgled, dear. There was no removal of property. It wasn't robbery."

I shrugged irritably. "You *burgled* an office, then—you burgled an office to entice a new client?"

She looked genuinely shocked. "Of course not. I did it to help you; to see if we could find information that would lead to a murderer; because I don't like Kenneth Wright; and—" her mouth narrowed—"and because if dishonest solicitors are allowed to operate, they weaken the rest of us and, pompous as it may sound, they destroy the fabric of society." Then she gave a small, catlike smile. "If, in the course of acting on those reasons, I bring in an extremely important new client, well, I won't turn him away."

I wouldn't have believed most people who made a speech like that, but I think any of Helena's friends would. She is amusing, she is tough, but she is also a person who believes in things like "the fabric of society." In a way, so do I, although I am less confident than she that it has not already been destroyed.

She went back to work and I made sandwiches. It was only five, but we'd skipped breakfast for burglary, and lunch had slid past without us noticing. Helena took a sandwich in her left hand, and went on making notes with her right, while I tried to be useful, tidying the documents back into their original order. Underneath them all was the diary. I flicked through it idly. Whatever foggy idea had made me go back to grab it had dissipated, ending up merely as a question: *Why would anyone keep a single engagement book?* It was odd, but was "odd" enough? On the spur of the moment I'd thought so. Now I wasn't so sure. Still, given that I'd stolen it, ignoring it seemed even sillier than my initial excitement.

So as Helena continued to write without a pause, I flicked through the diary. It was a diary. It had appointments. Not exactly a hot news flash. Why had Wright kept it? I made lists of dates, lists of initials, lists of names. Then I swapped them about, like some kind of jigsaw puzzle. But it was a jigsaw where all the pieces were the same color. I pushed them about again. And the colors clarified. I said, "Do you still have a copy of the manuscript?"

Helena looked up out of a fog of concentration. "Manuscript?"

"Kit's."

"On the third shelf above my desk, in a blue folder." She was already back at work, the words unreeling themselves under her pen.

I trotted up to her study and came back with the manuscript. I'd read it when Kit delivered it, but I hadn't begun to edit it, and I had only an imperfect recall of the details he laid out. After ten minutes I reached for a pen, too, and Helena and I sat in the gathering gloom, both writing as if lives depended on it.

It was near midnight when I sat back, easing my cramped back. Helena kept writing. "Mother," I said.

"Mmm. Just a minute."

"*Mother.*"

She caught my tone and stopped writing. She looked at me and paid attention properly. "What? What is it?"

"Wright killed Alemán."

She looked vaguely toward the files, small frown lines appearing between her brows.

"No, it's here. I took Wright's diary for 2007. It's all here." I pulled my notes toward me again. "Look." I went through the diary, showing how the entries matched up with the files we had taken that showed the extent of the property deals, and, more importantly, with the manuscript. "It's here. Wright has a series of appointments that are only indicated by a time. All the other appointments in the book are indicated either by name, or by initials. The ones that are indicated only by a time are always together in a bunch: two in one day, or three in two days, but never spread through a week. They are interspersed with other appointments, though, and those ones always have initials or abbreviations. The initials are sometimes straightforward, and I've matched up a few with the files." I nodded toward the copies of Wright's documents. "In the ones I can't match are two that recur: 'FStH' and 'Br.' They only come when he has the appointments that are indicated by time." Helena looked encouraging, so I went on. "The appointments link by date with the files. They are before each of the four big property deals that took place in Britain for Vernet that year."

"I don't understand, though," she said. "What's that got to do with murder? We know already from the files that he has been laundering money through the UK property."

My mother was quick, and she wasn't seeing it. I began to have doubts. "What do 'FStH' and 'Br' say to you?"

She considered. "'FSTH.' Nothing. 'BR.' Still nothing."

"Not 'FSTH,' all run together. 'FStH.' And 'Br.'" I spelled them out. Helena squinted at the book and gave a dubious murmur, so I prompted. "If 'St' is for 'Saint,' then how about Faubourg Saint-Honoré, where Vernet's offices are?"

"That puts him in Paris. We'll be able to check that, but surely it's not unusual that one of Vernet's British solicitors should go to Vernet's office."

"Not unusual, no, and he did that regularly. It's always in the diary as 'Vernet,' followed by a name or initials. And the day before 'Vernet' appears there are always travel times marked in. Wright usually went by train, but there's the occasional flight, too. That's always marked before and after a 'Vernet' entry. When 'FStH' appears, there's no indication that he's in Paris."

"Mmm," she said, thinking. "But how do you get to Alemán's murder from there? This still has money laundering written all over it."

"If 'Br' is 'Bristol' . . ."

"Where is this going, Sam? He can't have been in Paris and in Bristol on the same day."

"No, but he can have been in the Faubourg Saint-Honoré and at the Hotel Bristol—coincidentally, on the Faubourg Saint-Honoré—on the same day."

She nodded, not convinced. "Then what?"

"That confirms that he's in Paris. And it gives him meetings with people he's not willing to indicate even by initials, in a city he's not willing to indicate, although he does at other times."

"And then?" She was not doubting now, but not willing to jump to a conclusion, either.

"The days that he's there match up with either the commencement of the property deals for the most part, or with their failure, when Vernet pulls out suddenly and the money comes back from Wright's clean solicitor's account. There are no similar visits when the deal proceeds smoothly." I was getting more sure as I laid out the connections. "This is the important part, though. There are another three 'FStH' trips that don't link to any deals we've found in the files. The first comes the day before Alemán was killed. There's a notation next to it: '1/3.' The day after there's another meeting indicated by time, and another '1/3.' Then there's one final one, four months later, also a time and '1/3.'"

"A street and flat number? A meeting from one to three o'clock? I can't see why you're linking this with Alemán."

"Or one-third. A fraction. A payment that is made one-third on the day before Alemán died, one-third the day after, and one-third—"

She broke in. "How do you explain the last third, if that's what it is? If you're a contract killer, you don't wait months to be paid."

"You do if you're going to get more if the inquest produces a verdict of accidental death. The '1/3' is noted the day after the inquest. That's not all. A week before Alemán's death, there's an A with a circle around it. The next day, there's a meeting without initials."

Helena sat, thinking. Then she looked back at her notes, and spoke slowly, piecing it together. "Wright was not working with Intinvest in any of their money-laundering scheme. That's why Conway and Lambert-Lorraine are focusing on the false invoicing coming out of Eastern Europe. And that's why the material Diego Alemán brought them doesn't refer to the property scams. Intinvest is not involved in those. This is a separate operation, run by Kenneth Wright on his own, probably with someone inside Vernet."

I picked up again. "Exactly. Then Alemán comes to see Wright, which is the circled A entry. Either he has found out, and threatens to expose Wright, or he has found out and wants to be cut in on the deals. The next day Wright is in Paris meeting his contact, and a week later Alemán is dead. The inquest verdict has nothing to do with Wright's money laundering, but is simply a result of Vernet, entirely unknowingly, using their PR power to muffle any subsequent questions in order to protect their reputation. However, Wright and his contact have promised a bonus to their hitman if no charges are laid, and they pay it after the inquest." I knew I was on the right track now. "The clincher is the thing we've left out all along: the missing manuscript. From the beginning we knew that stealing it from the courier was not an attempt to destroy the work, otherwise Kit would have vanished earlier, or the manuscript would have been taken before it got to his typist. It was an attempt to *see* the book."

"And why does that point to Wright?"

It wasn't often I moved faster than Helena. "You told me, right at the beginning."

"I did?"

"What happens to a solicitor whose name is brought to NCIS's attention, money laundering is proved, or even just strongly indicated, and the solicitor is found not to have reported it?"

"Of course." Helena stood up. "If Wright was named in the manuscript, even if his tracks were covered substantially better than he has in fact managed to cover them—" she gave a contemptuous look at the papers littering the kitchen table—"even then, he would be reported to the Law Society, and probably struck off. It's more likely that they'd keep after him and he would, eventually, end up in jail."

"That's got to be the answer. The manuscript theft makes no sense otherwise. After the publication of Kit's book, Intinvest, or any money laundering run by professionals, would simply close up their operation at Vernet, and move on somewhere else. From what I heard at Conway's meeting, what Intinvest was doing was not unusual in method—it's not as if they wanted to keep the *way* they were washing the money secret. It didn't matter to them. It was business, and if this business folded, they'd begin operations somewhere else. And as far as consequences go, even if arrests are made, with an operation running out of Eastern Europe and Italy, they'll game the judicial system until everyone concerned grows old and dies in their beds. No one of any importance would ever go to jail. So why kill someone?"

Helena tilted her head, thinking. "How did Wright know about the typist?"

I thought, too. "Kit's burglary. It must be. He said he had no notes in the house, but I'm sure he wouldn't think a bill from his typist, or her name in his checkbook, would qualify as material that needed to be locked up at his solicitor's. There was an attempted computer hack at T and R, too. It may have been connected, or not. Why, if they had the manuscript from the courier, I don't know, but then, I don't know why I was burgled either, if they had the manuscript. Just to keep an eye on our e-mail? To see what else we knew? When they found no documents at Kit's, that might have been the next step."

Helena was pacing up and down, something I had never seen her do before. "So we're saying that Wright was responsible for the courier's death as well?"

"Got to be. There is simply no reason for Intinvest, Vernet, Conway—anyone else, in fact—to worry about the manuscript at that stage. Earlier, yes; later, absolutely. But not at that point."

Helena stopped. "We need to phone Jake. I'd like to warn Conway, but I can't. He'd take action, the Vernet contact will run, and the whole house of cards will collapse." She was putting on her coat.

"We need to call Jake wearing our coats?"

"No," she said tightly, "we need to put the diary back before we call him. It's the only evidence there is, and it was obtained illegally. Unless the police go in tomorrow with a search warrant and find it again, the case will never come to court." She looked at the diary I was still holding and handed me a dish sponge and a pair of washing-up gloves. "Sit down and wipe every single page. Don't forget inside the cover and the edges. Jake took your prints for elimination after your burglary, and all prints are now kept on file automatically."

I started to wipe. "How are we going to get back into the building?"

"Good question."

13

We were silent on the drive back to the City. It was still raining, and Helena drove carefully. An accident while in illegal possession of documents that proved murder seemed like a bad idea. I couldn't see a way past the security guard, and while one visit could be explained away, just, as coincidence, two would be disastrous, particularly when one was at two o'clock in the morning.

Although the streets were deserted, Helena parked two blocks down and one across from the building where Wright's office was.

"Do we have a plan?" I asked, hopelessly.

She nodded. "I'm going to get mugged."

"Oh. Is that going to be helpful?"

"It's weak, but it's the best I can come up with. I'll scream and run past the door. Arnie Leavitt is a good man. He'll come to the door, and when he sees me, I'll tell him I've been mugged, my bag is gone, and I've twisted my ankle. When he helps me to the car, you'll slip in and replace the diary. The whole thing won't take five minutes. If he stays to watch me drive away, I'll circle back and meet you there." She pointed to the corner behind us. "I'll make sure to hold him long enough for you to get out."

"Isn't there a closed-circuit camera?" I hadn't thought of this when we went in that morning, but it was all I could think of now.

Helena was amazed that it hadn't occurred to me earlier. "That's why I spent so long talking to Arnie this morning. I wanted to have a look at its range. If you keep your head turned to the right and down, your features can't be picked up in the front hall. There's nothing in the lift, and I stuck an adhesive label over the lens of the camera upstairs while you were open-ing the door. I think it's unlikely anyone's found out what's wrong with the fourth-floor camera yet—not on a Sunday."

"Can you keep the guard, Arnie, for long enough? Will it even *be* Arnie? That's a long shift."

I was asking dumb questions. Again. "I asked him this morn-ing. He does two eighteen-hour shifts, with twelve hours in between, then two days off. Weren't you listening?" And I had thought she was simply being nice. I took the gloves and the keys from her silently, and separated out the one I thought I'd used that morning, and stuck my hands in my pockets. Helena locked her bag in the boot, held the car keys in her hand and we went off. We walked silently around the block to come at the entrance from the far side. I felt Helena take a deep breath, and then gave a scream that made the hair on my neck stand on end. She sprinted away from me as I stepped behind a pillar near the en-trance, and stopped outside Wright's building, facing away from me. "Stop! Thief! Help!"

On cue, Arnie ran out. He didn't leave the shelter of the door-way, calling instead, "Who's there? What is it?"

"Arnie. Thank God! I've been mugged. Please. Help me."

"Wait a minute, Mrs. Clair. I'll just go and call it in."

I hadn't thought of that. Helena had. "Please, Arnie. I've been hurt. Help me, and then I'll call and give a description. He jumped into a van and he's gone."

If I had said something as feeble as that, no one would have paid any attention, but Helena has a will of iron. When she tells you to do something, she sends thought waves into your brain, until you think that what she wants you to do is exactly what you had decided to do from the beginning. Arnie was not im-mune either. He walked over to her, and after a minute's discus-sion put his arm around her to steady her while she limped off toward her car. I ran.

Those five minutes were the longest of my life. I swear that every gray hair I have from now to eternity will be caused by my career as a criminal. How people do this for a living I have no idea.

By the time Helena drove up to the appointed spot I thought I was going to be sick. She didn't say anything, but took me back to her house and made me tea with a generous slug of whiskey. She didn't ask me, she told me: "You're staying here tonight."

I was too cowed to fight. Wright, Kit, even my abortive foray to Gloria Ramsay's, were all combining to give me nightmares while I was awake. I couldn't imagine ever sleeping alone again.

By the time I came downstairs in the morning, Helena was half-way through a pot of coffee. The sun had finally broken through, and fresh, scented air was pouring in at the open window, the first really spring-like day we'd had. It was the kind of weather that after months of gray skies and sheeting rain makes Londoners think their climate is really pretty good after all, but I shivered when I saw it. Helena looked at me critically. "You look like you haven't slept for a week."

"You *slept?*"

"Why not?"

"Just a few minor details: murder, breaking and entering, planting evidence."

"Not the latter, I think. I'm not sure how a judge would rule, but since the diary was replaced where it had been earlier—"

I broke in on her legal musings. I wasn't up to a discussion on the finer points of evidentiary law. "Have you called Jake?"

She nodded. "He'll be here any minute."

There wasn't anything else to say, and we sat quietly, waiting.

Jake arrived, looking even more tired than when I'd last seen him. I kissed him on the cheek, gave him some coffee, and sat again.

He wasn't any more interested in social niceties than I was. "What is it that couldn't wait?"

Helena pulled out her notes. "First, you need to hear this from me, with no witnesses, and no notes." She looked sternly at the notebook in his hand.

Jake didn't budge. "Tell me."

"If there are notes, this will be useless to you." Helena was implacable.

So was Jake. He repeated, with an edge to his voice, "Tell me."

Helena had obviously decided that Jake was going to have to

know about yesterday, if unofficially and only in vague outline. "If you get a search warrant for Kenneth Wright's offices, you will find three files in a briefcase in a cupboard in the outer office. From those, you will be able to prove that Wright has been laundering money in phoney property deals in the UK for the past seven years. Here are summaries of the deals, and a précis of the case against him. It's all on this memory stick, which is not traceable."

Jake was not prepared for this. "Are you telling me you broke into his office?"

Helena remained serene. "No, I am telling you I have a memory stick summarizing the contents of some files. I have no idea where it came from. It was in an unaddressed envelope on the mat this morning. My fingerprints are on it, because I opened the envelope before I knew what it was. I am now handing it to you. This is the envelope." She pushed both across the table.

Jake made no move to take them. "I can't—"

She went on, in the same unhurried tone. "Furthermore, you will find an engagement diary for 2007 in the bottom drawer of his secretary's desk. There are notations in it that match the times and suggest locations for meetings linked to the property deals."

Jake slammed his hand down flat on the table, but Helena proceeded as if she were discussing the merits of full-fat over semiskimmed milk. "In the diary you will find an entry marked A, with a circle around it, the week before Alemán was murdered. The following week, the day before his death, there is an indication that one-third of something was passed from someone to someone else; a second third was passed the day after his death; and a final third the day after the inquest." She didn't hurry, and she didn't look away. Jake was mesmerized. "It might also be worthwhile to speak to Tiffanie Harris, or check his records, for a connection to the company whose courier was killed two weeks ago. That's more recent, and I assume therefore easier to jog people's memories. You might want to discuss with NCIS the penalties for a solicitor who does not report money laundering. I have been considering them, and Kenneth Wright has a great deal to fear from Kit Lovell's research. On a personal level, he has more to lose than anyone else."

She paused. Jake had sat back in his seat and was staring intently at her, not angry now, but thinking. She continued. "You can justify getting a warrant based on the anonymous information here. The diary, and what you find in it, will be a surprise to you, of course."

"Of course," he said absently, but he wasn't mocking her, just working through the information. He stood up, gently hoicking the memory stick into an envelope without touching it. "That's it for you two now. It's too close, and too dangerous." He looked over at me, and there was no smile at all. "No more Sherlock Holmes-ing. It's *over*."

"Me?" I pointed to my chest. "I'm Watson."

"You're an editor. Go edit something, for God's sake, and stay out of this." He waved an arm, indicating a vast world of literature that was waiting for me somewhere, well out of his way.

Literature. Shit. I looked at my watch. It was after nine. Shit, shit, *shit*. I was going to be late, and I needed to talk to David before the meeting at ten. I ran.

* * *

I got into the office five minutes after the meeting was due to start. Officially that is. Publishing meetings always begin late. I saw David coming down the hall toward the meeting room, and pulled him into my office.

"What—?"

"Sorry, David, but I've only just arrived, and we need to talk before the meeting."

He looked doom-laden: "we need to talk," the four words men most dread hearing. In addition, anything that couldn't be discussed in a meeting was bound to be contentious, and David hated contention. He had got to where he was by being everybody's pal—or by being spineless and rolling over and waving his paws in the air, whichever interpretation you preferred.

"Has Smith's been on to you?"

He shook his head. I put my head out the door and called to Miranda: "Did we get confirmation from Nadila yet?"

She looked up: "It's on your e-mail."

I found it and printed it, and handed it to David. "Here."

"Can't you just tell me . . . ?" He waved the e-mail at me.

"Read it. Then we'll talk."

It was four lines long, but it took David several minutes to master the contents. Or not to master them. "I don't understand," he said, at last.

"It's simple. I sent the manuscript of *Toujours Twenty-one* to Nadila Irani, who organizes author events centrally for Smith's. She loved it, and passed it on to her colleagues, who also loved it. They've made it their September Book of the Month."

"Loved it." He repeated the words as though they were code for something he couldn't quite grasp.

"Loved it," I repeated firmly, staring him dead in the eye, daring him to tell me how bad he thought the book was. He wouldn't. He was too much of a weed. "They thought it was a riot. I've had a lot of good feedback from readers of about the same age, too. This is going to be big."

"Big." I was still talking in code, apparently.

There wasn't a lot of time, and for the moment I didn't care about his support for the book. We needed to talk about Ben. "David, can we focus on the mechanics of the Book of the Month part for the moment, please? If you remember, we thought it was going to be Ben's book: *The Giraffe, the Elephant, and the Cat.*" I don't make up the titles. Honest to God I don't.

David had caught on. He looked terrified. "They want to *cancel*? They can't do that."

I nodded toward the e-mail. "It looks like they just have. I don't think they'll understand if we get stroppy about it, either. From their point of view, it should be all the same to us. They're substituting one of our books for another. And *The Giraffe* was never confirmed. I checked on Friday. Ben had a phone call from a friend at Smith's, tipping him off, but there was nothing official."

I watched David, not unsympathetically. It wasn't a publishing problem, it was a personnel problem. Ben would be furious, quite legitimately, that his book was losing a huge amount of publicity. As a first novel, it needed that kind of push to have any hope of succeeding. But in addition, and more importantly, Ben despised my books, and he despised me. This would be a very public humiliation, particularly as at the acquisitions meeting where *Toujours Twenty-one* was discussed he had gone on endlessly about this being the result of publishing "substandard literature"—that is, the rest of my list.

"*Toujours Twenty-one?*"

I played my cruellest card, and the one I knew I was going to have to show a lot. "Did you read it?"

He was vague. "Well, when it first came in . . ."

"Not, 'Did you look at it?' Did you read it?"

He caved in. "No. Only the first twenty pages or so. I hated it."

I nodded. "Nadila read it. All of it. So did the rest of Smith's. We've got a great comic novel here, David."

"But you said . . ." He trailed off. I'd never actually said I hated it.

I stood up. "Don't you think you should talk to Ben before the meeting?"

David stayed in his chair. He really loathed this kind of thing. Tough. That was why he was paid four times my salary. I said, "I'll tell everyone you'll be a few minutes late," and escaped down the hall.

I whispered to Sandra that it was all set, and then announced more generally to the people milling around the coffee machine that David had said to start without him. It was a good half hour before he joined us, and we'd worked our way fairly swiftly through the minutes in the absence of both him and Ben. David slipped into his seat just as Sandra started to update us on the publicity plans for the coming season.

When she got to September she hesitated, and David drew a deep breath. "I'd better step in here." She ceded gratefully. "We've had some good news and some bad news." I started to scribble furiously on my minutes. I didn't want to look as though I was gloating, particularly as I was. I drew a rabbit wearing a bow tie. It looked more like a cat, so I gave it a tail. "Unfortunately," David said, as if he were reading a ransom note that had been dictated by kidnappers, "unfortunately *The Giraffe* is not, after all, going to be Smith's September Book of the Month." Everyone looked up. This was more interesting than progress meetings usually were. "Instead." He stopped dead. He had the same problem saying *Toujours Twenty-one* that I always did. "Instead, Breda Mc-Manus's new book has been selected. We had confirmation this morning." He glared at me. Everyone else stared. The book we'd all been too embarrassed to discuss? I drew a house around the cat. It was too big, so I gave it a steeple and a bench for the cat to sit on.

David said, heavily, "Sam can tell you more."

"I can't, really. We only just heard, as David said," I smiled sweetly at him. "Breda's books have been chosen before, but we're thrilled that a comic novel from her is getting the same recognition." There, it was official: It was a comic novel. Now for reinforcements. "I know Sandra hasn't had much time to plan, but given the response we were hoping for, and the usual budget allocated for Breda's books, we're starting to shape up a very active campaign." There were nervous little murmurs. Sandra had known how good it was, too, and had budgeted for it. Mental realignments were going on all over the room. The only comfortable-looking people were the ones who had never pretended to read the book.

Sandra went through the plan she and I had scribbled out the week before. She was a good publicist, and it sounded as though a great deal of time and effort had been put into it, that she'd spent months assuming that this book was going to be her big title for the autumn. Just as she was finishing, Ben walked in, not looking at anyone. And in return, everyone else was suddenly riveted by Sandra's plans. No one wanted to look at Ben, for fear of seeming too pleased, or too sorry, for him. Neither would be welcome.

After that, the heart went out of the meeting, and we ran down the rest of the list in record time. I'm not sure what we discussed, and I don't think anyone else was, either. Everyone wanted to be out of the meeting: me to escape from Ben, the others to talk about him. When David gave his ritual cough before saying, "Well, if no one has anything else?" we all stood up as one. The usual chitchat and jokes were in abeyance as we headed for the door in a silent group. When Ben said, "Sam. Could we talk?" the others scuttled, like crabs when a stone is thrown into their rock pool.

It would have to be faced at some point, so it was good to get it over with. Even so, I stood near the door. "Ben."

He was having trouble formulating what he wanted to say. I looked closer and realized he was close to tears—tears of anger, I suspected. I took a step forward, putting out my hand. "Ben. It's only a book, Ben."

I couldn't have chosen anything worse to say. "Don't you fucking patronize me," he whispered.

Now I was angry, too. It was not my fault I was publishing a book that other people liked. It was not even my fault they liked it more than his. I have no competitive instincts about publishing. I know that a lot of people do, and Ben is particularly consumed: who is buying what, who is publishing what, is every bit as important to him as what he is publishing himself. He can only judge his own work by how others are doing. Well, fine, but I wasn't going to play. "I am not patronizing you," I replied tightly, mentally adding, *You little prick.* "You asked to talk to me. If it's only to abuse me, then I'm going. I'm busy. I have a big market-ing campaign to plan," I added cruelly. He flinched. "What do you want me to say? I'm sorry about the mix-up with Smith's." That was the phrase I'd chosen, and I thought it was inspired. It implied Smith's were incompetent, and it had nothing to do with either book. "But what can we do? It's happened."

"Just like Charles Pool happened?"

So that was what was eating him. Well, tough. "I don't know what you're talking about," I said, flatly.

"You don't. Funny, everyone else knows about it."

"Then why don't you go and talk to them. Because I have nothing to say. I've never met the man." Straightforward denial is always disbelieved, but the purpose of this rumor was long gone, and I no longer cared. Even if it had been true about me and Pool, what was it to Ben?

He wasn't going to back down. "It's—it's just unprofessional."

It took a supreme effort not to laugh. What a baby he was. But he was also a pain in the butt, and I didn't have the time or the energy for this. I started gently. "Ben, if I persuaded one of your authors to send their next manuscript to me instead of you, that would be unprofessional. However," I hardened my voice, "if I decide to fuck your entire autumn list—male *and* female— that is, I'm afraid, completely outside your editorial remit."

Ben had always treated me like I was a brain-dead senior citi-zen, gently knitting and dozing in the corner while he got on with the cutting edge of publishing. It was time he realized everyone over twenty-five wasn't senile yet. I smiled viciously at him, showing all my teeth. "Are we finished?"

I didn't bother to wait for an answer.

I stood in my office, breathing heavily, as though I'd been running. Miranda came in, saying, "You've had a—" She looked at me and changed it to, "Are you all right?"

I was still angry. "Ben thinks other editors fucking his authors is unprofessional." There, let that piece of childishness get around.

Miranda gave an explosive giggle. "He *said* that?"

I was already feeling better. "Apparently it's a new spin on publishing etiquette. I'm still not sure if it's professional to fuck your own authors or not. We didn't have time to cover that." I shook my head, as if trying to shake away an irritating wasp. "Never mind. What was it you started to say?"

"Nicholas Meredith has been ringing all morning. I didn't catch you before you went into the meeting, and he's called twice more since then. Oh, and a couple of your book fair meetings have moved. I've rescheduled them, and also a lunch. It's all in your book." She nodded to my desk diary, which to her—despair? amusement?—I insisted on still using, although I'd also accepted that we keep another, shared, online diary.

None of those dates mattered, and I didn't even bother to look to see what the changes were. Nick was always busy. If he was calling over and over, it was important. I called him straight back.

He didn't bother with any preliminaries. "Ian Childs had a peculiar phone call yesterday."

"From whom?"

"His ex-landlady. She said he'd sent people round to rent his old room. He thought she was drunk: She was crying, and shouting. He didn't know what she was talking about, but figured it had something to do with Nate Davies."

"It did. I was the 'people.' I went over there to see if—" I stopped. "Say that again," I demanded.

"What? Say what again?"

"What did you call Jonathan Davies? 'Nate'?"

"Yes, that's how he was known: Nathan from Jonathan. It's uncommon but not unheard of." Nick was, understandably, bewildered.

"What does he look like—Davies?"

"Thin. Tall—"

I broke in again. "About six foot, with long, slightly greasy dark-brown hair, a beaky nose, and bad skin?"

"That's him. Wait, I thought you said you had never seen him. Hell, I thought we were looking for him."

"We've found him." I hung up. I couldn't stop to explain it all to Nick. I sat staring at the wall in front of my desk. I had been followed by Jonathan Davies—also known as David Nathanson, who had barely troubled to give me a false name at Kay's. Why? Why was he following me, and why did he not care if I knew who he was? Nick and his tutor Oliver Heywood had not thought he was stupid. So either he meant me to recognize him, or he had completely lost touch with reality. He'd been a bit weird, but I hadn't thought any more than that.

Either my talking to him at the Lewises' party or my visit to Gloria Ramsay had triggered something. I sat turning it over for a good ten minutes, but I couldn't get any further.

I grabbed my jacket and told Miranda to tell everyone I was ill, and had gone home. When I got to the street I flagged down a cab and told the driver to take me to Roxfield Road. I had no idea what I was going to do when I got there, but if my just talking to his landlady had made Davies break cover, then it seemed worth paying a second visit. But as we drove up I hesitated. Everything looked so normal. Mothers were taking their children to the park, retirees walked their dogs, a woman festooned with carrier bags was heading back from a trip to the supermarket. Just an average day on an average street. I felt silly. I rang the bell before I could think better of this lunatic impulse.

The curtains moved, then Gloria Ramsay opened the same window she had talked to me through the day before. "Yes? Can I help you?" I turned around to face her, and she made a small noise, like a whimper of fear. I rarely have that effect on people, and it was startling. Her transformation from the lady librarian of the day before was even more so. She looked like hell. Her hair wasn't brushed, and it was sticking up in back, pressed into a peak by her pillow. She was wearing the same clothes as yesterday. I looked closer. It wasn't that she'd put them back on. She hadn't taken them off. The shirt was creased and limp, with makeup around the neck; the polyester suit was rumpled and twisted. Powder had clotted in the creases around her nose and mouth, and eyeliner had run into the bags under her eyes. Her whole face was swollen and red, as if she'd been crying for a long time.

I should have felt sorry for her, but I just became more determined. "We need to talk."

"No. I don't know anything. Go away." She slammed the window down, but I could see through a chink of curtain she was watching me.

I rang the doorbell. Nothing. I rang again. She opened the window. "Go away."

"No. Let me in." My face was fierce, and so was my voice.

She made the whimpering sound again and stepped back. I waited a minute, then put my hand on the bell and leaned on it. It shrilled on and on. After a full minute I stopped, and I said loudly, so that she could hear me through the window, "If you don't open the door *now*, I'm going to get the police." For what, I had no idea. I didn't think I'd need to.

I didn't. The door opened a chink, and Gloria stood behind the chain.

If the threat of the police got me this far, whatever she knew, I was determined to find out. "Open up." I sounded like a cop myself. Maybe it was contagious.

"What do you want? Go away."

I stared into her eyes, willing myself to bully this pathetic woman. "If you don't let me in in the next ten seconds, I will go for the police." I lifted my wrist ostentatiously. My watch doesn't even have a second hand.

She caved in. She pushed the door to enough to slip off the chain, and opened it another six inches, as though by making the entry narrow she'd keep the worst horrors out. I stood in the hall and let my eyes adjust. All the curtains were drawn in the sitting room, and the doors to the rooms at the back and upstairs were shut. The only light was filtered through the dusty fanlight. The hall was painted what had probably once been cream, but with age and cigarette smoke had turned a pale brown. The carpet was brown. The dust turned the light brown. It was like stepping into a boardinghouse fifty years before. Gloria Ramsay stood staring piteously at me, slowly rubbing her hands together. She couldn't be more than five foot, and she looked upward pleadingly.

"Tell me," I said, mimicking Jake this morning. I had no idea what I was talking about, but she didn't have to know that.

"Please. It's not my fault. I didn't know until yesterday, after you came. You must believe me."

"Tell me. I'll decide whether to believe you depending on the details." A faint hope was rising. This might just work.

"No. He'll kill me if he knows you're here. When you rang the bell he went up, but—" She looked sick at the thought.

"Up?" If I just echoed what she said, I might get enough to find my bearings.

"I didn't say that. No. You must go. Please. Now." She was quivering with fear, and making ineffectual little dabs at me, trying to push me toward the door.

"We're going up. Come on." I didn't wait for her, but headed for the stairs. She grabbed my arm but it was easy to shake her off. I had a quarter of a century and five inches on her.

There were three doors on the landing, all shut. The first was a bedroom, a spare room by the look of it. It was brown, too: brown corduroy curtains, brown candlewick bedspread, brown carpet. There was nothing there to accuse her of, apart from Decorating While Depression. That wasn't an indictable offense, so I closed the door and opened the next one. A bathroom. I closed it and approached the final door. Gloria redoubled her efforts. I paid her no attention.

As I put my hand out for the knob the door flew open. Standing there was Jonathan Davies. He looked even thinner and dirtier than he had at Anthony and Kay's. He also looked—it was hard to say. Exalted? I sniffed. Not dope. Maybe something else. Maybe crazy. What a cheery thought.

But he'd followed me first, not vice versa. I was buggered if I was going to let him scare me now. I moved forward, forcing him back into the room. The curtains were drawn here, too, and it was even darker than the hall. I was fully in the room before I realized there was someone else there.

I heard him before I saw him, a heavy, stertorous breathing, like an asthmatic in the middle of an acute attack. I flicked my eyes over quickly. I didn't want to be sandbagged by one of Jonathan's friends. Someone was on the bed, lying down. It took a full ten seconds before I worked it out in the dim light, then I pushed Jonathan aside and stumbled toward the bed. "Kit!"

He was lying on his back, with his eyes closed. His breathing didn't change when I called his name, and when I reached out and touched him it continued in the same labored way. I shook his shoulder. Nothing.

I spun around. Jonathan had moved toward the bed, and was looming over me. "What have you done? What's the matter with him?"

He smiled, and held up a hypodermic. Gloria whimpered again, and he inclined his head toward the door, without taking his eyes off me. "Gloria. Get out." She turned and ran.

I tried to move past Jonathan, but he blocked me easily. I called after Gloria's retreating back: "Gloria. Call the police!"

Jonathan giggled, which was the eeriest thing I'd ever heard. Up to now I'd been worried and angry. Now I was frightened. "What are you doing? Why have you done this?"

He giggled again and walked toward me, holding the hypodermic out with the plunger ready. I backed away, but couldn't get past him to the door. The back of my legs hit the end of the bed and before I could try to reach the window he was on top of me. I felt a prick in my arm, and we stared at each other, our faces as close as lovers.

14

I was swimming underwater, heading up to the surface. I could see the light above, and I was going up and up. Bits and pieces floated past me, bits of dreams, bits of my life, colleagues from work, Jake, Bim Lewis. That seemed perfectly normal, and I brushed past them, focusing only on the light.

I opened my eyes and there was Mr. Rudiger's concerned face. Of course. I'd been burgled and I was in his sitting room. I turned my head to look for the tree outside his window, but it wasn't there. Instead, Nick Meredith was standing with his back to the light, a worried look on his usually genial face. Not burglars. Mr. Rudiger was an impostor. I wasn't supposed to trust him.

I sat up abruptly, pulling away from his hand. The river came rushing back, and then I was sick. Someone was holding a bowl, and my head, gently stroking the hair back from my sweaty forehead. I finished and lay back. It was still Mr. Rudiger, and now Nick moved forward.

"What are you doing here?" I demanded fretfully. I looked around the cream-colored, anonymous room. "And where is 'here'?" I sounded petulant even to myself.

"You're safe now," came Nick's reassuring rumble. Except it wasn't reassuring. Why hadn't I been safe before? He saw that I had no idea what was going on, and filled in. "You're in hospital. You've been doped to the eyeballs with some sort of tranquilizer shit that Jonathan Davies gave you."

Now I remembered. "Kit?" I said.

"He's down the hall, in better shape than you, actually. Last I heard, he was offering his kingdom for a pair of trousers so he could go home and write a piece about it for the *Sunday News*."

I giggled weakly. That sounded about right.

"What are you two doing here?" I opened my eyes wide. "Mr. Rudiger! What are you doing here?"

He sat looking at me, smiling gently. He hadn't let go of my hand since I'd been sick. The door opened and Jake walked in. He was incandescent with rage. It came off him in great waves. He came over to the bed and loomed over me. "If you *ever* do that again—" He didn't finish.

I was ill, not brain-dead, and besides, being in hospital gave me rights. One of those was the right not to be bullied. "I don't know what happened, so I can't possibly say I won't do it again. Instead of shouting at me, why don't you tell me what the hell is going on? I went to see Jonathan Davies and then—" I didn't finish, either. The thought of the hypodermic and Davies' giggle was going to haunt me for a long time. "What about the dead man you pulled from the river?"

Jake rubbed the back of his neck wearily. "He's a dead man we pulled from the river. Unidentified. It happens. We've got a murder investigation, it just isn't Kit's. The DNA test results came in about an hour after you found Kit: no match with the sample from his sister." He shrugged. "As for you, you're lucky. You've got good friends." He nodded to Mr. Rudiger, who took up the story.

"When you didn't come home last night I was worried. You'd promised to come up and see me after work, and it wasn't like you, I thought, to forget. I rang, but there was no answer, and I was sure I hadn't heard you come in." He flushed slightly. "I usually know who is in the house."

Nick joined in, as a sort of Greek chorus to the action. "So he rang your office in the morning, and your assistant said you'd gone home ill the afternoon before."

"Which I knew was not the case," Mr. Rudiger picked up the story again. "She said you hadn't been in that morning, and that you hadn't rung. Now you had an appointment that you'd missed. It wasn't in character. I tried to ring your friend," he nodded toward Jake, "but he was out supervising an interview with someone they'd just arrested for murder—" I looked over at Jake and he nodded, putting his hand on my shoulder to tell me to wait. He left it there, warm and comforting. Mr. Rudiger continued placidly, "I couldn't explain the problem to the person in his office. He thought I was just a silly old man. He explained to me that young ladies today sometimes do stay out all night." He peeped at me demurely out of the corner of his eye, and I felt a laugh bubbling up. "But I knew that if that had been the case, you would have rung. You'd told me about your meeting with Mr. Meredith here, and his name was familiar to me—"

"As his was to me," broke in Nick. "I couldn't believe it when a voice said, 'This is Pavel Rudiger.' It was like someone saying to you, 'This is J. D. Salinger.' I mean—"

I overrode him. "Could we postpone this meeting of the Mutual Admiration Society while I get up to speed?"

"Sure, sure," said Nick, unabashed. "It was lucky that Pavel—" Nick was so proud to be able to use Mr. Rudiger's first name. He repeated, "that Pavel called me, because I had just had that weird conversation with you, and you'd hung up on me. He told me that you had disappeared. Following on from Kit's disappearance, it was more worrying than you just staying out overnight."

"Even if," I repeated solemnly, "young ladies today sometimes do."

"Then," said Mr. Rudiger, as though it were a routine event in his life, "Nick and I thought we should see what there was to be seen. So we went to Roxfield Road."

"*You* went to Roxfield Road?" I didn't mean to be tactless, but he said it as if, after two decades locked in his flat, zipping off to Shepherd's Bush was the equivalent of walking into the kitchen.

He looked proud, and more than a little pleased. "It was necessary."

"I'll say," I muttered. He stopped, so I gestured. "Go on, please."

"There is almost nothing to tell. Kay showed me how to call a taxi, and when I arrived Nick was waiting. We rang the doorbell and that poor woman answered. . . ."

"Gloria Ramsay," I said. "What happened to her? I asked her to call the police, but I doubt she had the nerve."

"She was standing on the doorstep, too afraid to leave, but too afraid to stay. We went upstairs and found you both."

Nick broke in. He couldn't wait any longer, he was so thrilled with himself. "I decked him."

"You what? You hit Davies?"

"Yup. I knocked him clean out, too. I haven't punched any-one since I was about twelve. If I'd remembered how much fun it was, I would have done it while he was at the LSD. He always was odious. Then Pavel called the police, and they brought you here. That's really all."

"All." I turned to Mr. Rudiger, who was still holding my hand. I put my other hand on top of his. "Thank you. I'm not sure what else to say. I know what it must have meant—how hard it must have been. Thank you."

He didn't answer, but he smiled and added his other hand to the pile, squeezing steadily.

Jake was getting restless. "Can you just very quickly tell me what happened, what you remember? We've got Davies, and we've charged him with abduction, but Kit has been unconscious for nearly a week. He doesn't remember what happened for several days before. The doctors say his memory might come back, but it might not."

I repeated what I knew, although Jake had had it all already. I didn't think he would take kindly to being reminded of that, though. "I knew Kit had been stalked by Davies. I guess after Kit ignored him, Davies escalated by charging him with harassment.

When that didn't work, either, he must have got crazier and crazier, and finally decided to abduct Kit. Where he got the drugs, I can't imagine—"

"We've got that," said Jake. "He was working at Boots as a shelf stacker. They'd had drugs pilfered while he was there, but no one was ever caught. He had access to everything: flurazepam, temazepam, Ativan, liquid valium. That's what you were shot full of. We're not sure about Kit yet. Once Davies had him, he didn't know what to do with him, so he just kept knocking him out."

"But that doesn't make sense. What was he thinking? Gloria Ramsay was completely under his thumb—and by the way, how come the police didn't tell the LSD that Davies was still living there?"

Jake flushed. "It was a minor complaint. There was very likely no substance to it. The officer made a phone call, and then didn't follow it up. Davies just told Ramsay to say she hadn't seen him for over a year."

I was embarrassed for him. "So Gloria . . ." I wasn't really sure what I wanted to ask. I just wanted to move away from the fact that the police had not done their job on the LSD investigation. It was over.

Mr. Rudiger helped out. "Poor soul. He had her convinced he was the Messiah returned."

I was uncertain. "That's a joke?"

Jake didn't smile. "Not a joke. She was, as you saw from the posters in her windows, a fundamentalist. She drank, and she was credulous, and she was lonely. Over the years Davies worked on her, and she began to rely on him completely." He shrugged uncomfortably. "It looks like he was drugging her, too, although the preliminaries are coming in clean. We'll see what samples from her hair show."

I was horrified. "You've arrested her?"

He was brusque. "What do you expect? She was living in a house with a man who had been abducted. Even if she didn't know before it happened, she did after. It's a small house. Kit couldn't have been there without her knowing. She's old, and she's sad. She'll be charged as an accessory after the fact, and at most she'll get probation, with luck compulsory psychiatric care. Davies will probably go for a psychiatric defense, too, but his treatment of her will make it hard to say that he was crazy. Stealing the drugs won't help, either. It'll prove premeditation."

The legalities brought my mother to mind. She was not hugely maternal in a television sitcom way, but that didn't mean she didn't care about me. "Where is Helena?"

Jake smiled for the first time since he'd arrived. "She's in my office, 'helping,' as we say, 'police with their inquiries.'"

I sat up sharply and was promptly sick again. After a minute I waved the bowl away weakly and stared accusingly at Jake. "You've arrested Helena too?"

"For God's sake, don't be ridiculous. For what? As far as I can figure it, the two of you spent the entire weekend systematically working your way through the penal code, going for the record: How many laws could be broken in forty-eight hours. But I can't prove it. She's helping NCIS clarify their case against Wright. Not," he added cheerfully, "that they need it really, since Wright's going to be banged up for murder for much longer than he is for money laundering."

"Really? The Alemán stuff panned out?"

Jake stopped smiling. "No, I'm afraid not. I doubt anyone is ever going to be charged with that. But we'll get him for the courier. The daft fucker used his own phone to ring the courier company and ask when the typist's parcel was scheduled to go out. Can you imagine?" He shook his head at the folly of the amateur criminal.

I yawned hideously. "Mmm," I said. "Lucky for you. Although it's weird."

"It wasn't luck." Jake was outraged. "And what is weird?"

I gestured vaguely at a world of weirdness. "A plonker like Wright doing his own clerical work." A thought struck me. "Do Selden's know?"

"I assume so. It's been on the news. Why?"

I sighed. "I would have loved to have been the one to break it to that pompous prick Hugo Littlewood. What a shame." I yawned again. While I was on the subject of Selden's, I really needed to let my office know where I was. I opened my mouth to ask Jake to ring Miranda. Then I closed it again.

Jake was watching me. "What have you just thought of?"

"Miranda keeps my diary."

He looked nervous, as though I had started speaking in tongues. I put my hand on his arm. "No, listen. Miranda keeps my diary." This did not appear to reassure him, and I was suddenly too fuzzy, and too exhausted, to figure out how to explain. But I needed to. I shook myself alert and tried again. "It's in her handwriting."

All three men looked at each other sideways. I knew that face they were all wearing. Then Mr. Rudiger broke ranks and took my hand. "Tell us," he said gently. "What about her handwriting?"

That someone was trying to understand helped. "Wright's diary," I said. "Do we know it's in his handwriting?"

Jake hadn't lost the humor-her look, but he was more comfortable now I was forming full sentences. He nodded encouragingly, and I tried to gather my thoughts.

"I often don't put my appointments in the diary. Miranda does. And publishing is not very hierarchical. Solicitors' offices are. Helena's secretary keeps her diary. Do we know what Wright's handwriting looks like? Do we know that his secretary didn't write those entries?"

Jake had shut down. I could feel it. He patted my hand. Good dog.

I contemplated acting in character and growling, but it didn't seem productive. Instead: "Talk to Tiffanie Thing—" I couldn't remember her name. "Just talk to her."

When I woke again, they were gone. It was late: The blind was drawn and the light was carefully shaded. I was feeling less nauseous than I had earlier, but my head still pounded. The room was designed to create the minimum impact: dim light, pastel colors, only one chair. Helena was sitting in it, with Diego Alemán and Patrick Conway leaning over her, talking softly.

I watched them for a while with that disengaged quality that comes with being ill. It was an unlikely grouping, but I wasn't really curious. Finally, I said, "Hey."

They looked up and turned to me. Helena smiled and kissed me, pleased to see me, but not overwhelmed by what I'd gone through. Conway boomed, "Welcome back, Sleeping Beauty," but when I flinched, he lowered his voice and looked solemn. "Sorry," he whispered. I thought the whispering might be worse than the cheery shouting.

I looked at Alemán. "Come," said Conway, waving him forward. "You haven't met Diego properly yet, have you?"

I widened my eyes. I'd met him, and I'd thought it had been proper. I looked back and forth to the two of them.

Diego stepped over to the bed and held his hand out formally. "I couldn't introduce myself last time. I'm Diego Alemán, seconded to the National Criminal Investigation Services."

I blinked. And waited.

He shrugged. "I was working undercover. I'm with Revenue and Customs. We'd seen the money going through Intinvest. We needed to find out where it was coming from, and where it was going to."

"You aren't a student at Birkbeck?"

He smiled, pleased that I hadn't even had a suspicion. "No. Rosie Stanley is my aunt, and when you rang Chris she thought it would be good for us to meet. Unfortunately, she forgot to tell me until after you'd arrived. I was working separately on tracing the Intinvest money, and we had been preparing a dossier on Vernet."

"Who," boomed Conway again, "have turned out to be law-abiding to a fault, and have been given a clean bill of health by NCIS and the Revenue."

"Rosie Stanley is your aunt?" I was focusing on the minor details, I knew, but the bigger picture had never interested me as much as it had Helena.

"My mother's half sister."

"Then you aren't Diego Alemán? You aren't Rodrigo Alemán's brother?"

"I am. Why can't a Spaniard have an English second wife? A first family brought up in Spain, a second in England? My mother is Spanish and her half sister English. It's not unheard of."

Of course not. I was a mongrel myself. But somehow you don't go round wondering if pleasant academic wives from north London might have world-famous couturier nephews who have been scandalously murdered. You also don't expect them to be as devious as Rosie had turned out to be. That slow, even schoolteacher's tone had had me totally fooled. Maybe I needed to rethink my views on north London. I certainly needed to rethink my views of Jake Field. He had, I'd been aware, been evasive about Diego Alemán, but that, I'd thought, was because he thought Diego was dangerous. Now it turned out he was a colleague, and Jake hadn't trusted me with the information. At least that resolved the question of why Jake hadn't been more curious about the meeting with Conway at Cooper's. He'd already heard all about it. Was he checking what I reported back? I pushed Jake's behavior to one side. I was going to have to think about it, but not now.

I went back to Diego. "I don't understand. Were you trying to talk to me because of what the book said about your brother, or because of your job?"

For the first time he looked embarrassed. "It was difficult for me. I had actually already decided that I couldn't work on the Vernet case altogether because of its links to Rodrigo. I had told Jake that, and I had told my own bosses that. That was why I was so shocked when I saw you at the Stanleys. Jake had said he'd put you off, and you wouldn't be trying to see me."

I sniffed. "Jake doesn't know everything."

"So it appears." He took a deep breath. "I knew from my own work that the inquest results on Rodrigo couldn't hold. But at the same time my mother was very distressed, and if it was possible for the book not to happen, I wanted it for her sake. The idea that Vernet would then be tainted, and Rodrigo by association—well, it was all too much. I was going to back out, until you popped up at the Stanleys."

"Yes, well, I wouldn't miss Rosie's lentil soufflé for the world."

Diego laughed out loud. It was the first time I had seen him even smile, and I realized he was much younger than I'd thought. "Isn't she a terrible cook?" he said fondly. "Anyway, once you appeared on the scene, NCIS thought it would be a good opening to apply pressure, so we went to—" he gestured to Conway—"to see what would happen."

I don't know if it was the information overload, or the thought of the lentil soufflé, but I'd suddenly had as much as I could handle. "What time is it? Are you allowed to be visiting this late?"

Helena hadn't spoken, content to let the others explain. Now she said, "You're in the Wellington. It's private. As long as we pay the bill at the end, we can do what we like. They asked me to let them know when you woke up, though. I'm going to ring for them now, and then we'll leave you until the morning. Will you be all right?"

I nodded, but couldn't look her in the eye. I couldn't say I was scared to be alone, but I was. I'd had nightmares about Davies earlier, and now I was afraid to go back to sleep.

Helena knew. She always knew everything. "I'll stay tonight, if you like."

I felt tears prick behind my eyelids. I knew it was the last thing she wanted to do, and also that she would do it in a heartbeat. I knew, too, that, scared as I was, I didn't want her there. Helena is a tower of strength, but towers aren't very comforting. "I'm fine, thanks. I'll see you in the morning."

She stared at me quietly, waiting, then when I said nothing else, nodded. I could see her thinking, *You are going to have to deal with this sometime, so it might as well be now.*

I made one last attempt to keep them. "One thing." They turned. I looked at Conway. "You lent me your plane."

He was puzzled.

"Why? I mean, what did you want from me?"

He was as guileless as a toddler. "I wanted you at that meeting, and you wanted to get to Galway. It was quid pro quo." He smiled. "Also, you were so pissed off in Paris. No one ever loses their temper with me. You have balls." He looked at me as though he'd just paid me a compliment. Of course, in his mind, he had. I'd just never wanted balls. Silly me.

But he meant well, so I let them go without commenting. Conway made a great drama out of helping Helena into her coat and ushering her out the door, his hand on the small of her back. I looked speculatively at the door. Well, well, well.

I was still considering the possibility of Conway and Helena—which, the more I thought about it, the more suitable it seemed—when the nurse came in and took my temperature and blood pressure, and inscribed both on my chart with all the solemnity of a temple acolyte performing a sacred rite. God, I hated hospitals. Just as she was leaving, Jake reappeared, together with a porter pushing a cot bed. She nodded. It didn't surprise her. It surprised hell out of me. "I'm staying here tonight," Jake announced, without preamble.

I sat up. "Why? What's—? Where's Davies? Did he get out on bail?" I asked accusingly. If he had, my tone said, I was holding Jake Field responsible for the failures of the entire criminal justice system.

He made shushing gestures. "No, it's fine. He's in jail, and awaiting psychiatric evaluation. He won't be out before his trial. I just don't think you're ready to be alone."

"But it's uncomfortable. You're exhausted. You don't want . . ." I trailed off.

He looked disgusted. "Thanks, Jake," he said and then answered himself, "Oh, not at all, no problem."

I was ashamed. "Thanks, Jake," I echoed meekly.

"Oh, not at all, no problem," he parroted back. "Now shut up and go to sleep." He turned off the light.

I waited. He didn't speak, but he wasn't asleep, either. "Tiffanie?" I said neutrally into the dark.

"Go to *sleep*," he snarled. So I did.

* * *

I spent the next day becoming increasingly bored, teasing the nurses, and generally making a nuisance of myself. Helena didn't reappear, which I thought un-maternal. Jake didn't either, which was even worse.

I was eating the sludge that passed for dinner when the two of them showed up together. "Have a nice day?" I said snottily, spooning up what appeared to be library paste.

"Nell," said Jake. So he was back to "Nell." Did that mean we weren't sleeping together anymore?

I turned to her. For the first time in my life I saw her completely dazed, as though one of her own files had got up and told her how to organize a defense. She just shook her head.

"Hello? Is someone going to tell me what is going on, or do you just plan to wander in from time to time, look puzzled, and leave me to my glue?"

"We've arrested Tiffanie Harris," said Jake finally.

I considered this for a moment, carefully building a moat from the mush in my dinner tray. No one said anything, so finally, "Tiffanie Harris," I echoed, concentrating on my plate.

Jake was staring at me accusingly. I hadn't looked up, but I didn't have to to know that he was. "She was laundering money. And she arranged for the courier to be hit. And, we assume, the break-in at your flat, although we're holding off on that for the moment."

I nodded sadly. I have no idea why knowing about Tiffanie was making me feel guilty, but it was.

Jake's tone agreed. This was all my fault. "Yes," he said, as if I'd been contradicting him for hours. "Yes, it was her handwriting,

OK? Wright made a deal with the Crown Prosecution Service, and is trading his evidence for immunity."

"So the two of them—" I ventured, finally meeting his eyes.

A lifted eyebrow said, *So, you don't know everything.* Everything? I couldn't even recognize a comic novel when I'd acquired one.

I didn't bother to protest, however, and he went on, talking to the wall rather than to me. "Not the two of them. Harris was running the laundered money through Wright's account to make it look like Wright's deal. She was blackmailing him with the fact that no one would believe it was her, since it was his office, and his account. Cooper's had begun to worry about the number of aborted deals, which said 'money laundering' to them, but they couldn't find any evidence—unsurprising, since he wasn't doing anything. All the same, they were nervous enough to get rid of him. It was only then, or so he claims, that he decided to cut himself in on the deal. In return for taking Harris with him to his new office, he made her kick back a percentage." He finally looked at me. "How did you know? The handwriting in the diary I get, but how did you make the leap?"

I considered. How had I known? I thought of the three men standing over me the night before. They all knew I was a perfectly intelligent human being, but the moment I was unable to articulate, they were united without a word spoken, no benefit of doubt entered their minds. So, "She was a woman. And she was in a subordinate position." I tried not to sound accusing. "Men don't pay attention to women. They rarely wonder what women do, and they never wonder at all what they think. If you're a secretary . . ." I shrugged. "Cooper's didn't believe

Wright even though they must have known he was a—" I thought back to my single encounter with the man—"a dim-bulb blowhard. I never met Tiffanie Harris, but it's clear now she is very intelligent. But she is a secretary, and she spells her name with an 'ie.'" I carefully didn't look at Helena. "When it was a choice between the two, everyone automatically assumed the man was in charge. Was smarter, was the one who would be running a successful money-laundering scheme."

I thought about it some more. "And then there was Wright phoning the courier company. He just wouldn't have. That's what men like him have wives and secretaries for—to do the boring jobs men think are beneath them. Wright doesn't pick up his dry-cleaning, or buy his own loo paper, he doesn't book couriers. Men like him don't."

Jake nodded. "They were both women. We've got the contact in Vernet, too, and it was Alemán's assistant, Devora Vargas. The two of them were running it together, and when Alemán came to see Wright, they knew that the fraud had been uncovered, and arranged for him to be killed. Vargas's brother is in jail in Marseille, and that's the most likely how they found a contract killer. All seemed fine, then, until Kit's book came along. Harris was afraid the information it contained would put NCIS back on the trail, and so she arranged for someone to hold up the courier. That was all she'd planned, but the courier's bike skidded in the rain. That's what she told Wright, anyway. And now Wright is petrified, and is telling us everything he knows."

We sat silently for a few minutes.

"How old is she?" I asked suddenly.

"Late thirties, early forties. Your age, give or take." His mouth quirked, but he didn't add anything else.

Neither did I. I didn't think he'd missed the point. Not too much. Or he wouldn't too often. Probably.

Epilogue

I'd been back at home for a few days. I'd read, and dozed. I wasn't ready to go into the office yet, and deal with the curiosity of my colleagues. Mr. Rudiger made me meals, which he brought downstairs with all the pride of a child taking its first steps. After his trip to the hospital he had not gone outside again, but my flat was now apparently an extension of his domain upstairs, and thus safe to visit. I was grateful. He was a good cook, and I welcomed the company. It meant I didn't have to think too much.

It was late afternoon. I was lying on the sofa, reading my favorite book in the whole world, *Gentlemen Prefer Blondes,* for probably the twentieth time. Comfort reading, mashed potatoes for the mind. Bim was playing in the garden with Kay, and his squeals of pleased laughter blew in the window with the spring-like weather. I was as close to calm as I'd managed to achieve for a while.

It was all superficial. The doorbell rang, and I jumped so

violently my book flew across the room. Kay was in the garden, and it was too embarrassing to run up and tell Mr. Rudiger I was afraid. I had to answer it, and my palms were starting to sweat. I sat waiting, but the bell went on and on. By the time I got to the front door I was pretty sure who was on the other side. No one else in the world rang a doorbell that aggressively. But I couldn't risk opening the door. I stood frozen on the mat.

The bell kept ringing. I had to do something. My first attempt was useless. My voice had completely vanished. I cleared my throat and tried again. "Yes?" I called through the door.

"Stop being silly, Sam, and open up." I was right. Kit.

I opened the door and we stood looking at each other. I'd seen him briefly in hospital, but he had gone home sooner than I had. He'd had a week more of Davies' ministrations, but it had cleaned itself out of his system much faster than it had from mine.

"You've lost a lot of weight," I ventured.

"The newest spa treatment: Get a wacko to abduct you." He was preening, really quite pleased with himself.

We went in, and I made coffee. When I brought it in to the sitting room, Kit took his cup and said cheerfully, "Now, I'm here because I want to talk to you about something serious."

I nodded.

"Being abducted is one thing, but being unconscious for a week just makes me feel foolish."

I nodded some more. I had no idea where Kit was headed.

"So," he said, clapping his hands together briskly. "I'm going to tell everyone that Davies was a crazed sex attacker, and I can't say what happened during that week only because it was too perverted for public consumption."

I stared at him. Then, "Are you serious?"

He smiled benevolently at me.

"You are. You're serious. You're going to make this into a comic turn." I hadn't laughed for a week, but I couldn't stop now. I was heading toward hysteria. Kit began to get worried, and went into the kitchen to get me some water. By the time he came back, I was more or less under control, but still shaken by giggles. "A crazed sex attacker." Just saying it set me off again.

"Sam. Pay attention."

With an effort I straightened my face. "I am. You weren't unconscious, you were the recipient of kinky sex, your stalker's deviant lust object."

He looked pleased. "That's it. OK, hon, I've got to run. Talk to you later."

He was gone, and I sat smiling at nothing, feeling better than I had in weeks.